SYLVIA PIERCE

Down to Puck
Buffalo Tempest Hockey, Book Two
Copyright © 2017 Sylvia Pierce
SylviaPierceBooks.com

Published by Two Gnomes Media

Cover design by Two Gnomes Media

V10

E-book ISBN: 978-1-948455-70-1
Paperback ISBN: 978-1-948455-00-8

CHAPTER ONE

Kyle "Henny" Henderson had been yelled at by a lot of women in his life, but there was only one he'd ever really listened to. Only one who'd ever gotten him to say those three little words.

Yeah, I promise.

That was nearly four weeks ago, and he'd stuck by it. Twelve games later, and he hadn't started a single fight on the ice. No major penalties, no injuries, no media shit-storms. February had been a banner fucking month for the Buffalo Tempest right winger—even his agent had complimented his good behavior.

Yeah, well. Looked like *that* happy little streak was coming to an abrupt end tonight.

His best friend Bex would have his ass for it later, but Henny didn't have a choice. No matter what he'd promised her, he would not—*could* not—let a world class fuckstick like Greg Fellino take cheap shots at his team.

Not without a little payback.

Ignoring the guilt churning in his gut, Henny spit out a mouthful of blood and skated into the fray, popping his mouth guard back into place. He was pretty sure his teeth had survived Fellino's hit, but that wasn't earning the bastard any points in Henny's eyes. Dude was bad news any way you cut it. In five years, he'd already cycled through three different NHL teams, honing the fine art of dirty play. Henny couldn't believe the guy hadn't been booted out of the league.

But, he figured, long as Fellino kept putting points on the board, his team would protect him.

Just like the Tempest protects you.

Henny shook off the thought. He wasn't the one going after innocent players. He was just defending his men. And his teeth.

"You good?" Walker Dunn, starting center for the Tempest, smacked a gloved fist against Henny's shoulder as he skated past.

Henny gave a quick nod, then pivoted on his blades to catch a short pass from his left winger, Roscoe LeGrand. Fellino was on him again like a dog in heat, but Henny saw it coming this time, deking left before tapping the puck back to Roscoe. Fellino tried to drive him against the boards—another late hit the refs totally ignored—but Henny spun away and slid out behind him, passing up a perfectly fine opportunity to charge the sonofabitch.

It was pretty damn magnanimous of him, and he hoped Bex'd seen it. She couldn't make every game—worked a lot of nights managing her mom's pub—but she was here tonight, right behind the glass, shaking her "BRING IT, #19!" sign. Ever since she'd moved back to Buffalo this summer, she'd been making a new sign for every game, all bright colors and glitter. Henny had them all tacked up in his workout room at home.

Girl sure knew how to light a fire under his ass. Always had.

The puck was back in Henny's control again, and after snaking around Miami's grinder, he saw a damn near perfect shot. He pulled back, then smacked that bad boy right between the goalie's skates, bringing the Tempest to a three-two lead.

His eyes immediately cut to Bex. She was on her feet with the rest of the crowd, pumping that sign in the air, wild auburn curls bouncing. Her crazy smile untied a few of the knots in his gut. The last three years in California had done quite a number on her, but if she was smiling like *that*, she was getting better. More every day. And if she was getting better, then maybe—eventually—she'd be okay.

The crowd was jacked tonight, cheering for Henny

from one side of the arena to the other. Roscoe slid over and smacked him on the helmet, but over in the box, head coach Gallagher and the rest of the stiffs looked unimpressed.

Again his insides churned, but he shut it down. Fuck 'em. He'd take those silent scowls over another lecture any day of the week.

After the goal, Henny lined up with Dunn and Roscoe for the next face-off, pumped as hell. They were halfway through the third, ten minutes left on the clock. If luck was on his side tonight, they'd score another goal or two, lock in the win, and he'd be done in time to grab a beer and burger with Bex.

Just had to find the right moment to nail Fellino's ass to the wall, and all would be right with the world.

"Let's zip this up, boys," Dunn said, waiting for the puck drop. Soon as it hit the ice, he was on it, dodging Miami's center as he rocketed across the ice. He passed the puck to Roscoe, who shot to Henny, back to Dunn...

And Dunn fell on his ass.

Fucking Fellino. Bastard had tripped him up with his stick.

Dunn was back on his feet in an instant, but he'd lost the puck to Fellino's winger.

Henny waited for the refs to call the penalty, but when it came to Fellino, apparently the officials were asleep at the wheel.

He chased the action down toward the Tempest goal, where Dimitri Kuznetsov—a.k.a. Kooz—was doing a bang-up job keeping those pricks out of the net. Kooz was tough as shit, but Fellino was relentless, attacking the puck like a rabid animal until he finally knocked it in.

Shit.

Tied with eight minutes left to play, the teams lined up for the face-off. Fellino managed to beat Dunn this time, sweeping the puck down the ice for another shot at Kooz.

Roscoe and Henny forced him into the corner, where the three men duked it out. After their brief scuffle, Roscoe slid out from the tangle of bodies, puck cradled in his stick.

The look in Fellino's eyes was pure rage. He shoved off the boards, charging back toward Roscoe on the hunt for blood. Roscoe tried to pass to Walker, but Fellino got right in there again, swiped the puck from Roscoe's control.

Not tonight, asshole.

Henny was close on Fellino's heels, shadowing him as they barreled down the ice. Soon as they got close to the boards again, Henny saw his opportunity. Grabbing his stick with both hands, he crashed into Fellino and checked his ass.

Damn, that felt good.

The ref's whistle pierced the noise of the crowd and stopped the play.

You have got *to be kidding me.*

"Buffalo penalty, nineteen, Kyle Henderson," the ref announced. "Two minutes for cross-checking."

"Wake the fuck up!" Henny shouted, but there was no point in arguing. These refs had shoved their collective heads up Miami's ass at the start. And no, Henny's hit on Fellino wasn't exactly above board.

Worth it, though.

Brooding in the box, Henny chanced a look to his left, scanning the seats for his best friend. He couldn't see Bex up close from this vantage point, but he felt it right down to his bones—the heavy weight of her disappointment. The worry and sadness in her eyes. He hated that look. Hated being the reason for it.

He shook his head, staring out across the ice to watch the Miami power play. He couldn't even look in Coach Gallagher's direction. He'd get an earful soon enough.

Henny blew out a frustrated breath. Yeah, the boys would always have his back, just like he had theirs. But things hadn't been so hot with the coach and management this season. He'd been warned more times than he could count; every screw-up felt like a nail in the proverbial coffin.

Fuck 'em. If the suits wanted to drop him, he'd make it easy for them. Retire early. Escape to a tropical island, find some hot little chick in a black bikini to rub suntan lotion on his back.

And so what if he loved Buffalo? Loved his friends and the life he'd built here? If the team didn't want him anymore, he'd bounce, long before they had the chance to do it for him.

You didn't leave Henny. He left *you*. It was a rule to live by, one he'd adopted as a teenager after his parents gave up on his delinquent ass and sent him packing. He had Bex to thank for keeping him off the streets—she'd convinced her mother Laurie to take him in their junior year of high school, and after a brief but rough adjustment period, he finally straightened out. Laurie had even helped him get a hockey scholarship for college, and the rest was pretty much history.

He hated the idea of leaving them, especially now that Bex was back in town. But he wasn't about to stick around where he wasn't wanted. Where he was only bringing everyone down.

What the fuck is wrong with you? Get your head out of your ass.

Henny blinked hard, swigged some water. Out on the ice the guys were holding their own despite his absence. Forty-five seconds left on his penalty. Forty. Thirty-five.

Miami was down near the net again, Kooz and the Tempest defense battling the onslaught. The boys managed to clear the puck away from the net, redirecting everyone back into Miami territory. Kooz took advantage of the break in the action, reaching for the water bottle he'd stashed on top of the net.

Seconds later, the Miami offense was back in the zone with the puck. Out of the tangle of sticks and skates and jerseys, one player shot forward. No puck, no plan, just another dirty-ass move in the works. Henny saw it play out in his mind a half-second before it happened on the ice.

Fellino slammed straight into Kooz.

The hit was hard and high, blew Kooz's helmet clean off. The goalie was down, scrambling like a crab to get back in front of the net, just in time to block Miami's shot.

And once again, Fellino was in the clear. Not an official in sight.

Both Tempest defensemen chased the bastard, but that wasn't enough. Not for Henny.

Ten seconds left on his penalty. The guys on the ice were no more than a smudge of color. He couldn't find the puck, couldn't hear the roar of the fans, couldn't feel anything but the pounding of his heart, the rush of blood and adrenaline coursing through his system.

Six seconds. Five. Four.

Everything narrowed down to this. A single purpose. A mission with only one possible outcome.

Three.

Two.

One.

Henny stepped out of the box.

Then, he fucking *charged*.

He was dimly aware of Roscoe and Walker circling behind him, picking up on his energy, on his intentions, but he pushed harder, faster, speeding away from them.

Never mind the penalties. The fines. The suspensions. He shot across the ice like a missile locked on his target.

Ten feet. Five. Three. BOOM.

He didn't even feel the impact, just heard the brutal clash of equipment, the roar of the bloodthirsty crowd, everyone already out of their seats and gunning for a fight.

Henny was nothing if not a crowd-pleaser.

With Fellino pinned to the boards and momentarily stunned by the hit, Henny tore off his gloves and grabbed a fistful of Fellino's jersey, taking a swing with his free hand. Fist connected with jaw, the force of it splitting the skin over his knuckles. Again. Again. His hand went numb, but still he didn't stop. Not until he felt the bony fingers hooking into his shoulders, yanking him backward.

The official shouted something in his ear, but Henny wasn't done. Far from it. With a surge of new energy he charged back in and took another swing. Another hit, blood trickling down his hand, the crowd roaring, another official zooming toward the fight, his own guys fighting off the other team. He lost his helmet, felt the icy air on his sweat-soaked head only seconds before he saw Fellino's eyes narrow.

Henny tried to pivot, but it was too late. Fellino's gloved fist connected with Henny's jaw, snapping his head back into the glass. His vision swam, then darkened. He slumped down on the ice.

He vaguely heard the penalty calls—a major and a game misconduct. He'd be ejected, sent back to the locker room alone, leaving his team to clean up the mess.

Fellino was slumped on the ice next to him, groaning and bleeding.

Henny managed a pained grin. He'd gotten his man, laid that bastard out on the ice in front of both teams, all the coaches, all the managers, the whole damn stadium, and everyone watching at home. And the best part? Fellino was ejected, too. Fucking *finally*.

He should've felt vindicated.

But there in the black pit of his stomach, the only thing Henny could find was shame. It burned its way up into his throat, into his mouth.

Blood and ash—that was all he tasted.

"Let's go, one-nine." One of the linesmen hauled him up. "On your feet."

As they escorted him off the ice, Henny chanced a final glance at Bex, bracing himself for her anger but desperate to see her beautiful face anyway. To know that no matter what, she had his back.

But there behind the glass, all he found was an empty seat.

Bex was gone.

CHAPTER TWO

Bex Canfield was going to kill that man.

It was after eleven when he finally strolled into Big Laurie's Pub, dark hair still damp from the post-game workout and shower, chest puffed out like a damn peacock.

Bex finished wiping down the beer taps and tossed her rag into the sink, drying her hands on her apron. She was glad the bar was mostly empty now—Henny looked like he was still gunning for trouble, and she wasn't in the mood to referee a fight. She'd seen enough of that on the ice tonight.

Instead of acknowledging him, she shifted her attention to the liquor display, making sure that each bottle faced forward, tallest ones in the back row, shortest in front. So what if she'd been counting down the minutes until he walked through that door? Henny didn't need to know that. His ego was big enough already.

"Cocky prick," she whispered, biting back a smile. Why was it so hard to stay mad at him?

"Mmm." Fiona, Bex's cocktail waitress, set down her serving tray at the end of the bar, staring at Henny as he hung his coat on the rack up front. "That cocky prick makes my lady parts tingle. Good lord, look at those forearms."

"Please don't pee your panties on account of his arm porn."

"Only if he asked me to." Fee gave Bex a playful wink, then leaned across the bar and lowered her voice. "Too bad he's only got a hard-on for you, babe."

Bex rolled her eyes and gave Fee the finger, but that was all the fight she had left for that tired old argument. She needed to save her strength for her best friend. Jokes aside, he was heading down a dark road faster than she could follow, and she needed to reign him in. The conversation was long overdue.

Henny strutted up to the bar and sat down like he owned the place, all muscle and hard angles and that damn attitude that would eventually get him thrown out of the league, even if it *had* earned him the title of NHL's sexiest athlete. What had the newspaper coined him last week? The Bad-Boy Bachelor of Buffalo? God. She cringed to think what all the bunnies were saying about him on the hockey forums.

"Don't say a word," he said, resting his arms on the bar. He was wearing a black cashmere sweater, sleeves pushed up to the elbow, and okay *fine,* the man had *really* nice arms. But muscles would not save him from Bex's wrath. Not tonight.

Bex folded her arms over her chest and stared him down. "You're in *serious* trouble."

"I've been beat up enough for one night, thanks." He finally met her gaze.

He was definitely sexy in that make-a-good-girl-go-bad kind of way, but when he fixed those ocean-blue eyes on her now, Bex saw only Henny. *Her* Henny. Not the macho, bad-boy NHL star who'd broken as many hearts as he'd broken records, but the sweet, big-hearted friend she'd known for twenty-five of her thirty years on this planet. The one who'd walked a mile out of his way every day all through grade school just to keep her safe from the junior high bullies who'd once chased and catcalled her. The one who'd taught her how to drive stick and check the oil and change a tire. The one who'd cut short his vacation in Spain this past summer and hopped a plane to San Francisco instead, packing up her tiny apartment and bringing her back home to Buffalo when she'd barely had the strength to get out of bed.

Six months had passed since *that* move, most of

which was still a blur. But every day since then, Bex had gotten a little stronger. A little better. All because she had a friend like Henny who cared enough to show up, give her a hug, and then promptly kick her ass.

Now it was her turn.

She ducked out under the server's entrance at the end of the bar and hopped up onto the stool next to him, her knees brushing against his thigh as she looked him over. The team docs had taped some of his fingers together, stitched up a small cut near his hairline. His upper lip was puffy, his jaw red and swollen beneath a few days' stubble, and there in his eyes—just behind the still-smoldering rage—were a thousand regrets.

"Let me see," Bex said softly. Taking his big hand into hers, she ran her fingers lightly over the tape, tears stinging her eyes. Hockey was a brutal sport, and he'd been playing since they were kids, but she'd never get used to seeing him so banged up. "Oh, Hen."

"I'm good," he whispered, squeezing her hand. "Really. I'm okay."

Bex nodded, stowing the worst of her fears. At least he wasn't seriously hurt. "Eva figured you'd show up here."

"She called?"

"Just after the game," Bex said. Eva was the team's skating coach. They'd become fast friends after Henny had introduced them a few months back, and Eva often

15

texted her after the games—sometimes to meet up, some-times just to say hi or get Bex's opinion on the latest wedding plans. She and Walker Dunn were getting married later that summer.

"*Women*." Henny gave her hand another squeeze. "If I'd known you two would make a habit of gossiping about me, I wouldn't have introduced you."

"Well, us womenfolk do talk about other things on occasion, Kyle Henderson. Believe it or not, the sun doesn't rise and set on you." Bex's teasing smile lasted only a second before melting into a frown. The truth was, most of their recent texts *had* been about Henny. "She's worried about you. We all are."

The way Eva had put it, it was as though Henny had been erecting a wall this season, one brick at a time. He was showing up at every practice, playing every game, scoring enough goals to keep justifying that insane salary. But he was mostly going through the motions, drifting out of reach from the people who cared for him. Bex had sensed it, too; even in the relatively short time she'd been back in Buffalo, she'd watched him pulling away. Already he was spending less time with his friends, less time at the team's social and charity events, less time even on hookups—a first since high school.

Something was definitely going on with him, but she couldn't figure out what. He claimed to love hockey. He was one of the top paid players in the league, still skating at the top of his game. He had a good group of friends. And even though his schedule kept him busy with constant travel, practice, and games, he'd still managed to find time for Bex and her mom.

So what was missing?

"I'm fine," he said, his voice soft and reassuring. But Bex saw the lie in his eyes, that now-familiar darkness settling into their blue-green depths.

"Hen, just tell me what's going on with you. You can't keep—"

"You tell *me* something, beautiful." Henny tugged on one of her curls and turned up the megawatt smile, melting a bit of her anger. "What's a guy gotta do to get a beer in this place?"

"Don't even try that charm on me," Bex said, finally releasing his hand. She hopped off the stool and ducked behind the bar again. "For your information, we are officially in a fight."

"I thought I wasn't allowed to fight?"

"Yes, and that's working out brilliantly, isn't it?" She filled up a pint of Labatt Blue from the tap, then set it down on a cocktail napkin in front of him. "Are you *trying* to get fired? Or put into a coma? Or killed?"

"Is this, like, a multiple choice thing or—"

"It's an I'm-going-to-kick-your-ass thing. Henny..." She closed her eyes, took a deep breath. God, he was infuriating. There was so much she wanted to say to him, so many warnings and what-ifs and can't-you-sees. But that was just it—he *could* see. Eva might think that Henny was lost or confused, but Bex knew better. Henny knew *exactly* what he was doing—always had. Nothing about him was ever accidental, and that scared the hell out of her.

Because for the first time in more than two decades, she couldn't figure out his end game.

"Why did you go after Fellino like that?" she finally asked.

"He was screwing with my boys."

"Isn't that part of the game?"

"He's dirty, Bex. Needed to be taken down a notch."

"You could've put him in the hospital. Was that your plan?"

Henny's eyes lowered to his beer, hands wrapped around the glass. His jaw ticked, but he said nothing.

Before she could press, Bex was called away by a customer claiming the jukebox ate his twenty bucks.

By the time she got it sorted and returned to her spot behind the bar, Poison was blaring out "Every Rose Has Its Thorn" and Henny had finished his beer.

She was beginning to think he'd leave without answering her when he finally said, "That's why you bailed? Because of what I did to Fellino?"

"They ejected you from the game. No point in sticking around after that." Bex put her hands on her hips, trying to look tough, but she couldn't lie to him. Resigned, she said, "I have to close with Fee tonight. Mom's still in Florida." Her mother had taken off a few weeks ago to go stay with Bex's aunt, who was recovering from a double mastectomy. She'd left Bex in charge of the pub. They really needed a second cocktail waitress —another bartender and cook, too—but right now they couldn't afford new hires. Bex was working on a plan, but until things got rolling, she'd have to pick up the slack.

Henny drummed his fingers on the bar, a grin lighting up his face. "So where's my sign?"

"Maybe I chucked it."

"Maybe you're full of shit."

She rolled her eyes. "It's in the car. But you're not getting it until you tell—"

"Got time for a bite?" Henny nodded toward the booths behind the pool table at the other end of the pub. "I'm starving."

"You deserve to go hungry tonight, jerkface," Bex said. But she ducked into the kitchen and put in an order with Nico anyway.

"Black-and-bleu burgers, huh?" Henny said when she came back out. "That's new."

"To match the shiner I'm about to give you." Bex raised a fist, but she wasn't fooling anyone. No matter how badly he'd fucked up, Henny could always bring the smile right back to her face. She felt it now, stretching from ear to ear as Henny grabbed her fist. The tape on his fingers felt rough and foreign against her skin.

"I don't know why I put up with you," she said.

"Because you love me." Henny kissed her fingers. "Now shut up and feed me, woman."

CHAPTER THREE

Ten minutes and three 80s rock ballads later, Bex grabbed their food from the kitchen and headed over to their usual booth, gesturing for Henny to follow.

In the four months she'd been working at her mother's place, this had become an unspoken post-game routine, another familiar comfort in a lifetime of familiar comforts they'd shared together. Some nights, half the team was with him, everyone piled into booths or shooting pool with the locals, singing right along with all the retro rock tunes this town seemed to love so much. Other times it was just Henny and his closest teammates, Walker and Roscoe.

But once in a while it was just him, and those were the nights Bex savored. Even though they were living in the same town again, just like when they were kids, they didn't get to spend much time together. Henny did his best to make it happen, but Bex was usually working nights, and Henny was either on the ice, on the road, or sleeping in preparation for the ice or the road.

Bex sighed, her heart heavy. Despite the fact that he'd made time for her tonight, he'd broken his promise, and she wasn't letting him off the hook so easily. They had a deal: he'd stop fighting and screwing up on the ice, and she'd start taking action on her plans for the pub. So far, she'd been keeping up her end of the bargain. Couldn't say the same for Henny.

"What'd Gallagher say?" she asked, stuffing a sweet potato fry into her mouth.

Henny grabbed his burger. Then, "Strongly suggested I sit out morning practice, get my act together before tomorrow night."

"What's tomorrow night?"

He wolfed down half the burger in a single bite. "Wow. This is *really* fucking good."

"Henny!" She kicked him under the table. "What happens tomorrow night?"

"Phone hearing."

Bex winced. Hearings could go either way. Fellino wasn't seriously injured, which would work in Henny's favor. But it wasn't Henny's first offense. He'd been racking up fines and penalties this season, and the

Department of Player Safety wouldn't look favorably on that. "What does that mean for—"

"It means I get to sleep in tomorrow, so you're buying me another beer." He took a monster bite of his burger, then another, chasing it with a handful of fries. "Damn, girl. This burger has best-seller written all over it."

"Glad it passes the Henny test."

"It passes *every* test. This is seriously good, Bex. What else you working on?"

She got him a fresh beer, then gave him an update on her plans.

"I checked out the building records downtown, talked to a bunch of the locals and regulars," she said. "This town is definitely ready for an upgrade."

Big Laurie's was the perfect location, too. Not too far off the highway, not stuck in the middle of all the downtown hotspots. It was also far enough away from the university district that they didn't have to worry about underage drinkers or the obnoxious frat crowd. There were a few other local dives nearby, but if Bex had her way, Big Laurie's would be the only one of its kind in the immediate neighborhood. A few key expansions and upgrades would allow them to offer a bigger menu, book bands on the weekends, even host special events, all while maintaining the hometown feel the place was known for.

"All in all, the perfect storm of opportunity," she finished up.

Henny stopped inhaling food long enough to smile. "You know what I love about you? No matter what's in front of you, you just tackle it. All the way. You're a fucking badass, Bex."

Bex lowered her eyes, picking at the fries on her plate. She didn't feel like a badass. More like a scared little girl who'd run back home to Buffalo after letting a man stomp all over her life. Sure, she got all excited about her grand plans for the place—her mom was barely breaking even on it now, and soon she'd be retiring. She had to sell the place or she'd lose her shirt. Bex would love nothing more than to be that lucky buyer, to pick up where she'd left off with her catering business in California, to follow through on all of her big ideas. But at the end of the day, that's all they were. Dreams and plans that lived only in her imagination.

"If I was such a badass," she said, "I wouldn't be in this mess. I wouldn't even be in Buffalo."

Beneath her smile, Bex seethed with fresh anger, unable to dislodge the image of her ex from its permanent position in her brain. Over their three years together, he'd lied, schemed, and smashed her heart, draining her bank accounts and destroying her business in the process. If it wasn't for Henny, Bex was pretty sure she would've stayed curled up in her bed forever.

Bex blinked away fresh tears. Buffalo was supposed to be her fresh start. Not her dream life—certainly not what she'd planned for herself after culinary school and California—but a nice reset. And so far, it really had been. She enjoyed working at the pub, and she was secretly proud her mom had handed over the reigns while she was down in Florida. She'd made a few good girlfriends, occasionally went on a date with a cute guy, and her best friend was back to being a permanent fixture in her life.

But fresh starts couldn't erase the past, no matter how fast you ran to get ahead. And no matter how great her business plan was, no matter how big and bold her dreams, no bank would ever approve her for a business loan. Those were just the cold hard facts.

When Bex finally looked up at Henny again, she found him watching her intently, thumb rubbing his lower lip, the space between his eyebrows creased. It was the same look he'd given her in the ambulance when she'd fallen off her bike in junior high. The same one when she'd had a pregnancy scare her freshman year of college—false alarm, thank God—and didn't want to tell her asshole boyfriend. The look that said simply, *I'm in your corner. I've got you.*

"Hey." Henny's voice was gentle, warm, and she knew he was reading her thoughts. Henny could always tell when she was obsessing about the past. "That part of your life is over."

"The effects of it aren't," she said. She'd never told him all the ugly details about the breakup and financial mess, but he knew she'd lost her business, and it was pretty obvious she wasn't rolling in cash.

"Let me help you," he said. "I could put up the down payment, or just buy it outright from your mom. We'll put it all in your name."

"I'm not taking your money."

Henny shrugged. "A loan, then. No interest, take as long as you need to pay me back."

"Hell no." She blew out a breath. "The only thing that'd ruin our friendship faster would be sleeping together."

Henny nearly choked on his beer.

"See?" She pointed at him with a French fry. "Better let me do the thinking, okay?"

"You always were the brains of the operation."

"*And* the looks."

"Touché."

She raised a brow, popping the fry into her mouth. "You got the balls, Hen. Don't complain."

"Nah. Pretty sure you got those, too." He inhaled the last of his burger, pausing only to steal a few more fries from her plate. Through a half-full mouth, he said, "Will you at least let me set up a meeting with my finance guy at Bluepoint Bank? Miguel can take a look at your plans, see what your options are."

"Henny—"

"The other option is to put me to work. I might be out of a job soon anyway."

"Can you even pour a drink?" she teased.

"Hire me and find out."

"No way. This bar would fill up with screaming women flashing their boobs and flinging their panties at you faster than your slapshot."

"You say that like it's a bad thing."

"It is."

Henny grinned. "My money or my smiling face, babe. Which one do you want behind the bar? How about both?"

"How about piss off?"

"You might as well say yes now. You know I always get what I want in the end."

"Charming. I bet you say that to all the girls."

By the time their laughter subsided, Bex had come to a decision. Henny was right—talking to a financial advisor couldn't hurt. Maybe there was some special grant program for local business owners. Ones who'd lost their shirts for trusting idiots who'd promised them the moon and delivered a bill instead.

"I'm not taking your money," she said, "and I'm *defi-*

nitely not hiring you. But I'll think about Bluepoint. That's my offer. Take it or leave it."

"I'll take it. For now." Henny balled up his napkin and dropped it on the plate, barely stifling a yawn. Nothing like a little food coma after a big game. "You off soon?"

Bex shook her head. "Another two hours."

"Want me to stick around?"

"I'm a big girl now, Kyle Henderson. You don't have to walk me home from school anymore."

"Yeah, yeah." Henny got out of the booth and reached for his wallet, but she swatted his hand. It was a familiar game.

"Let's go, Brawler." She looped her arm through his and led him to the front. "I'm officially kicking you out."

She waited as he slid back into his coat and fished out his keys, both of them stepping aside to let a customer in.

"Hello, beautiful," the man said, cutting between them and deliberately brushing against Bex's chest.

Great. Her least favorite regular. And she hated when anyone else called her beautiful. That was Henny's line.

"Hey Logan," she managed. "Be right with you."

He winked at her and took his usual seat at the bar, flipping through his phone like he had many important messages to check.

"He's totally looking at porn," she said.

"Sure you don't want me to stick around?" Henny asked.

"For Logan?" Bex laughed. "He's annoyingly harmless. No, you go home. Sleep. Pub's closed tomorrow, so I'm around if you need me."

"Closed?"

"Fee's uncle is coming in to work on the bathroom pipes. Said we need to shut off the water. I'm not sure what he'll find in there, so I'm playing it safe."

"Smart." He pressed a soft kiss to her forehead, his warmth lingering on her skin even after he pulled away. "I'll check in as soon as I know anything."

"The *minute* you know anything," she said, "my phone better light up."

One more kiss on the cheek, and then he was gone.

Before giving Logan the time of day, Bex joined Fee at the booth to finish clearing their table. Beneath Henny's plate, she found a hundred dollar bill folded into a napkin with two hearts drawn on it and a message underneath.

Nice try, slick. —H

Fee snickered as she stacked the plates onto her tray. "You're right, babe. He doesn't like you at *all.*"

"Would you stop? Seriously?" Bex handed over the money. "Go put this in the tip jar."

"What about the love note? Does that go in the tip jar, too?"

"It's a napkin. It goes in the trash." She gave Fee a gentle shove toward the bar. "Just for that, you've got Logan tonight."

The moment Fee walked away, Bex slid the note into her apron pocket, biting back her smile.

Oh, Henny.

One of these days, she really *was* going to kill that man.

CHAPTER FOUR

After the hearing, Henny didn't bother with a phone call. Just showed up on Bex's doorstep with a six-pack of beer in one hand and a bag of tortilla chips in the other. It was Friday night, the ass end of a shitty week, and the best he could hope for now was a little company and a few Bex-inspired laughs to distract him from his thoughts.

She opened the door, all shiny and hopeful and glad to see him, and something shook loose in his chest.

Holding up the Coronas, he managed half a smile. "I brought beer. And all my usual charms."

She looked like a teenager—baggy sweats, messy bun on top of her head, baby blue eyes looking up at him all sweet and innocent. For a whole twenty seconds, she seemed happy. Really, truly happy.

But one good look at him must've told her the state of things. Her face fell, and suddenly he felt like a dick.

She doesn't need this shit. Not now.

"Sorry. If you're doing your own thing tonight," he said, "we can—"

"Oh, shut up." She grabbed his arm and dragged him into the house, closing the door behind him. "You *are* my own thing. Now tell me what happened at the hearing. I've been pacing this house all night!"

He handed over the goods and stripped off his wet coat and boots, leaving a pile of late February slush on her doormat. "Four-game suspension."

"Damn." Bex frowned, and he resisted the urge to smooth out the little wrinkle of worry that pinched her eyebrows together. "That sucks, Hen. I'm sorry."

"It was the right call," he said, running a hand through his matted hair. It was damp and cold from the slushy weather. Totally matched his mood. "I screwed up."

The punishment wasn't unexpected, but it stung. Four games was a lot of time off the ice, a nice chunk of change out of his salary, and another black mark on his record. It was also a major headache for the team.

"You tell the guys yet?" she asked. "Eva's been texting me all afternoon."

"Gallagher was calling them as I left. Dunn just texted me."

"Text him back and let him know you're here," she said. "Eva's worried sick."

Henny braced himself for another lecture, but after a beat, Bex just shook her head and wrapped him up in a hug. She pressed her ear to his chest and sighed, and for a while he just held her, lips pressed to the top of her messy hairdo, inhaling her sweet, tropical scent.

"I'm glad you're here," she finally said, pulling out of his embrace. Immediately he missed the warmth of her, the familiar feel of her body tucked under his arm, but she rewarded him with a bright smile. Bouncing on her toes, she said, "I've got just the thing to fix you up. My cure-all trifecta of goodness."

He gave her a dubious stare. "Which is…?"

"Nachos, cheap tequila, and Netflix documentaries about the end of civilization, of course."

Henny laughed. "That's your cure-all?"

"Trust me. Once you see how bad things *really* are in the world, you can acknowledge the utter meaningless-ness of life and the total insignificance of our own petty problems."

"Sounds like new-age hippie bullshit to me."

"It's cheaper than therapy."

Following her into the kitchen, Henny sent a quick text to Dunn, Roscoe, and Eva: *Nachos @ Bex's place. Crashing here tonight. Cancel the APB.* By the time Bex had pulled everything out of the fridge for the nacho prep, he already felt a lot less sucky than he had on the drive over.

Being at Bex's was like hitting the reset button. He loved this house. A little too warm, stuffed with mismatched furniture she'd rescued from neighborhood yard sales, magnets covering the entire fridge, plants growing on every damn windowsill.

The whole place smelled like her, too. Like a smoothie on the beach, with just a hint of something spicy and mysterious. Something that was all Bex.

While she browned the beef, Henny cracked open two beers and pushed a lime wedge into each bottle, the tension in his shoulders easing.

"I miss this," he said, handing her a beer.

"It's just Corona." Bex clinked their bottles together, then took a sip. "They sell it on every corner."

"You know what I mean."

She pressed a hand to her heart and sucked in a breath. "Is Buffalo's Bad-Boy Bachelor actually admitting that he misses me?"

"I don't know about *that* asshole, but me? Yeah. Maybe I do." He leaned against the counter next to her, watching her cook. It'd been a long time since they'd hung out like this, just the two of them, nowhere to go in the morning, no postgame or pregame workouts, no team meetings on the docket. Much as he loved the guys, Bex was the only person in his life he'd ever felt totally himself around. No pretense, no holding back. No bullshit.

"Say it again," she teased.

"Sorry, no idea what you're talking about." He tipped back his beer, stifling a laugh.

"That's what I thought." She turned back to stir the beef. Then, so soft he almost didn't catch it, "Miss you too, jerkface."

Bex never gave him a hard time about his schedule, but he really did wish he could spend more time with her. Not just hanging out, but doing things for her—stupid shit like taking out the trash, shoveling the front walk, scraping the ice off her windshield. Yeah, she was a total badass who could handle just about anything life threw at her and still come out swinging. But Henny liked taking care of her. Liked being there for her, whether it was reaching the glasses on the highest shelf at the bar or just holding her tight when she needed a good cry.

Thankfully, the latter hadn't happened in a while.

It'd been six months since her breakup with the asshole that'd just about destroyed her, and she'd come a long way since those days. But the memory of her lying in her bed back in San Francisco, numb and shocked, totally despondent, not eating... *Jesus*. It still had the power to blast a truck-sized hole in his chest. That image would *never* leave him.

"Take a picture if you love looking at me so much, stalker." Bex stuck out her tongue and crossed her eyes.

Still, he didn't turn away. He loved having her back home, a five-minute drive away instead of a five-hour flight, and he'd look at her for as long as he damn well pleased.

But depending on how things shook out with the Tempest this season, their proximity might not last.

That fucking thought was keeping him up nights.

Henny blew out a tired breath. What the hell was he doing with his life? Seemed like whenever something good happened, he found a way to sabotage it. After years of living on opposite coasts, seeing each other only on the occasional holiday, he and his girl were finally back in the same zip code. Yet here he was, acting like a man who *wanted* to get booted off the home team.

And he had no idea why. When the Buffalo Tempest picked him up from Detroit six years ago, Henny was thrilled to move back home, back to the city he knew like none other. But a restlessness had taken root inside him this season. An itch. It made him hot and jittery, wound tight as a drum. He knew it was no good for him—could see disaster looming on his horizon every time he pushed things too far on the ice, locked horns with Gallagher, blew off the media. Yet he felt powerless to stop it.

Right now, the only thing that made sense in his life was the woman standing right next to him, cooking up her cure-all nachos. He leaned close, tucked a lock of hair behind her ear—same errant curl that'd been falling out of place since they were kids.

She turned to him and frowned, reaching up to rub the crease between his eyes. "I do *not* like that face."

"Tough break." He grabbed her hand, pressed a kiss to her palm. "It's the one I got."

"Hey, what happened to the tape?" She glanced at his hand, then his forehead, realization dawning in her eyes. "And the stitches? Henny, you can't just—"

"Good as new." He wiggled his fingers in front of her face, ignoring the stiffness he still felt. Punching Fellino hadn't been his brightest idea. "I heal fast."

"You really are impossible." Bex opened her mouth to say something else, then apparently changed her mind, nodding toward the knife and cutting board in the dish rack instead. "You're on prep. Green peppers and onions. I want small chunks, not strips. After that, mash up the avocado with some garlic and the rest of the fresh cilantro."

"Which one's cilantro?" He ran a hand over the leafy plants on the sill behind him. "You got a jungle growing here."

"Blue pot, not the red."

Side by side they worked, silent except for Bex's soft humming and the sizzle of peppers and onions frying in the pan.

He liked that he didn't have to put on a show for her.

Didn't have to act like the bad boy or any of those other bullshit titles the media had given him. He hated that shit. Hamming it up for the paparazzi didn't help his game, and it sure as shit wouldn't fill up that gaping void in his chest.

Not even a roll in the sack could fix that anymore. He'd stopped trying months ago.

When all the prep work was done, including a not-so-terrible batch of fresh guacamole that might've included basil instead of cilantro, because who the fuck could really tell the difference anyway, Henny went into the living room to browse Netflix while Bex assembled dinner.

"Here we go," he said, settling on what he hoped was a suitably terrible documentary. "Nuclear Waste: A Love Story."

"Aww, Henny! Who knew you were such a romantic?" Bex came out with a tray full of all the fixings—salsa, sour cream, Henny's guacamole. Then she brought in a steaming dish loaded with cheesy, heart-attack-inducing goodness… except for the healthy-looking crap on the bottom.

"What the serious fuck is that?" Henny grabbed a fork, poked at the mountain of chips.

"Nachos," she said brightly.

"Why are there leaves underneath?"

"It's a bed of steamed organic kale, and you'll shut up

and take it like a man." She passed him a paper plate and sat down next to him on the floor, their backs against the couch. "You're an athlete, Hen. You can't live on fried food and cheeseburgers."

"Says the girl who lives on fried food and cheeseburgers."

"I'm a bartender. It's practically research."

"Why didn't you research how to make nachos? Because this sure as shit ain't it."

"Sorry you feel that way." She pulled apart a clump of chips dripping with melted cheddar and jalapeños. "More for me."

"Give me *that*." He snatched the chips out of her hand and loaded up his plate, leaves and all.

They were the best damn nachos he'd ever tasted, and by the time he'd finished scarfing down his third helping and learned all he could stomach about the contaminated state of the global water supply, his week of a thousand fuck-ups was damn near forgotten.

When Bex handed him another beer and insisted on handling all the cleanup herself, he got to his knees, grabbed her hands, and said, "Marry me."

"Or I can just stick a fork in my eye and call it a night."

"Heartbreaker." He dragged himself off the floor and stretched out on the couch, wishing he could take off his pants. "Tell you what. I'll make breakfast tomorrow. Pancakes, eggs, hash browns, the works."

"You know how to cook? Since when?"

"Maybe I didn't go to culinary school, Chef Canfield, but I can make the *fuck* outta breakfast."

"You've got yourself a deal, one-nine."

Between the nachos, the overly hot living room, and Bex's soft humming at the kitchen sink, Henny was cruising right into rapid onset food coma. Damn cell phone buzzed in his pocket, though, shattering his bliss.

He unlocked the screen—group texts from the Dynamic Duo, Dunn and Roscoe.

DUNN: *Hey, Slick. How are those "nachos" working out?*

ROSCOE: *And by nachos he means sex.*

Henny snapped a picture of his middle finger, then sent it back to them.

DUNN: *Dude. Seriously?*

HENNY: *Would you rather a shot of my balls?*

ROSCOE: *You know Dunn's taking bets, right? Kitty's up to a thousand bucks.*

DUNN: *That's just for the first kiss. Pool goes up accordingly.*

HENNY: *You know what else goes up accordingly? My foot. Up your ass.*

DUNN: *Save that kinky shit for the bedroom.*

"You guys are like a pack of teenage girls." Bex swooped in and snatched the phone out of his hands. He hadn't even heard her shut off the sink, but now she loomed over him, water soaking the front of her shirt, thumbs sliding across his phone screen. "What could possibly be so urgent?"

He tried to grab it back, but she was faster than him, already on the other side of the living room before he even sat up.

"Your friends are such pervs!" She continued scrolling through, then cracked up. "Okay, we need to find Roscoe a woman. He's obviously got some pent-up stuff going on there. And Dunn? That boy needs to keep his eyes on his own paper."

Henny pinched the bridge of his nose. The guys always gave him shit about Bex, but he didn't like her seeing it. "Ignore them. They're cavemen."

"*Rich* cavemen. A thousand bucks? Just for a kiss?" She flopped back on the couch next to him, enveloping him in a wave of her tropical scent. Her knee rested against his thigh, warm through his jeans. "Can we split the cash? Because I'd totally kiss you for five hundred bucks. Hell, I'd do it for a cool hund-o."

"How about I give you a cool hund-o to never say cool hund-o again?"

"Done and done." She tapped out a rapid-fire message, the glint in her eyes wicked.

"What are you up to now?"

"Just told them we're down for a three-way with

Roscoe. He'll be here in ten minutes." She flashed him another crazy grin, then lowered her eyes to his crotch, wriggling her eyebrows. "We should probably change into something a little more...accessible. Be right back."

Tossing the phone into his lap, she hopped off the couch and scooted down the hallway into her bedroom.

Henny's mouth went dry, stomach threatening to revolt.

She *had* to be fucking with him. And if she wasn't, and Roscoe had agreed to it... *holy shit.* There wasn't a grave deep enough to bury that sonofabitch...

"You should totally see your face right now." Bex poked her head out from the bedroom doorway down the hall, laughing her ass off. "You thought I was serious. Oh my God, Henny. Gross!"

"Oh, please." *Thank fucking God.* "I knew you weren't serious. I'm—"

"My clothes are soaked and it's way too hot for sweats. Sometimes you are *such* a weirdo."

"Whatever." Henny didn't get embarrassed. Not ever. But his face was feeling pretty damn hot at the moment, his stomach twisting up into his throat. "Dunn and Roscoe are a pain in my left nut."

"I can't *believe* you thought I'd be into a threesome. With *you* guys." She was out of sight now, opening and closing dresser drawers. Henny tried not to focus on the fact that she was stripping on the other side of that half-open door, casually tossing out words like *threesome*.

The night was *not* going according to plan. He was here to blow off steam about his suspension, kick back with his best friend. When the fuck did he start thinking about her naked?

The phone buzzed in his lap. He'd forgotten all about it. He saw now that there was nothing in the messages about a threesome. Just Dunn and Roscoe, shooting off more of the same stale jokes.

"For your information," Bex went on, "if I was going to hook up with someone on the Tempest, there's really only one candidate."

Henny did *not* want to know.

"Check me out." She sauntered up the hallway in a Tempest jersey that came down past her hips, and for a split second Henny thought he'd seen *his* number curving over her chest.

His heart dropped into his stomach again.

Is she saying… Is that… Are we…?

When she reached the living room, Henny got a clear view of the number.

Not a one-nine. A *seven*-nine. Dimitri Kuznetsov.

"Are you fucking kidding me?" he asked. "Kooz? You got a thing for *Kooz*?"

She closed her eyes and let out a soft moan, running her hands down over her hips in a way that had Henny thinking very bad thoughts. Thoughts he should *not* be thinking about his best friend.

What the hell did she put in those nachos?

"Russian hockey players make me weak," she purred.

"All the more reason to stay the fuck away from them."

"I can't. They're like my Kryptonite."

He grabbed his beer off the table, chugged down the rest in two gulps. "Then consider me your lead suit."

"You're no fun. You dragged me all the way back to Buffalo. The least you could do is hook me up with your hot Russian teammates."

"First of all, I didn't *drag* you, I accompanied you. And second?" He headed to the kitchen, grabbed another beer from the fridge. Two of her magnets crashed to the floor, and he stuck them back on the door with more force than necessary. "Never gonna happen."

"Why not?" She stuck out her bottom lip, a move that brought him back to their high school days, to Bex running off on some crazy dare as Henny tried desperately to save her ass from self-destruction.

Come on, Henny! I can totally climb that water tower! Stop telling me what to do!

"Because the second he touches you," he snapped, "I'm breaking both his goddamn hands. Ever hear of a goalie who plays without hands? No? That's because they can't. End of fucking story."

Henny slugged his beer, trying to ignore the burn in his gut. Bex was always saying shit like that, messing with him, pushing his buttons. So why was it needling him so hard tonight?

Because you saw her in another man's jersey.

He dropped back onto the couch, blood simmering. Another man's jersey? No, that wasn't it. Not by a long shot.

The truth was way fucking worse.

It wasn't just that she was wearing Kooz's jersey. It was that—for one ridiculously hot second—Henny had dropped his guard and let himself imagine she was wearing *his* jersey. Nothing *but* his jersey. And once that image had entered his mind, it lodged itself in there, good and fucking tight.

Bex sat down on the couch and elbowed him in the arm, nearly spilling his beer. "Cheer up, Gloomypants. We've got tequila, remember?"

A grin split her face, big and bright, no trace of the awkwardness *he* was feeling. Christ. Fucking Roscoe and Dunn. He should delete them both, off his phone and right out of his life.

Instead, he turned off his phone and chucked it to the other end of the couch, out of sight. Those guys could talk all the shit they wanted. Fact was, Henny and Bex were strictly friend zone. No way, no how, not in the most frozen outer reaches of hell would they ever be more than that, no matter whose fucking jersey she wore.

"The good stuff?" he asked now, plastering on a smile.

"Define good." She hopped up and scooted back into the kitchen for the booze. "This stuff is so cheap it doesn't even have a name."

"Perfect."

She came back with the bottle, a couple of shot glasses, a plate of cut limes, and a small bowl of salt. Damn girl never half-assed anything.

Sitting next to him again, she poured out two shots. "Ready?"

Henny looked at the stuff spread out on the coffee table, trying to remember the order. Lime first, then salt? Or tequila, then lime? One tequila, two tequila...

Fuck.

"The only time I ever had tequila was in Mexico, straight out of the bottle," he admitted. "There a trick to this?"

"Seriously? Okay, your college education was obviously subpar." Bex made a fist, holding it up between them. "First, you lick."

"What?" Henny shifted on the couch. His pants were getting more uncomfortable by the minute. Tight. Straining. This was not good.

"I can't believe you've never done this," she said. "Watch."

Her tongue darted out, slowly licking the spot between her thumb and forefinger, and holy *fuck* he never wanted to be anything so badly as he wanted to be that spot. He felt it all the way down to his balls, a shock of heat and pleasure so intense it was as if her velvet-soft tongue was teasing the head of his cock, driving him right over the fucking edge.

He wanted to excuse himself to the bathroom, to the kitchen, to the garage—anything to clear his muddy head and stop the aching throb of his cock against his jeans. But Bex was watching him intently, sweetly, waiting for him to follow along.

Henny licked his hand.

It did *not* help the situation below the belt.

"Next, a little salt," she said, grabbing a pinch from the bowl and sprinkling it over each of their hands. "Then you pick up the lime."

He followed her instruction, eyes never leaving hers, praying she wouldn't look at his lap.

"When I say go," she said, "pick up the shot glass with your free hand. Then you lick the salt, down the shot, and suck on the lime. Got it?"

She'd lost him at *lick* and *suck*, but he nodded anyway, dumb fucking idiot that he was, copying her motions. The tequila was cheap and warm and terrible, and it burned like gasoline all the way down.

Maybe it'll burn a hole in your fucked-up mind...

"Another," he said, spitting out the lime.

She poured another round and repeated the whole process. This time he didn't watch as she licked her hand, just did his own shot as fast as he could, then gestured for another one.

Three shots in, he was starting to feel pretty nice. Four, and his dick was securely back in hiding, right where it needed to remain for the rest of the night. Come morning, he'd hop in the shower, rub one out, whip up the best damn pancake brunch they'd ever fucking had, and forget all about the unwelcome thoughts that had invaded his brain tonight.

"Not so bad, right?" Bex laughed, her words running together. "Gets more the better you drink."

He shook his head, making the room tilt. *"Better* the *more* you drink. And no, it doesn't."

"You're smiling, right? That means my trifecta worked." Bex reached for his arm, but instead of the punch he'd expected, she grabbed him, curling her fingers around his bicep. The warmth of her touch radiated through his Henley.

She was smiling up at him, her eyes glassy, cheeks pink. She stroked his arm. A little piece of lime clung to her bottom lip.

"You've got…" Henny reached for her face, swiping his thumb along the bottom edge of her lip. Before he could pull away, that soft little tongue darted out again, licking the lime from the tip of his thumb.

Oh, fuck…

Henny rocketed up from the couch, nearly knocking over the bottle on the coffee table. The room wobbled beneath his feet. "Be right back."

He darted into the bathroom and shut the door behind him, his whole body buzzing and hard, his dick standing at attention once again. Leaning over the sink, he turned on the tap and splashed cold water on his face until his cheeks went numb and his dick calmed the hell down.

Staring at his pathetic reflection in the mirror, he gripped the edges of the sink and took a deep breath.

No more naughty thoughts about your best friend. None. No good can come of it. You're grown-ass adults and this isn't funny and you need to shut this shit down, pronto.

Back in the living room, Bex was waiting for him right where he left her, beaming up at him with that dimpled smile he loved so much. A few more auburn locks had come loose from her bun, and now they hung loosely around her face, brushing her shoulders. He wanted to touch them. To untie that bun, glide his fingers through that hair, pull her close…

He sat down next to her, blinking hard. Everything

around him was off-kilter. Too warm. Too... everything.

"Do you know what time it is?" Bex asked.

"No."

"Time... for another round!" Bex laughed as she reached for the bottle, but she was still looking at him. He couldn't tear his eyes away, either. Seconds passed like hours. And then, just as she narrowed her eyes and her smile started to fade and things were hurtling toward awkward-as-fuck territory, another very bad thought invaded Henny's head.

What would happen if I kissed her?

Instinctively his eyes lowered to her mouth. Her smile was totally gone now, her lips parted slightly, tongue touching her teeth like she was about to ask a question but couldn't find the words. Everything in the room faded away except this one thing, this ridiculous moment that had sucked him into another dimension where Bex wasn't his friend at all, but some gorgeous stranger who'd invited him home for the night.

He stared and stared and stared, unable to look away. Unable to see or hear or feel anything but this. Bex, her dark pink lips, soft and pillowy. Sleet lashing the windows outside. The ticking of the oven she'd forgotten to turn off. The sound of his own heartbeat pounding in his ears, and the soft whoosh of her breath quickening under his watchful gaze.

All he had to do was lean in, take his shot.

It could be good between them. Oh-so-fucking *good*.

Six inches was all that separated them.

Five.

Three.

Hey, dickhole. That's your best friend you're eye-fucking there. How about you calm the fuck down?

"Whoa." Henny nodded, blinking rapidly. Slowly the room came back into focus, time speeding back up again. "Sorry. I, uh. Yeah. Little buzzed over here."

"Thought I lost you for a minute." Bex was still looking at him kind of funny, one eyebrow cocked higher than the other.

"Hit me," he said, holding up his shot glass.

"You sure?"

Henny closed his eyes, trying to erase the image of those luscious lips. Had she wanted him to lean in? Was she picturing the same damn kiss in her mind, wanting it just as bad?

Stop it.

He needed to numb himself with another drink and pass the fuck out before he did something really, really stupid.

When he opened his eyes, he shrugged and flashed her a grin that was a hell of a lot more blasé than he felt.

But fuck it.

"Yeah," he said, nodding toward the bottle. "Why the hell not?"

CHAPTER FIVE

Morning light blazed through the window, nudging Bex awake. She wasn't quite ready to open her eyes, and the rest of her senses came back slowly, tugging her from a hazy dream.

A headache loomed at the base of her skull. She was dizzy, still a little drunk, and *so* not ready to move.

Must've been some night...

Her body was heavy and way too warm, arms and legs tangled up with those of the man she'd brought home. She couldn't quite tell where she started and he began.

He was still passed out, his face pressed between her boobs, silky hair tickling her bare skin. She shifted beneath him, enjoying the sudden press of something hot and hard against her thigh.

Hello, morning wood.

The man groaned softly in his half-sleep, and Bex let out a satisfied sigh, wondering if they had time for a little romp before she headed out for the day. A proper orgasm was the fastest cure for a headache she—

Wait…

I didn't bring anyone home last night. I never bring anyone home. It was just me and…

Her eyes flew open, heart hammering in her throat as she jolted fully awake, the events of last night crashing through her mind like a car wreck.

Nachos.

Tequila.

Henny.

Oh, God. Henny.

Bex peered down at the man nuzzling her chest, sliding her fingers into his dark hair and brushing it back from his face, praying he was somebody else.

Anybody else.

No dice.

Her best friend was fast asleep, his mouth parted, breath hot on her bare flesh.

The room tilted sideways, her head thudding as her heart dropped right into her stomach.

This was bad. Beyond bad.

Henny grumbled and rolled over onto his back. Bex held her breath, but he was still sound asleep.

Gingerly, she lifted the sheet and scanned her body.

The shorts, hockey jersey, and bra she'd had on last night were noticeably absent, the flesh beneath her breasts pink from the press of Henny's face. She was still wearing her blue lace panties, but that didn't mean they hadn't come off at some point last night.

Or that Henny hadn't simply worked around them.

Steadying herself for the killing blow, she cut her eyes to Henny.

Completely naked.

And still hard.

And... wow. Double wow. Her best friend was packing some serious mojo. It was the biggest, smoothest, most perfect cock she'd ever seen, like something sculpted by some old Italian master. The sheet tented over him when she let it drop back into place.

Holy hell.

Surely if that monster had been inside her last night, she'd be able to feel it this morning.

Taking a steadying breath, she did a quick mental inventory. Her entire body ached, but she could blame the cheap tequila hangover for that—not a night of wild sex.

Right?

Silent as a mouse, she trailed her hand down her stomach, slipping inside her panties to better investigate the situation. The brush of fingers over her clit sent a shock of desire through her core, so unexpected she almost cried out. She was slippery and needy, though it was impossible to tell whether it was her body's natural response to having a warm, hard man in her bed, or whether it was leftover from last night.

Her head swam. She tried to remember something from last night—anything—but all she got was a blur. A flash, then it was gone. The headache crept across her brain, burrowing in like an animal.

It was no use. Bex had no idea what had happened in this bed. All she knew was that now, despite every warning in her heart, she almost... *almost*... wanted it to happen again.

She skimmed over her clit once more, and this time her thighs clenched.

God, that feels good...

"Holy fuck." Henny's voice startled her, and she yanked her hand out of her panties and turned to meet his eyes, her cheeks burning.

He was watching her, his own eyes wide with shock, followed by confusion, followed by—most unmistakably —arousal. Raw, unguarded lust.

Her breath hitched. "I was just..."

"Yeah. I noticed."

Henny sat up against the headboard, the sheet falling down to his waist. His bare chest rose and fell rapidly, muscles rippling as he shifted away from her. Bex waited for him to crack a joke, to admit this was all some elaborate prank, to spoon-feed her the logical explanation she was so hungry for.

But Henny only gaped at her.

"How did this happen?" he demanded.

"I was hoping you could tell me." Her gaze swept over the firm ridges of his abs, landing in his lap. He was still hard beneath the sheet, a realization that sent another bolt of desire through her core.

But still, Henny offered no explanation. No jokes. Nothing.

"Turn around," she said. It was a little late for modesty, but she was hanging on by a thread, looking for control anywhere she could get it.

Henny swung his legs out over the side of the bed, his back to her as he raked a hand through his hair. She tried not to notice the adorable way it stuck up in the morning, or the way his sculpted shoulders flexed, or the way her own body still pulsed with heat.

Keeping one eye on Henny, she rose from the bed and yanked her robe off the door hook, wrapping herself up good and tight as she headed out of the bedroom in search of answers. And a hot shower. And coffee. Lots and lots of coffee.

She stumbled on something in the hallway, catching herself on the wall. "Fuck!"

"You okay?" Henny called out.

"Yeah." She glanced down at her feet. "Found our clothes."

The living room was a disaster, too—couch cushions on the floor, salt spilled across the coffee table, the empty tequila bottle tossed into the pot of her poor snake plant.

Tequila. Never again.

Standing in the middle of her living room, Bex got a flash—a memory? A dream?—of Henny pulling her into his lap on the couch, kissing her neck. Nibbling her ear. Both of them laughing.

"I'm still hungry," he said.

"Too bad you ate all the nachos."

"Guess I'll just have to eat you…"

No. It had to be a dream. It wasn't a memory. Not a real one. She and Henny would never, ever cross that line.

All evidence points to the contrary, sweetie.

Bex headed into the bathroom, hoping a searing hot shower would help clear her head.

It didn't.

When she finally returned to the bedroom, Henny was still sitting on the edge of the bed with his head in his hands.

"Whatever happened last night," he said to the floor as she entered, "I don't remember anything." He blew out a breath and finally turned to look at her, guilt etching new lines into his face.

Tightening the tie on her bathrobe, Bex forced a grin she wasn't entirely feeling. "Ouch. Guess I need to work on my game."

Henny didn't laugh.

"Hey," she said, softer now. Her first instinct was always to comfort him, to erase those lines from his face, but she held back. She wasn't upset with him—they'd gotten themselves into this mess together, after all—but she wasn't ready to touch him yet. The moment felt fragile as a bubble, like if either of them said or did the wrong thing, their entire relationship would pop right out of existence.

"If it makes you feel better," she said, "I don't remember anything either."

"Nothing?"

"Just..." *Your hands in my hair. Your mouth on my neck. Guess I'll just have to eat you.* "...the tequila. Everything after that is a blur."

He held her gaze for a minute, assessing. Then, finally, "I'm clean, Bex. Haven't been with anyone in... well, a while, and I just had a checkup with the team doc. But I'm pretty sure we didn't use a—"

"I'm on the pill."

Henny blew out another breath, nodding.

"And I haven't been with anyone since—"

"I know," he said, holding up his hands. "It's okay. We're good."

Typical Henny.

Bex tugged the towel from her hair, squeezing out the excess moisture and wrapping her curls up in a quick bun. Henny just sat there, spacing out on her bed.

She shouldn't be surprised. Sex had always been an off topic for them. She could joke with him to an extent, but he'd usually shut it down before she went too far. And even though there hadn't been many men in her life, Henny never liked hearing about them. Not in detail.

Still, she wished they could sit down and *talk* about this.

Turning to face him again, she said, "Henny, I was—"

"I'm—"

"But—"

"You're—"

"Sorry." Bex held up her hands. "You go first."

"I was just gonna hop in the shower. Is that… okay?"

No, it's not okay, Henny. I'm pretty sure we had sex last night but I can't remember and everything is about to fall apart and I really, really can't deal with this right now and you're asking me about the shower? Seriously?

"Bex?"

"Huh?" She blinked back to reality. "No. I mean yeah,

of course. Go ahead. You remember where the towels are, right?"

Remember where the towels are?

God. Bex was pretty sure she couldn't get any more pathetic.

Henny didn't move from the bed, just continued to watch her, waiting. "Um..."

"Oh! Sorry. I'll just... I'll make us some food. In the kitchen. Out there." She clamped her mouth shut and scooted out to give him some privacy, not that it mattered anymore.

Because they'd seen each other naked.

Because they'd almost definitely had sex.

Because everything was a disaster of epic proportions.

While Henny showered, Bex made some extra-strong coffee and popped a couple of sesame bagels into the toaster. Last night, Henny'd promised her a big breakfast today, but she didn't think either of them could handle it.

What had they done?

It's just Henny. Come on, girl.

She let out a soft sigh, staring at a magnet on the fridge—a stuffed pink shrimp she'd gotten at the Bubba Gump restaurant back in San Francisco. She'd picked it out for Henny a year ago, thinking he'd get a good laugh, only she'd never sent it to him.

Now, it seemed to be laughing at *her*.

Bex closed her eyes. So they'd had a few too many shots, fooled around, possibly slept together. No need to get all soap opera on each other. They weren't teenagers anymore. They were thirty-year-old adults, and they'd seen each other through the best and worst times of their lives, emerging unbroken every time.

This would be no different. Another funny story in the lifelong history of Bex and Henny, no more or less significant than the time they dared each other to eat worms, the time they ditched their respective prom dates to go watch a meteor shower together, the time they got two weeks' detention for recreating the *When Harry Met Sally* orgasm scene in the school cafeteria.

They just had to get through this awkward morning, maybe take a break from seeing each other for a few days, then everything would go back to normal.

So what if the thought of sleeping with Henny sent a warm current rippling through her body.

So what if she was tingling and breathless.

So what if she was wet again just thinking about his hands on her body...

"You good?" Henny appeared in the kitchen doorway, damp hair curling over his ears. He was dressed in last night's clothes—rumpled jeans, light gray Henley that clung to his muscular chest.

Stop noticing his muscular chest!

"Why wouldn't I be?" Bex turned around, stretching up on her tiptoes to grab a couple of mugs from the cupboard above the sink.

"Jesus," Henny whispered. Suddenly he was right behind her, his breath hot on her exposed nape. With the lightest touch, he ran his thumb down the back of her neck, making her shiver. "You, ah... you might wanna wear your hair down today. Or put on a turtleneck. And a scarf."

She turned around to face him. "Why?"

Henny's eyes were dark, his pupils dilated. He touched the back of his neck, his chest rising and falling rapidly. "There's something..."

Bex stalked into the bathroom and grabbed her compact, angling herself to see the back of her neck in the mirror over the sink.

There, right where the ghost of his touch lingered, was a purplish bruise ringed with small red marks.

Teeth.

Oh my God. He bit me.

A bite like that could only happen one way.

From behind.

Bex closed her eyes as another flash shimmered into focus behind her eyelids...

Bex, pressed up against the wall in her bedroom, her bare nipples aching and hard. Henny, one huge hand pinning her wrists over her head, the other tangled in her hair. He slid his leg between her thighs, growled in her ear, told her all the things he wanted to do to her. Bex had never been so turned on, so needy. She arched her back in response, moaning as he licked and sucked the tender skin of her neck and back, crying out in sheer ecstasy when he finally bit down.

Her core pulsed as the memory replayed…

"I'm sorry," Henny said from the doorway. "I guess things got a little… intense."

Her compact hit the floor, the small mirror popping out.

"You're lucky that didn't break," Bex snapped. "The last thing I need is seven years of bad luck." She stormed past him, but Henny was faster, grabbing her arm and spinning her back around.

"Hey," Henny said. Then, softer, "It's *me*. *Us*."

Bex sighed. Henny was right. She was acting like she'd woken up with a stranger, not a man she trusted with her life.

"It's crazy, but it's over," he continued. "We were drunk. We did… whatever we did. Doesn't mean anything has to change between us. Right?"

She nodded automatically, but was that even possible? Sex *always* changed things, no matter what the circumstances. Would they ever be able to hang out, have a few drinks together without thinking about last night? Without worrying that it might happen again?

Without *wanting* it to happen again?

Taking a deep breath, she locked all those thoughts away and pulled him into a hug. Forget not touching, forget the fragile bubble. They'd been friends for too long for something like this to come between them.

"Just... don't be weird, okay?" she said, her words muffled against his chest. He smelled different today, like her soap and shampoo instead of his, but it was still Henny. Still her best friend. "I can't handle it if you get weird on me now."

His chest shook with a small laugh. "I'm not the one being weird, Bex."

Okay, maybe he wasn't being weird, exactly. Just distant. But that almost bugged her more. Why wasn't he freaking out? Whether he could remember it or not, was the idea of sex with her really so inconsequential to him? Was sex in *general* inconsequential to him? How many women had he been with? How many mornings had he woken up just like this, hazy and hungover, eager to make his escape?

Slow down, crazy train.

"Sorry," Bex said, finally drawing herself up. She was being ridiculous. Henny was the only man in her life who'd never disappointed her, twenty-five years and counting. That wasn't about to start now. "You're right."

He flashed his trademark smirk. "Care to put it in writing?"

"Don't push your luck."

"Listen, I need to take off," he said, checking his phone. "Gotta hit the gym, then run some errands. You guys opening the pub today?"

"Fee's uncle gave us the green light on the plumbing, so we should be okay."

"I'll stop in later. Sound good?"

The knot inside her chest loosened, and Bex finally allowed a smile. Working out? Stopping in at Big Laurie's? That was all normal. Normal was good. Normal was just perfect.

"Good," she repeated, nodding for emphasis. She wasn't sure whether she was trying to convince Henny or herself, but she was already feeling a little better about the whole thing. Meeting Henny's eyes again, she said, "So we're... okay?"

He cupped the back of her head, stroking her ear with his thumb. The gesture was meant to be comforting, but now it made her shiver. Suddenly she was noticing things about him she'd never paid much attention to before—the violet ring around his ocean-blue irises, the brush of his calloused fingers on her ear, the perfect cupid's bow of his full lips—lips that had probably closed around her nipples last night, sucking and teasing...

He pressed his forehead to hers and closed his eyes.

"We are *always* okay," he whispered.

After a beat, he pulled back and kissed her forehead —something he'd done hundreds of times. Maybe even thousands. It was a gesture so familiar she couldn't remember a time when he *hadn't* done it.

So why, after all these years of hellos and goodbyes, was she suddenly trembling?

CHAPTER SIX

"Don't tell me we lost the bet." Walker skated up to Henny the moment he stepped onto the ice, punching him in the shoulder. "What the hell are you doing here? Thought you were on house arrest."

Henny took a slug of Gatorade. He was cotton-mouthed and dizzy as hell, but after a failed attempt to work out at his home gym, he found himself driving over to the practice arena. Gallagher hadn't really said one way or the other about practices during his suspension, so he'd decided to take the chance.

Forcing a grin, Henny said, "Guess I'm just a sucker for your love, Walker Dunn. Where's Gallagher?"

"Conference call," Dunn said. "Eva's in charge."

"You must *love* that," Henny said.

"I let her have her way on the ice, she let's me have my way in the bedroom. Win-win."

Henny grunted. "Don't let her hear you say that. You'll be sleeping with the dog."

"Speaking of having your way in the bedroom, how was *your* night, sunshine?"

"Fine." Henny finished the Gatorade, then chucked the bottle into the trash. "I need to warm up. Catch you in a few."

After a couple laps around the rink, Henny slid back into formation with Dunn and the rest of the guys, lining up for Eva's power skating and edgework drill combos. Her particular brand of torture was exactly what Henny needed today. Something hard, painful, and punishing to blast the lingering booze from his system and obliterate all thoughts of Bex.

Naked.

Touching herself.

In her bed.

Next to him.

Jesus.

His dick bulged at the memory, even as his brain warned him to cut it out. He hadn't even *begun* to process what had happened between them. The fact that neither of them could remember the details might've been a blessing... if only Henny hadn't woken up to an eyeful of her sweet, creamy flesh...

Lock it down, asshole.

Refocusing on the ice, he watched as Eva demonstrated the newest drill, then launched himself toward the other end of the rink with the rest of the pack. The snap of cold air made his eyes water, but he pushed on, slashing over the ice, pumping harder and faster, getting himself into the zone.

The slash of blades, the hum of the ice machines, the shouts of his teammates, Eva's shrill whistle... the sounds of the Tempest practice arena were familiar and comforting, but no matter how hard he worked, all thoughts led back to Bex.

How the fuck did we end up in bed last night?

He replayed everything he could recall, but things got real fuzzy after the tequila. Was there a kiss? He remembered looking at her mouth, remembered the shot of desire he'd felt when she licked the lime from his thumb. There were a few more shots after that, her laughter, the silky brush of her hair in his fingers, the taste of her skin... Did she climb into his lap? Had he grabbed her, pinned her against the wall as she begged for more, or was that a dream?

Fuck. Putting the pieces together was like trying to hold water.

"Feel free to join us any time, nineteen!" Eva shouted from the goal line. The rest of his team members were already lined up for another drill, leaving Henny in the dust. He'd completely missed the whistle.

When he got into the lineup, Dunn nudged him.

"What the fuck happened last night? Looks like you went three rounds with a yeti and lost."

"Smells like it, too," Roscoe said. "Weren't you with Bex last night?"

"So you're my secretary now?" Henny asked. "You need to know my schedule?"

Dunn and Roscoe exchanged a look, but before Henny could defend himself, Eva was shouting at him to get moving.

Whatever.

He took off down the ice. On the outside, he was all sharp turns and adrenaline, pushing himself faster and harder, keeping up with Eva's demands. But inside he was in knots. Guilt burned a hot path straight to his gut.

He'd gotten his best friend shitfaced, in all likelihood fucked her senseless, didn't remember a goddamn thing, then bailed on her before breakfast because he didn't have the balls to sit down and talk it out like a man. If some other asshole had done that to her, he'd make damn sure that guy wouldn't mess with her again. Hell, that guy wouldn't even be able to *walk*.

But now that guy was him.

How the fuck was he supposed to kick his own ass?

He skated over to the bench and grabbed a water bottle, pouring it over his face and mouth. When he shook it off and opened his eyes, Dunn and Roscoe were standing in front of him, gaping.

"You two want my autograph?" he snapped.

Dunn kicked ice into his face. "You wanna tell us why you're being such a dick?"

"Nah, I'd rather just be a dick in peace. Keep the mystery alive." He was about to skate away, but Eva was gunning for them across the ice, her eyes lasering in on Henny.

Great.

"Are you ladies done chitchatting?" she asked. "Or do you need a few more minutes to powder your delicate asses?"

Henny cracked a smile—first real one all day. He took great joy in the fact that even though Eva was engaged to Dunn, she busted his balls just as hard as she busted everyone else's.

"Thirty-eight, forty-six." She thumbed toward center ice. "I want you two working on your edges. We've got a tough matchup with Carolina tonight, and we're down a starter." Then, glaring at Henny, "You should probably call it a day, nineteen. Gallagher's heading over soon, and he's in no mood for your shit."

"Eva," Henny began, but before he could say another word, she held up her hand, eyes blazing.

"I'm not in the mood for you, either," she said. "In case that wasn't clear."

"Over the Fellino shit?" he asked. Yeah, it was a dick move on his part, putting the team in jeopardy by getting himself suspended. She had a right to be frustrated, but this seemed a little over the top, even for her. "I know I screwed up, but he attacked my boys. Even knowing the outcome, I wouldn't change a thing."

Eva said nothing, just continued to glower. "Are you leaving?"

"No. I need the workout."

"Then get to work," she snapped.

The knots in his gut tightened. "Eva, am I missing something here?"

"Don't you pretend like you don't know what's going on," she said, jabbing a finger into his chest.

"But… I *don't* know what's going on."

Eva huffed. "Just for that you're all getting another round of passing drills. And you, Walker Dunn, are sleeping with Bilbo Baggins tonight."

Henny actually laughed at that one. Bilbo was her seven-year-old daughter Gracie's St. Bernard—big fucking drool monster.

She skated away, leaving the air temperature about twenty degrees colder.

Roscoe followed, close on her heels. "Eva? What about me? Do you still like *me*?"

"Great," Dunn said to Henny. "Thanks a lot, asshole."

Henny kicked the ice, heart hammering in his chest as he finally figured it out. This wasn't about Fellino and the boarding call at all.

"Fuck," he said to Dunn, who stood by his side despite the evil glare from his fiancée. "I told you we shouldn't have gotten those two together."

"What two?"

"Eva and Bex," Henny said. "They must've talked this morning. Christ."

"What's up with Bex? I thought—" Suddenly, Walker's face fell. "Dude, did she see our texts last night? She knows we're just fucking around, right? I never meant—"

"I think we fucking did it."

"You... Wait." Dunn pulled off his helmet, took a step closer. "*What*?"

"You need a drawing? Me and Bex. Pretty sure we had sex last night."

"*Pretty* sure? Dude."

Roscoe skated back over with three sticks and a puck. "Eva's on a rampage. Better get—"

"Henny and Bex finally left the friend zone," Dunn said, taking his stick from Roscoe. That motherfucker had the nerve to smirk.

Henny blew out a breath. "Now that we're all caught up, I gotta go. Good talk."

"But what's this 'pretty sure' shit?" Dunn asked.

"I don't remember it," Henny said. "Neither does she. We were drinking, and then... who the fuck knows? We woke up in her bed this morning hungover as shit."

He left out the rest of the details of that little wake-up call.

"Jesus," Dunn said. "How much did you drink?"

"Don't ask."

"Let me get this straight," Roscoe said. "You finally slept with Bex, making all of our dreams come true, and you don't fucking *remember* it?" Roscoe grabbed a handful of Henny's hair, gave him a good shake. "You sure *you* weren't the one who got his bell rung against the boards?"

"Touch me like that again, and you'll get *your* bell rung." Henny jerked out of his grasp, a fresh wave of dizziness crashing over his head.

"Last chance, boys," Eva shouted. "Passing drills. Now. Or you're all getting written up."

The three of them geared up again and started their punishment drills.

"So what happens now?" Dunn asked, passing the puck to Henny. "Friends with benefits, or...?"

Henny slapped it over to Roscoe. "You think I'd let it happen again?"

"Why not?" Dunn asked. "You two are tight as hell. You're both adults. You're obviously into each other. Why does it have to be some big fucking deal?"

Henny laughed. "So you're the relationship expert now, Dr. Ruth? As I recall, you got your panties in quite a bunch over your little ice princess there, crying into your whiskey on Christmas while Roscoe and I consoled your weepy ass."

"I can vouch for that," Roscoe said. He banked the puck around the corner, sending Dunn chasing after it. Dunn nailed it back in Henny's direction.

"She's not into it," Henny said. "Neither am I. Last night never should've happened."

Dunn and Roscoe exchanged another one of their special little looks, then Roscoe said, "Dude. Pretty sure last night was years in the making."

Henny shook his head. It was pointless to explain—they wouldn't understand. No one did. Just because Bex was smart and funny and knew almost all of his secrets... Just because she'd been there for him in all the ways that mattered... And yeah, just because she was fucking beautiful... So what? That didn't mean he wanted to fuck her. Didn't mean he wanted their friendship to be anything more than that—friendship.

Did he?

Did *she*?

Oh, fuck. What if she had feelings for him, and he'd just been too dumb to see it all these years? What if she thought *he* had feelings? What if all this shit had already wrecked their friendship?

His head was spinning again.

"Well apparently Bex told your fiancée the whole story, so if anyone knows anything, it's Eva." Henny slapped the puck over to Dunn as they made their way back toward the rest of the group. He hated himself for what he was about to ask, but he was at a total fucking loss, grasping at straws. "Maybe you could talk to Eva, find out where Bex's head is at?"

"Noooo." Dunn barked out a laugh, slamming the puck down to the blue line where second-line forward Lance Fahey was waiting to scoop it up. "There's not enough room in that dog house for both of us, my friend."

"Plus," Roscoe chimed in, "Dunn's a cuddler. Kind of invasive if you're not into it."

"Look," Dunn said, "I'm the last guy to advocate talking about your feelings. But maybe you should, you know, talk about your feelings. Sit her down, lay it on the line, see if there's more to this than friendship."

"There isn't," Henny insisted. "I don't have feelings for her—not like that. We're—"

"Incoming!" Out of nowhere, a blue-and-silver burst shot across the ice, crashing into Henny from the side.

Just one of the guys fucking around, but today was *not* the day. Henny twisted around and grabbed the guy's jersey, slamming him against the boards.

The guy was laughing his stupid ass off.

"I come to check you out," he said, his damn Russian accent like a jackhammer to Henny's skull.

Kuznetsov.

Russian hockey players are my Kryptonite...

He tightened his grip on the jersey, shoving Kooz harder against the boards.

Eva blew her whistle.

Fuck. Henny was losing his shit. Backing off, he released Kooz, smoothed out the wrinkles in his jersey. "Sorry. Bad day."

"Hey! Don't turn into mush on me, nineteen." Kooz flashed him a smile that left no doubt as to why Bex had a thing for the Russian goalie.

Asshole.

"Just friends, huh?" Dunn shook his head, skating away with a smirk the size of Texas plastered across his smug face.

"One question." Roscoe clapped Henny on the back. "When can we start calling you guys Benny? No good? How about Hex?"

If this shit wasn't so supremely fucked, Henny might've laughed at that one. "Whenever you want your ass beat. That'd be a good time."

"Rain check? I've got drills to finish." Still laughing, Roscoe skated off.

Henny let him go. Didn't matter what the guys

thought. Playing it cool was the only way to go here. The only way to not make things worse.

So as confused and—unfortunately—turned on as Henny was, that's what he'd do. Play it cool. Move on with his life. And forget this whole mess had ever happened.

CHAPTER SEVEN

"Any cleaner and we'll be able to do surgery in here." Fee reached across the bar and took the rag from Bex's hand, tossing it into the bucket behind them.

"We're a food and beverage service establishment, Fiona. Clean is the bare minimum."

Fee folded her arms over her chest and smirked.

Bex huffed. "We can't afford bad Yelp reviews over an unclean area."

"Yelp reviews. Got it." Fee sat on a stool and popped her elbows up on the bar. "Is Yelp our entire marketing strategy, then?"

"Laugh if you want, but online customer reviews are critical for social proof." Bex grabbed a stack of papers from under the bar—charts and graphs, a few notes, the marketing plan she'd been working on before she'd started cleaning. "Read page seven. Studies show that negative reviews can actually prime people to have a bad experience, so even if it's not technically bad, they'll still believe it was. Then *they* leave negative reviews, and on and on, and soon it becomes an endless cycle of one-stars. Businesses have been doomed by lesser things, Fee."

"Social proof. Bad reviews. Doom, doom, doom. Got it." Fee shuffled the papers into a neat stack, setting it back on the bar. "In the meantime, whenever you're ready to tell me what's *really* going on, I'll be right here. Waiting patiently. Not making a mess."

Bex blew out a breath, her emotions rising up again like a wave. She'd tried to stop thinking about it, but her mind was completely wrapped up with Henny. After the most awkward goodbye ever, Bex hadn't heard a word from him all day. It's not like he *had* to check in with her. It's just that usually, he did. Especially on days when he didn't have a game.

Bex stared at her phone screen. "Can you text me? I think my phone service is screwy."

Fee took Bex's phone away. "Your brain is screwy. You're totally obsessing. What is going on?"

It was a long moment before Bex could make the words come out of her mouth, and even then, she had a hard time completing the sentence. "Henny and I... I'm pretty sure we..."

"Oh." Fee's eyes widened dramatically. "Oh! Oh my God! What happened?"

Bex told her the story. It didn't take long, considering she didn't remember most of it.

"And now it's just... it's weird," Bex said. "He said everything was cool this morning, but how can it be? He's probably home right now planning his escape from me."

"Bex. Henny's a good fucking guy, and I don't say that often. Do you honestly think he'd ditch you over a night of drunken sex that neither of you even remembers?"

No, she didn't think that. Not really. But it wasn't that simple. Whether they'd remembered it or not, something happened between them. They'd crossed the formerly uncrossable line, and there was no going back. Things would continue to get awkward. Then they'd start avoiding each other—cancelling plans, making excuses, hiding. Bex hated confrontation, so she'd simply pull away. Henny couldn't deal with rejection, so he wouldn't chase her.

She explained all this to Fee.

"And one day," she continued, her throat tight and raw from holding back tears, "I'll be picking out tomatoes at Wegmans and someone will bump into me, and I'll look into his eyes and smile, letting him pass right on by, and later on I'll be like, hey, I think I used to know that guy. And I'll get this weird pain in my chest but I won't know why and then I'll cry myself to sleep and—"

"Hey." Fee reached across the bar and grabbed her arm, giving her a comforting squeeze. "It's possible you're overthinking this. Just a little."

"I'm not." Yeah, her brain liked to kick into high gear, project into the future, worry about crazy things that hardly ever came to fruition. But this was different. There's no way things would stay the same between them. Sometimes, you just couldn't go back, no matter how hard you wished for it.

"We've been friends since grade school. He lived with us for the last two years of high school." Bex grabbed a knife and cutting board and got to work on the day's citrus prep, trying to calm her breathing. "And now it's all wrecked."

"In all that time, you two never thought about... something more?" Fee asked.

"Nope." It was the truth. For the first ten years of their friendship, boys weren't even on Bex's radar. Then in high school, they watched as all their friends paired off, hooked up, and quickly crashed and burned. She and Henny had a pact, even if unspoken—nothing like that would ever come between them, would ever put their friendship at risk.

"You never fooled around? Not even a kiss?"

"No, Fee. I'm telling you. It's not—it *wasn't* like that

with us."

Despite what everyone thought, the last and only time she'd seen Henny naked was in high school, just after graduation. They'd wandered away from the beach party and dared each other to strip down and wade into Lake Erie, only to discover later that a fellow prankster had swiped their clothes. They ran all the way back to her car, giggling and freezing their assess off, fighting over a musty old blanket she'd found in the back seat. They couldn't even talk, their teeth were chattering so hard. When they got back to Bex's house, her mother caught them trying to sneak inside—Henny with his hands covering his junk and Bex wrapped up like a wet burrito—and immediately assumed the worst.

It took years for Bex to convince her mother that nothing had happened between them, and some days she still wasn't sure Mom believed it.

After that, she had no interest in seeing Henny again without his clothes on, and she *knew* he felt the same way. And if she hadn't known it before, he'd made it perfectly obvious that morning, bailing before he'd even touched his coffee or bagel.

Henny never said no to food.

Fee offered a gentle smile. "Has it occurred to you that maybe you two have actual feelings for each other, and *that's* why you ended up in bed together?"

"Feelings? For Henny? No." Bex chopped a lime into

pieces so tiny, they were practically liquid. "No way. Eww. Just... no."

"Did you... did you just say *eww*? About Kyle Henderson?"

"Yes. And I'll say it again. Eww!"

"We *are* talking about the same guy, right? NHL's Sexiest Player for, like, ten years running?"

Bex rolled her eyes, reaching for an orange. "Of course he's hot. Of course he's built like a Greek god. And fine, he's basically the perfect mix of sweet-as-pie and stubborn-as-an-ass. And don't even get me started on those eyes. Or his stupidly long lashes. Or that hair. But those are just facts—totally objective."

"Oh, totally."

"Besides, he's a hockey player. Way more angst than they're worth."

Fee arched a brow. "Eva would probably disagree."

"Walker and Eva are exceptions to the rule. They're completely obsessed with each other."

"I don't know, Bex. That glow she gets when she's looking at her man?"

Bex pointed at Fee with the knife. "Exactly. Obsessed."

"Whatever you call it," Fee said, "I've seen it on *you* every time Henny walks into the bar."

Bex's cheeks flamed. What was Fee talking about? She shook her head so hard it ached. "Hardly. It's just...

always hot in here. I'm probably sweating. That's not the same thing as being obsessed *or* in love."

Bex hadn't known Walker and Eva that long, but whenever they were together, you couldn't help but feel their love. It was the special, real-deal, once-in-a-lifetime kind of love. The kind Bex had stopped believing in when her last relationship imploded.

But the way Fee was looking at her now, like she knew some secret Bex just couldn't get clued in on…

Was it possible she had feelings for Henny? *Those* kind of feelings?

Her stomach fizzed at the thought, but she immediately dismissed it. Her body, which had always been a pretty good indicator about people, had become completely unreliable since last night. Now, whenever she thought about her best friend, it was like all her wiring short-circuited, sending jolts of electricity zipping up and down her spine. And inside her chest. And… other places.

Purely physical. That was all. It *had* to be all. Because one thing Bex was sure of? She didn't crawl back to Buffalo after her epic relationship disaster just to take more risks, especially with the people she cared about. Henny's friendship was not something she'd ever gamble on—not if she could help it.

"I'm just saying you should keep an open mind," Fee said, swiping an orange slice from the cutting board and popping it into her mouth. "Yes, you've been besties since before you had your first orgasm, but so what? People change. Relationships evolve."

"Or they go nuclear. We've seen it play out in this bar a hundred times. Hello, Love Hurts?"

Last month, some dickhead biker thought he'd drop a bombshell on his wife during a game of pool—he was filing for divorce. Poor girl bawled her eyes out, and he just continued chalking his cue, calling his shots like nothing was wrong. Bex and Fee had started calling him Love Hurts because of the song playing on the pub jukebox at the time. It was like something out of a terrible movie.

Bex shook her head, remembering the poor wife. "If that's what marriage looks like—"

"I'm not telling you to propose to the guy, Bex. I just wouldn't be so quick to shoot down the possibility of something more—however tiny it may be." Fee lowered her voice, her eyes suddenly sparkling with mischief. "Especially since he's walking in that door right now. *With* flowers."

"What?" Bex's head whipped around so fast, her neck cracked. Sure enough, Henny was standing in the front entryway, kicking slush off his boots and balancing a huge bouquet in his arms.

"And there's the look." Fee pointed at Bex's face and

smirked. "I'll just go... put on some mood music. Let you two talk."

"Fee, don't you dare!" Bex reached forward for Fee's hand, but it was too late. Fee was already on the other side of the room, studying the CDs in the jukebox. Seconds later, the unmistakably nostalgic piano chords of Journey's "Don't Stop Believing" floated through the air.

Bex glared at Fee. *Laying it on a little thick there, girl.*

"Hi," Henny said, all awkward and adorable. Beneath his jacket, he wore a dark gray V-neck sweater that clung to his muscular chest and made his blue-green eyes stand out like the lake on a clear summer day. His hair was rumpled, curling up at the ends like it usually did when he went outside with wet hair.

Bex couldn't hide her smile, but she did her best to camouflage her relief. It was starting to be a regular feeling with Henny, and she wasn't sure she liked it. "Hi yourself."

"Journey, huh? I was just, uh..." He looked at the jukebox, then back to Bex, thrusting the flowers across the bar. "These are for you."

The bouquet was lush and vibrant, full of her favorite flowers—bright orange tiger lilies, white peonies, and peach roses.

She searched her memory, but couldn't recall a time when Henny had given her flowers. She'd had her appendix out in college, and he'd brought her donuts and Burger Hut and fuzzy pajamas with pockets, and never had a more perfect gift existed. But… flowers?

She filled up a clean plastic pitcher with water and set it on the bar, then unwrapped the flowers from their tissue paper so she could trim the stems. "What's the occasion?"

"I wanted to thank you," he said. "For last night."

Her eyes snapped up to meet his, her body instantly rigid. *Thank you? Seriously?* "Last night wasn't a favor, Hen."

"For the nachos, I mean. And the movie." He wrapped a hand around the back of his neck. "Definitely took my mind off the suspension."

Bex arched a brow. "Is that why you ran out this morning?"

"No, I decided to hit practice today," he said, clearly eager to get back to neutral ground. "Just missed seeing Gallagher, which was probably for the best. Eva was running the show."

"She told me."

"Yeah, I wondered if you guys texted or something."

"Why? Did Eva say something?"

"No, I—"

"You assumed I'd run to her with all the details?"

"Did you?"

"Did you tell Walker and Roscoe?"

The air crackled between them, and suddenly Bex

was back in high school, boiling over with a melodramatic flare so ridiculous it almost made her laugh.

Of course he'd talked to Walker and Roscoe, just like she'd talked to Eva and Fee. How could she be upset?

Bex knew her fears were completely unfounded, but that didn't make them any less real. Especially not when Henny was looking at her that way, his eyes turning stormy in the dim light of the pub.

"Bex," he said, suddenly serious. "We need to talk."

Her heart thudded in her chest. Desperately, she tried to remember the symbolism of tiger lilies and peach roses. Friendship? Love? Loyalty? Was this the best-friend breakup bouquet? Or the let's-give-this-dating-thing-a-whirl one? Or maybe it was the I-sure-wish-I-remembered-fucking-you-last-night, let's-try-it-again-sober one? Did they even make a bouquet for that?

Frozen in place, she wrapped her hand around the stems and grabbed her citrus knife, waiting for Henny to spit it out.

"I, uh…" His eyes roamed the room, back to the juke-box, the pool table, finally settling on the papers she'd left on the bar. He thumbed through the stack, reading over her marketing notes. "What's all this?"

Really? We're playing this game now?

"Just some stuff I've been working on for the pub," she said.

He flipped through a few more pages, nodding his approval. "Wow. You did all this research?"

"Yep."

"You really need to set up that appointment with my guy."

"Henny, can we just—"

"I'll call him right now." Henny pulled out his phone. "I'm sure he'd love to meet you."

"Stop. Please, stop." Bex appreciated his support, but Henny did *not* come in here today with flowers and that tight sweater and those impossibly blue-green eyes and that manly, sexy, freshly-showered scent that was doing very naughty things to her insides just to talk about her marketing plans.

Why was he stalling?

The longer he stood there, not saying anything, letting the awkward tension between them thicken like pea soup, the more upset she got. Why couldn't he just say it? Whatever *it* was? Good or bad, she needed to hear it. They needed to clear the air and move forward.

She looked at him expectantly. Blinked her eyes. Cleared her throat. And still, the man was infuriatingly silent.

"So, did you need anything else?" Bex gripped the knife and whacked off the bottom of the flower stems.

Henny flinched.

"No. I mean, yeah. I just..." His eyes darted up to the

ceiling, then back down again. "Like I said. Thanks for the nachos."

Thanks for the nachos? Is that what the kids are calling it these days?

She whacked at the stems again. And again. And once more for good measure. Because if she stopped chopping, if she stopped moving, if she looked up for even one second and saw pity in those ocean-blue eyes, she was going to lose it.

Chop. Chop. Whack.

"Bex."

Whack.

"Look at me. Please," Henny said, soft and sad and vulnerable, nothing at all like the bad-boy hockey star everyone else usually saw.

She finally looked up, not bothering to hide the tears that glazed her eyes. What was the point? He had to know this was ripping her apart inside. How could it not?

"I screwed up," he said. "Believe it or not, sometimes I make mistakes."

Her heart hit her stomach. It shouldn't have hurt like that, but it did. "So you're saying it was a mistake?"

"The worst."

She gave the stems another whack, narrowly missing her thumb.

"Wait, no!" Henny said. "I meant *me*. The way I reacted this morning. That was the mistake."

Henny took away her knife, then covered her hands with his. His touch was warm and strong and familiar, but she was anything but comforted. The feel of his callused hands only served to remind her of last night. Of what they'd done. Of what she'd missed.

Hands in her hair, on her ass, gripping her thighs...

"Last night was *not* a mistake," he said, squeezing her hands. "Most likely, it was pretty great. But yeah, I could've handled it better."

"Me too," she admitted, blowing out a breath. "Guess I got a little freaked. Okay, a lot freaked." She glanced at the stem graveyard on her cutting board. "I'm being a total psycho, right?"

"Only about twenty percent psycho."

"What's the other eighty?"

"Just... my girl." Henny grinned, the lines of his face smoothing out the tiniest little bit. "Right?"

Bex's stomach did a little flip. Fee's earlier advice echoed. *I'm just saying you should keep an open mind...*

She took a deep breath and searched his eyes, letting the possibilities run wild.

Could we be together like that?

She tried to imagine going on a date with him. Cooking dinner for him. Waiting outside the locker room after a game to give him that first victory hug. Watching the away games on television, rooting for her man as excitedly as she did at the home games.

She pictured him hanging out with her at the bar, waiting for her to close up for the night. Encouraging her to meet with his finance guy. Cutting the grass at her mom's house in the summer. Checking in on both of them whenever he could.

In other words, all the best-friend stuff they'd been doing all along.

That settled it.

Just because they'd accidentally had sex—sex they couldn't even remember—didn't mean they were relationship material. Certainly not *capital-L Love* material. People who believed that a night of drunken debauchery led to wedding bells obviously watched too many movies.

Looking at you, Fee.

Bex arranged the flowers in the beer pitcher, admiring her handiwork. They were a little short on account of her overzealous knifing, but the blooms were gorgeous—bright bursts of color floating above the lush white peonies.

"Sunshine in a vase," she said, moving them to the register area, out of reach of the rowdy customers that would soon file in. Turning back to Henny, she said, "I don't want anything to come between us. Especially not sex."

"It won't. I would never let it, Bex. I promise." His face was sincere, eyes full of the familiar mix of protectiveness and intensity she'd come to know and love about him.

"So, we're moving forward?" she asked. "Putting this whole thing in the rearview?"

"After we douse it in gasoline and torch it."

"With a flamethrower." Bex laughed, the muscles in her neck and shoulders relaxing for the first time since she woke up in Henny's naked embrace this morning. He was back. *They* were back. Friends to the end, just like always.

"That's my girl. Hundred percent Bex." Henny leaned across the bar and gave her a very platonic, very normal kiss on the forehead. "Okay, I need to pack. Gallagher wants me on the team flight after the Carolina game tonight."

"When are you playing?" she asked. The Tempest had an away week coming up, but Henny was still riding out his suspension.

"Not till Toronto, but I'll be practicing with the team so everyone's ready when I get back in the lineup."

"Stay out of trouble, Kyle Henderson." Bex narrowed her eyes. "I'll be watching every game."

"You'd better be." He held her gaze a moment longer, then knocked on the bar twice as if that settled things.

Seconds later, Heart's "Barracuda" was on the jukebox and Henny was out the door.

Bex buried her face in the flowers, inhaling their sweet scent. She'd officially survived their first post-awkward-forgotten-sex reunion, and it was everything she could've hoped for. The air was cleared. The reset button on their friendship firmly pressed. And, she thought, admiring the bright blooms, she'd gotten some gorgeous flowers out of the deal.

So why did it feel like someone had just scooped out her insides?

CHAPTER EIGHT

The Toronto Mavericks' stadium was stuffed to the gills with insane, rowdy fans that would love to see Henny take a beating. Henny didn't care. Couldn't afford to. It was the third of five games on the road for the Tempest —Henny's first night back on the ice since the suspension—and letting the home team's crazy fans throw off his game was not an option.

He was doing a fine enough job of that on his own.

Midway into second period, Gallagher called for a line change, yanking Henny off the ice with Roscoe and Dunn.

It was an unusual call for the coach—the starting lineup was tight as hell, and they usually worked together like a well-oiled machine. The only time they changed it up was if one of them got hurt—or if he was having a seriously off night.

There on the player's bench, Gallagher steamed. "Get your head in the game, nineteen, or your ass is on the bench for the rest of the game. And you two?" He glared at Dunn and Roscoe. "Collect your boy and keep your line together."

Gallagher returned his attention to the ice, leaving Henny to stew in his own mounting shame. Behind them, a group of assholes with faces painted in Mavericks' red and gold banged on the glass.

"Aren't Canadians supposed to be nice?" Henny asked, flipping them off.

"Not on game night," Roscoe said. "Come on, Hen. This ain't your first rodeo."

Dunn grunted. "This rate, it might be his last. What the fuck, nineteen?"

Henny yanked off his helmet, shoved a hand through his sweat-drenched hair. "I'm just a little off my game tonight."

"You think?" Dunn snapped. "Brilliant observation, Watson. Hey! If this hockey thing shits the bed, you might have a shot as a private dick. Emphasis on *dick*."

Dunn grabbed a bottle of Gatorade, not meeting Henny's eyes.

Henny couldn't blame him. Tempest was up by one, but they should've been up by at least four. Henny'd been playing like shit all night, missing key passes, taking sloppy shots, giving up the puck more times than he could count.

"First game back in a week, sold-out crowd, on the road...." Roscoe shrugged, busting out his "good cop" grin. "Bound to be a little rusty."

Roscoe, the eternal fucking optimist. Complete opposite of Dunn, who was so worked up his face was turning purple. "This has nothing to do with the suspension and everything to do with—"

"Don't." Henny held up his hands. He didn't need Dunn to spell it out for him. Not like he could forget about her.

Fresh pain jabbed his heart. He hadn't spoken with Bex in days. After the flowers, he'd gone back to avoiding her, looking for excuses to miss her calls and texts.

Joke was on him, though, because those calls never came. She was avoiding him, too.

A week on the road was supposed to put things back in perspective. Time apart should've helped Henny clear his head, get his focus back on the game and his rapidly disintegrating career.

But he was a wreck.

"Fuck yeah, Kooz! That's how it's done!" Dunn was on his feet, shouting across the ice. Looked like Kuznetsov had just made a crazy save. Henny hadn't seen shit. He forced himself to locate the puck, watching as Fahey skated it down the ice.

Fahey and his wingers played a tight game. Like Henny and his boys, the second-line offense had great synergy, reading each other's movements and playing to each other's strengths as they stormed the Toronto goal zone. The Mavericks goalie was tough as hell, but he wasn't fast enough to stop Fahey's over-the-shoulder shot.

The crowd roared in frustration. Tempest was up by two now, and Dunn and Roscoe cheered. Henny wanted to join them. He wanted to be happy for his team. He wanted to get back on the fucking ice. But his mind kept looping back to Bex, again and again and again.

He'd gone over to the bar that day with every intention of clearing the air. But no matter how hard he'd tried to pretend everything was normal, Henny just couldn't look at Bex the same way. For twenty-five years they'd been friends. *Best* friends. They'd shared a bond that transcended all others. Even his team—guys he'd do just about anything for—came second to Bex. And the women he'd been with in the past? Hell, none of them could hold a candle to her. Not where it really counted.

Yeah, any man could see she was gorgeous. It's not like Henny couldn't acknowledge a simple fact. But before the other night, hormonal high school fantasies aside, he'd honestly never entertained thoughts about being with her like that. Bex and Henny were friends. The best. His mind simply hadn't allowed for any other possibilities.

But now, whenever he thought of Bex—pretty much every five seconds—his gut twisted, and it wasn't just guilt. Seeing her at the bar the other day had nearly undone him. She was different. Everything was different.

Fuck.

What was happening? Was he just being protective, feeling guilty for putting her in that situation, especially knowing she'd been through hell and back with her ex?

Or did he have feelings for her?

Bex was the most important person in his life. But when he remembered the soft feel of her skin on his face that morning, the curve of her bare shoulder when he'd woken up next to her... Hell, he'd never been so turned on in his life. Even now, hundreds of miles away from her, he was hard as fuck.

He was totally hot for her, and there wasn't a damn thing to be done about it.

Second period ended with a buzz, jerking Henny back to the present. Fahey had scored another goal. Henny hadn't even realized it.

Get your head in the game, asshole.

Henny took a swig of Gatorade, forcing himself to stay in the moment.

Hockey. Toronto. Start of the third.

Across the bench, Gallagher eyed them up, assessing.

"You good?" Roscoe asked.

Henny nodded, strapping his helmet back into place. Yeah, he was good. Fine. Had to be.

"Do *not* fuck this up." Dunn smacked him on the helmet, finally meeting his eyes. His snarl twisted into a smile, and Henny blew out a breath. "Let's rock these motherfuckers."

Dunn signaled to Gallagher that they were ready to roll, and seconds later, the starters were back on the ice, lining up for the third period face-off.

By some monumental effort, Henny shoved aside all thoughts of Bex for the rest of the game, channeling all his energy into beating the Mavs. One minute into the third, he scored his first goal of the night, then assisted Roscoe on another soon after. In the final minute of the game, refs nailed the Mavs' left winger for high-sticking, and Henny scored again on the penalty shot, closing out the game with a six-three win.

The boys were pumped. Gallagher and the suits were marginally appeased, but Henny couldn't complain about their lack of enthusiasm. Tonight could've just as easily gone the other way.

After a brief recap, the team hit the visitors' gym for the post-game workout, then headed into the showers. It was still fairly early in Hogtown, and after the excitement of the win, the single guys were ready to check out the scene, clock in a few hours of fun before their morning flight to Minnesota.

Wasn't too long ago that Henny would've lead the charge.

But tonight, there was only one woman on his mind.

And he was done pretending he could go for more than a day without hearing her voice.

CHAPTER NINE

Bex hadn't heard from Henny since the "Thanks for the Nachos" incident. She was beginning to worry that the flowers had meant goodbye rather than gratitude, when her phone finally buzzed with his text.

Part of her wanted to ignore it, but as usual, one word from her best friend and her anger melted away.

HENNY: *You see me out there tonight?*

BEX: *Out where?*

HENNY: *Very funny. Hope you made a new sign for me, woman.*

BEX: *Oh, you had a game tonight? I can't be expected to keep up with your sporting events. I'm a busy woman, Henderson.*

HENNY: *Too busy for this face? Doubt it.*

He sent her a selfie, all goofy-ass smile and crazy eyes. He was in his hotel room, dressed in a faded black

Radiohead shirt—they'd gotten matching ones at a concert in New York City during one of their college Christmas breaks. His hair was sticking up everywhere, rumpled and adorable, and her fingers curled inward against her palm, itching to touch him.

She closed her eyes, remembering the scent of his skin, the warmth of his kiss on her forehead. The press of his face on her chest, his hair tickling her breasts.

Opening her eyes, Bex took a deep breath, fingers hovering over the phone screen. Then, before she could talk herself out of being honest…

BEX: *I miss that face, Henny. I miss YOU.*

HENNY: *Yeah. I've been kind of a schmuck. :-(*

BEX: *Pro tip? Stop ghosting on me, schmuck. One of these days I'm going to kick your ass. Also, I've been a schmuck too. :-(*

HENNY: *Tell you what. I'll bring you some more flowers, you give me my sign, we'll call it even.*

Bex smiled. The roses from his bouquet were hanging over her dresser, drying. Every time she walked into her bedroom, she caught a whiff of their sweet scent and thought of Henny.

Not that she needed external stimulation to think of Henny. He was pretty much the only thing on her mind lately.

BEX: *Next time say it with chocolate. You heading out with the guys tonight?*

HENNY: *Trying to ditch me already?*

BEX: *Ha! I've been trying to ditch you since the 90s.*

HENNY: *Guess you need to try harder. I'm not going anywhere. Uh, recent dickishness notwithstanding. Promise.*

Bex responded with a smiley emoji. He'd already made that promise in some form or another three times now. She didn't doubt his intentions, only his follow-through. Or her follow-through. Things were getting ridiculous.

She wasn't ready for the conversation to end, but she didn't know what else to say.

A minute passed. Then another. She was about to call it a night when the phone rang with his ringtone.

Bex hit the answer button and smiled. "If you're calling for bail money, I can't help you."

Henny cracked up, the sound going right to her heart. God, she'd missed that laugh.

"No bail money, babe. Not for me, anyway. I'm all alone in my hotel room tonight."

"Should I even *ask* what you're up to?"

"Truth?"

"Always."

"Trying not to think about you."

Bex's stomach did a little flip. Before she could stop herself, the words were out. "Same here."

"Yeah? How's that working out?"

"It's not." She closed her eyes, listening to the soft

sounds of Henny breathing, trying to match the steady rhythm to her own.

"God, I'm glad to hear your voice," he said.

"Hmm. Rough night on the ice?"

"Something like that."

"You looked good, though," she said, glad to be back on familiar ground. Hockey. His moves on the ice. Not their relationship and missing each other and thinking about each other and all the stuff they were so obviously avoiding.

As far as strategies went, avoidance was a good one.

Right?

"Got through all three periods on your feet," she went on. "No time in the penalty box. Look who's out there bustin' a move, not getting suspended!"

"Last time I got suspended, I got nachos."

"Among other things." Bex laughed. She had to. Because if they weren't going to talk about what happened, they had to at least joke about it, or they'd never move past it. "So, how'd everyone feel against the Mavs? Their new center is looking pretty good."

"Definitely one to watch." Henny sighed. "Hey, can we talk about something else? I need to get hockey off the brain. Tell me about your day."

"You wanna hear about my boring-ass fight with the bar plumbing?"

"You know I do."

"Another pipe burst overnight. Fee and I were greeted by a flooded bathroom this morning."

"Everything okay? I thought Fee's uncle fixed all that?"

"Different pipe. He got it patched up right away, but I was on my hands and knees all day cleaning."

"Wow. Only you could make plumbing sound sexy."

"Oh, sexy is an understatement when it comes to me. Shall I tell you what I'm wearing?"

"A guy can dream." Henny laughed, but she sensed there was more to the joke, a flicker of heat sparking up beneath the easy, familiar surface. "Long as it's not Kooz's jersey."

"No." Bex was pretty sure she'd never wear that jersey again. She couldn't even remember why she'd ever found the goalie attractive.

"Tell me," he teased. Or maybe he was begging.

She dropped her voice to a sultry, smoky tone. "I'm wearing my red flannel pajamas—the ones with little Scottie dogs all over them. They have buttons, but I'm going to let you in on a little secret." In a scandalous whisper, she said, "They're really just snaps."

"Mmm, I love snaps. Tell me more."

"I'm also wearing a pair of dark blue hiking socks with a hole in the heel, and my anti-glare computer glasses, which I somehow managed to get peanut butter on."

"Peanut butter?" Henny cracked up. "Now you're *really* driving me wild, dirty girl."

Bex returned his easy laughter, but his words left her feeling warm and fizzy, her body buzzing with an unfamiliar current. Her laughter faded, and the silence stretched between them, nothing but breath and heat and anticipation.

"Bex," he finally said, low and smoky in her ear. "I wish you were here."

"In Toronto? We went up there in the fall, remember? With Mom and—"

"No." A beat passed. Another. Then, "In my bed."

She shivered at his admission, the moment between them delicious and forbidden. They were playing a dangerous game, but here in the dark after all those nights of radio silence, Bex wanted to *keep* playing. To see how far they could take it before one of them backed off.

"What would you do to me?" she asked. Far from sexy, her voice was shaky now. Trembling.

"Are you..." Henny cleared his throat. "You seriously asking me that?"

Maybe it was the distance. The darkness. The strangeness that had fallen between them since that night, eradicating the boundary between "just friends" and the "something else" they'd become. From the moment she'd woken up next to him in bed, Bex had known there was no going back—not to the easy, comfortable friendship they'd always had. She had no idea what that meant for the future, but for right now? Tonight?

"Yes." Bex stretched out on her bed and licked her lips. "Tell me."

She heard rustling on the other end of the line, and she imagined him sliding between the cool, white sheets of his hotel bed, leaning back on the downy pillows. She wondered whether he was in his sweatpants or shorts. She wondered whether his eyes were closed, whether the lights were off, the blinds drawn tight, the television muted, flickering soft blue light over his skin.

But mostly, she wondered whether her best friend was as turned on as she was.

"I would take my time with you," he said, voice thick with something she didn't recognize, but liked. A lot. "Slide my hands down the front of those pajamas, popping each snap until I had you unwrapped for me like a present."

As if under a spell, Bex trailed a hand over her fake buttons, popping them and letting her shirt fall open.

"You'd arch your back and press yourself against my hands," he said, "begging me to touch you. To take you into my mouth."

Bex nearly came at the rough sound of his words, low and sexy and dangerous, each one sending a pulse of heat to her core. Unbidden, she cupped her breast, gently tugging her nipple. It stiffened instantly, aching for more. Aching for him.

Henny was right. If he were here right now, she *would* beg him for it.

"Please," she whispered. "Don't stop. Keep talking."

"Are you touching yourself for me?"

Bex bit her lip, suddenly shy. She'd never been particularly modest in bed, but this was different. This was Henny. *Her* Henny. Could their friendship survive this? Again, her thoughts started to spin, threatening to pull her out of the fantasy, but she didn't want out. She didn't want to overanalyze and worry and fret.

She wanted to keep playing.

She wanted more.

Shoving aside the fears, she trailed her hand down her stomach, then slipped it inside her panties. She was hot and wet. Needy.

In a soft voice, she made her confession. "Yes. Are... are you?"

"Am I what?" he asked. Teasing. Gentle. Inviting her into this game, one sinfully sweet word at a time.

Heat crept across her chest, her neck. "Are you touching yourself?"

"Do you want me to?"

Bex closed her eyes, flashing back to that morning in her bed, the forbidden peek beneath the sheets. She'd tried her best to forget it, but the image of his strong, solid body and massive, hard cock was permanently seared in her memory. She imagined him now, gripping himself tight, hardening just for her.

A whimper of pure pleasure escaped her lips. "Yes."

"Say it, Rebecca. Tell me *exactly* what you want. Exactly how you like it."

The sound of her full name on his lips made her melt, unleashing a flurry of delicious phrases in her mind. *I like it when you stroke yourself. I like your big hands in my hair, rough and messy. I like your mouth between my thighs…*

But as much as she wanted to, Bex couldn't make herself say the words out loud. She'd never been into dirty talk before—it always left her feeling awkward, anything but sexy.

But Henny? God, she was red hot and throbbing for him, his every word turning her into butter. She couldn't imagine what he'd feel like right here, in her bed, stone cold sober, saying these things to her. Waiting for her to tell him how she liked it.

"Tell me," he whispered.

"Hen, I don't… I've never done anything like this before," she confessed. "On the phone, I mean." Her cheeks heated. Not with embarrassment or awkwardness, but excitement. She *wanted* this. Wanted him to take her somewhere new and uncharted.

He didn't speak right away, but she heard him

shifting around, the sheets rustling. When he finally spoke, his voice was tender. "Do you want me to stop?"

"No!" Bex giggled softly. "I mean… maybe just… Can you take the lead?"

"Close your eyes," he said, still gentle. Easing her back in. Protecting her, just like always. "Picture me there with you, helping you the rest of the way out of those pajamas. Watching you."

"Touching me," she finally said. "I want you touching me."

His breath quickened in her ear, the sound sending shivers down her spine. In a low growl that made her shudder, he said, "Where?"

She slid her fingers deeper inside her panties and spread her legs. "Between my thighs. Inside my panties."

"What do you feel like?" he asked.

"Slippery. I'm so wet, Henny." She dipped a finger inside, then pulled out, coating her clit in her juices, massaging herself with gentle circles. She'd never gotten so close to the edge on her own before—not without a lot more effort. "You're driving me wild."

"Jesus," Henny whispered. Bex wondered if he could truly hear her—the soft, barely audible moans, the thud of her heartbeat, the desperate sucking sounds her body was making. All of it conspired to reveal her secrets.

"Henny!" She gasped, shocked at how quickly it was happening. "I'm right there. I'm going to—"

"Shh," he murmured. "Not yet, beautiful. I want you to stop."

God, she didn't want to. But she wasn't ready for this night to end, either. She wanted to see what else he could do to her.

Obeying, Bex slid her hand out of her panties. Between her thighs, she throbbed with unrequited desire.

"I'm taking my time with you tonight," Henny said.

"Henny," she whispered again, her hand twitching, desperate to return to her soft, wet heat. Here in the dark, Henny's deep voice in her ear, it almost felt real. Henny, touching her. Kissing her. Caressing her into a state of pure bliss. "Touch me. Please don't stop."

"No. No more touching. For the rest of the night, I'm only using my mouth."

Oh, fuck.

"I'm starting with a kiss. Sucking your bottom lip, grazing it with my teeth. Kissing my way down your neck, down to that little scar on your collar bone."

She ran her fingers over the small white ridge just inside her left shoulder, courtesy of an exposed screw on an abandoned set of monkey bars she and Henny had discovered in fifth grade behind the old Shop-N-Save. She was surprised Henny had remembered, that he'd even noticed the mark. Mostly, her clothes covered it up.

Except for that night…

"I'm not done yet," he continued. "I'm kissing your soft skin, your shoulders, my tongue tracing the curve of your breast. Buzzing your hard little nipples with my lips."

She ran her fingers over her nipples again, imagining his mouth on her flesh, the hum of his deep voice, the scratch of stubble and teeth. She wondered what he was like in bed—the real deal. Would he play rough, or take it slow? Would he talk to her like this, or just take charge?

Bex decided she didn't care. She wanted him. However, whenever. Her entire body was aching for him.

"Are you still wearing those pants?" he asked.

"Yes."

"Lose them. I want you naked now. Nothing but that soft, beautiful skin for me to taste."

She set the phone down, tearing her clothes off in record time.

"Okay," she breathed, settling back onto the bed, pressing the phone to her ear.

"Are you naked for me, beautiful?"

"Yes."

"You taste so fucking good," he said. "Your soft belly. Your hip bone. Open your legs, baby. Let me see that gorgeous pussy."

Again she obeyed, spreading her thighs, imagining Henny guiding her every move.

"You're so beautiful, Bex," he purred. "Let me taste you."

"Yes," she panted.

"My cock is so fucking hard right now, but I can't stop kissing you. Licking you. Making sure you're hot and wet and ready for me."

"I'm ready," she whispered. "I'm so close. I want you inside me."

"Are you sure?"

"It's all I can think about since that night. I want... I want you to fuck me, Henny. Hard. Fast. Deep."

Bex's cheeks flamed. It was possible she'd revealed too much, but she was too close to the edge to care. Right now, all that mattered was Henny. His voice. His hands. His mouth.

"Jesus, Bex," he said, his voice suddenly strained. He was losing control, too.

The realization filled her with a sense of power. Heat. Hope.

Despite his orders, she couldn't hold back. She needed the friction of her touch. She needed to come.

Sliding her fingers between her thighs, Bex arched her back, stroking herself again, frantic and hot.

"You feel amazing," she said. The boundary between real and imaginary—just like the one between friendship and something else—was obliterated. She was in too deep to stop now. "I love the way you touch me. The way you kiss me. The way you make me come."

Henny groaned, the sound as wild and desperate as she felt. "If I was there right now, you'd be in so much fucking trouble. I wouldn't be able to stop myself."

"I can't hold back. I'm right... I'm right there."

"Don't hold back," he said. "My tongue is deep inside that gorgeous pussy, and I want to know *exactly* what you taste like when you come."

Bex gasped as the orgasm crashed through her body, her thighs trembling, stars dancing behind her eyelids as Henny whispered dirty, delicious promises in her ear.

Seconds later, breathing hard and fast, Henny growled like an animal, deep and powerful, his raw, unguarded passion making her tremble all over again.

He'd made that sound for her. *Because* of her.

Bex had never felt so alive.

Seconds passed between them in silence, their breathing finally returning to normal.

"You okay?" Henny finally asked.

"Better than okay," she said. Her own voice was thick and syrupy. She was still in a trance. A happy, golden trance from which she never wanted to wake. "That was... wow."

"Mmm." Henny hummed into the phone, and she pictured him running his thumb back and forth over his lips. Then, after a beat, "Will you do something for me?"

She laughed. She was still naked, spread out on her bed, unable to move. "Something *else*? You're insatiable."

"You don't know the half of it."

"I'm starting to get the picture." Bex laughed. "What can I do for you?"

"Well, two favors, actually. First, burn Kooz's jersey. I'll get you one of mine."

"Deal. What's the second?"

"Stay with me? Just until I pass out?" Henny's voice was softer now, sleepy. "I want you to be the last thing I hear before I fall asleep."

CHAPTER TEN

"I can't believe we pulled that off tonight," Dunn collapsed into the seat next to Henny on the charter plane. They'd just wrapped up their final road game and were heading back to Buffalo.

Henny wasn't in the mood for another lecture, but he'd fucked up tonight, and Dunn seemed determined to rub his nose in it.

They won the game, but it was sheer dumb luck more than strategy. Defense had been tight—Kooz was on point tonight, as usual. But the offense was sloppy, and most of that was Henny's fault. Dunn and Roscoe had picked up the slack, and together the team pulled through.

No thanks to Henny.

"You pulled it together in the second," Dunn said, "but you're head is somewhere else."

Henny didn't deny it. This thing with Bex had him all twisted up, torn between wanting to keep her protected in their innocent little just-friends bubble, and wanting to tear off her panties with his teeth and fuck her into oblivion.

They'd spoken a few times since the phone sex night, but not about that. Just bar stuff. Hockey stuff. Bullshit TV stuff. They'd talked about every damn thing under the sun except the one thing Henny couldn't get off his mind.

Christ, he couldn't even think about it without getting a fucking hard-on. That night on the phone was so unexpected. And she'd been so responsive, so eager, so fucking hot.

He hadn't told the guys about that, but they knew something was up.

Henny blew out a breath, trying to shake loose the grip she had on him. "The past week... This shit with Bex has me wrecked, dude."

"Past week?" Dunn shook his head. "Try six months."

"What are you talking about?"

"You've been in a funk ever since she got back. Connect the dots."

"What dots? She's my best fucking friend."

"And you're sleeping with her now."

Henny clenched his jaw, reigning in his temper. "Look, she's gone through hell the past couple years. I'm

trying to be there for her, help her get her shit together."
A familiar pain stabbed Henny's chest, the same feeling
he always got when he thought about San Francisco. No
matter what Bex had said, Henny still blamed himself—
he should've called her more often, made more time to
visit, gotten to know this jackoff boyfriend. Maybe he
would've seen the warning signs, saved her from the
sonofabitch before things got bad.

After news of the breakup and Bex's emotional state
had reached them in Buffalo, Bex's mom Laurie had
agreed that bringing Bex home was the best move. After
a few days in California, Henny was able to convince Bex
it was for the best, too. He'd helped her pack up, settle
things with the landlord, and find a new rental house in
Buffalo.

As far as Henny could tell, she was doing great—
making friends, enjoying her work at the pub, excited
about the future for the first time in a long time. But he
still felt responsible for her. Protective. If that was
messing with his head, he'd take it. Beat out the alterna-
tive any day of the week.

"Yeah, she's on my mind," he continued. "I worry
about her. Want her to be okay. That's all there is to it."

Dunn shook his head. "I'm not buying it."

"Good. I'm not selling it."

"Jesus, Hen. It's crystal fucking clear to anyone who
knows you. Anyone who's spent more than thirty

seconds with you two in the same room. Just about the only one who doesn't see it is you."

"Doesn't see what?"

Dunn leveled him with a glare. "You're into her, asshole. I don't know if it's always been that way or just now that she's back, but this shit's been going on long before you two ended up in bed together, and your head's a mess."

Henny crossed his arms over his chest and looked out the window, away from the penetrating heat of Dunn's gaze. The plane climbed into the sky, leaving the runway lights far behind. "So you're my shrink now?"

"No, Henny. I'm your friend. I'm also the guy bailing you out on the ice every night, trying to keep our team on track for the playoffs and keep your ass in the starting lineup."

"You don't know what the fuck you're talking about. We're just friends."

"Yeah. Okay. So what are you doing tonight? Heading home to get some rest before tomorrow's practice? Watching your films from the week? Prepping for the Philly game?"

"Yeah, something like that."

"Great. I'll round up the boys. We'll meet at your place."

Fuck. He'd walked right into the trap. "I was gonna grab dinner at the pub first."

"Which pub was that?"

"You know which pub, dickhole."

"Sweet. I think the boys and I will join you. Watch some of this 'just friends' stuff in action." Dunn slammed his seat backward and shut his eyes. "In the mean time, I suggest you polish up your resume. You're gonna need it."

"Polish *this*, fuckface." Henny flipped him off, but there was no more anger behind it. He wasn't pissed at Dunn or any of the other guys. Not even the coach, who'd been cold-shouldering him for weeks. They had every right to call him out on his shit—he was putting the whole team at risk, and he needed to work his shit out before things spiraled any further.

Yeah, something was definitely fucked up in that head of his. But Dunn was wrong about Bex. That wasn't why he was all messed up. Couldn't be. He'd known her too fucking long. If things were gonna happen between them, they would've happened long ago. High school. College, even, on any of their holiday breaks. Would've been so easy to go down that road—a few drinks, holiday cheer, a warm body on an ice cold night. But thirty-year-olds who drank too much tequila and fell into bed together? Total fucking accident.

And as for the phone sex? Fine. Hot as hell. Definitely *not* an accident. But that didn't spell feelings either. Just a one-and-done good time they'd obviously both needed to get out of their systems, and now that they had, things would be right as fucking rain. He'd see her tonight, grab a burger and a beer like old times, and prove to Dunn and everyone else that he and Bex were nothing more than capital-BFF friends.

Big Laurie's was rocking tonight, but Henny had no trouble spotting Bex. Inside the dark and crowded pub, she was a bright light behind the bar, mixing drinks for a group of girls in fake wedding veils.

"Damn, I love bachelorette parties," Roscoe said.

"Bachelorettes?" Kooz elbowed his way between Henny and Dunn. Must've been the magic fucking word, because seconds later Roscoe, Kooz, and his D-men—Jarlsberg and Kenton—were shoving ahead in to the crowd, making a beeline for the ladies and leaving Henny and Dunn in the dust.

"You need an escort or something?" Henny asked Dunn. "Want me to hold your dick?"

Dunn laughed. "Just looking out for you. Shall we go see your quote unquote *friend*?"

Henny's eyes hadn't left her. She pushed the girls' drinks across the bar, laughing at something one of them said, and his heart damn near exploded. God, he'd missed her. Not in the way he was used to missing her, but with his whole damn body. Heart. Mind. Hands. Mouth. All of it. He'd never wanted to touch her so badly. To inhale her sweet, summer scent. To do all the dirty, sexy things he'd teased her about on the phone…

Fuck, this is bad.

Henny was totally staring at her, his cock throbbing in his jeans. Denying Dunn's accusations at thirty thousand feet in the air was one thing. But standing here in the pub, seeing that smile light up her face, remembering the sounds she'd made for him on the phone… That was a different story entirely. One that had his dick on high alert, eagerly awaiting the happily ever after.

"You good?" Dunn's hand on his shoulder snapped him back to reality. "'Cause right now you're looking at her like you're Gollum and she's the fucking precious."

Dunn was right, as usual.

Henny needed a drink. A good, stiff one.

He needed to stop thinking about words like *stiff one* around his best friend.

"I got this, Gandalf. Thanks." Shaking off Dunn's hand, Henny stalked through the throng to prove just how *not* affected he really was.

Yeah. Good luck with that.

CHAPTER ELEVEN

Bex's heart fluttered, adrenaline flooding her body as Henny and the entire starting lineup crowded into the doorway.

That much muscle and power in one room would give anyone jitters, but Bex barely noticed the other guys. Every one of her senses was trained on Henny. Dressed in dark jeans and a black button-down shirt that clung to his muscles, stretching tight in all the right places, he moved through the crowd with purpose. His blue-green eyes locked onto hers as he approached, and when she finally smiled, he grinned at her like a wolf.

Bex's thighs clenched tight, desire pulsing through her. She'd been over it in her head a hundred times since that phone conversation, all the reasons why this thing with Henny—whatever it was—was a terrible idea.

She'd planned to tell him as much as soon as he got back into town, just to be sure they were on the same page.

But now that he was standing in front of her in that tight shirt with those mischievous eyes and that soft, full mouth... *holy hell.* All she could think about was the sound he'd made on the phone that night. The deep, primal lust coursing through his voice as he told her all the hot, dirty things he'd do to her in bed.

As if he could read her thoughts, Henny lifted a flirtatious brow, making her stomach swoop. She stared unabashedly, emotions roiling, waiting for him to give her an indication—*any* indication—about which way things were going.

But Henny seemed determined to remain unreadable. Sexy, cocky, and impossibly neutral.

"I see you brought backup," Bex finally said. She refused to let him know how badly he was getting under her skin.

Henny shrugged. "Not one of my better decisions."

"Pretty sure the wedding party disagrees." She nodded toward a table across the room, where the Tempest defensemen were doing shots of whipped cream off a woman's neck while her friend wrapped Roscoe in a feather boa.

"Jesus," Walker said, joining Henny at the bar. "We're here five minutes and Roscoe's already wearing feathers? This can't end well."

"Don't you party animals have an early practice tomorrow?" Bex asked.

Walker grinned. "Now that you mention it, Bex, we *do* have an early practice. But someone here—not naming names, but his initials are Kyle Fucking Henderson—insisted on seeing you before heading home."

"Dick." Henny punched Walker in the arm. "I told you, I wanted to grab dinner."

"Because the stuff we ate on the plane wasn't enough."

Henny grumbled something else just under his breath. Bex couldn't hear, but it made Walker laugh.

"Whatever you need to tell yourself to sleep at night, bud," Walker said.

Ignoring him, Henny turned those intense eyes back on Bex. He leaned across the bar, up close and *very* personal, brushing his lips over the shell of her ear. His breath was hot and soft on her skin. "You look beautiful."

She closed her eyes, inhaling his clean, masculine scent. It was still Henny, but the smell of his skin had a very different effect on her now than it did a week ago. He started to back off, but she didn't want him to pull away. She wanted everyone else in the pub to pull away instead, leaving them alone to finally finish what they'd started.

Henny settled back on his stool, filling Bex with a

longing that made her jittery and anxious. She reached for her bar rag and wiped down a spot in front of them, then remembered Fee teasing her about how clean everything was. She tossed the rag into the sink and folded her arms over her chest instead.

"So," she said. "You boys want something from the kitchen?"

"What are my chances of getting one of those black and bleu burgers?" Henny asked.

"You're still playing this game?" Walker shot Henny a death glare, then shook his head. Smiling at Bex, he said, "Okay, then. Let's make it two."

"And sweet potato fries," Henny said.

"Same," Walker said.

"I'll take a beer when you get a second." Henny glared at Walker. "You up for that, gramps?"

"Let's do it. Hell, why not order shots, too?"

Henny held up two fingers. "Jägermeister."

Walker scoffed. "What are you, seventeen?"

"What are *you*, sixty?

"Two beers, two shots of Jäger coming right up." Bex scooted over to the liquor setup and grabbed the bottle. She got the feeling there was trouble brewing in Tempest bromance paradise, but Eva had taught her early on not to ask questions. Those boys could bicker like old ladies and damn near come to blows, and five minutes later they'd be hugging it out, promising to name their kids after each other.

Bex was grateful Henny had guys like Walker and Roscoe in his life. Grateful that he'd *let* them in. After everything that had happened with his own family situation when they were kids, Henny played his cards close to the vest, never letting anyone too close to his heart. It took him years to warm up to someone, and even then it could be a painfully slow process. But with Henny, once you were in, you were in. You couldn't ask for a more loyal friend.

But what about a lover?

The thought flooded her with desire, but Bex shook it off. Now was not the time to get all hot and bothered—not with a full bar, a bachelorette party that was getting crazier by the minute, and five hockey players to keep track of, two of which may or may not be in a fight.

She poured the shots and beers, then ducked into the kitchen to put in the food order. By the time she returned to the bar, things had thankfully calmed down between the boys—they were laughing now, signing napkins for one of the bridesmaids.

At least they're not autographing her boobs.

Dismissing a sudden spark of jealousy, Bex checked on her garnishes and ice tubs, then did a quick scan of the pub. Kooz and his D-men had drawn an enthusiastic crowd around the pool table—locals loved when the

Tempest boys joined in for a few rounds—but it looked like Fee had everything under control. The bridesmaids seemed content to take pictures of the hockey players. Back at the main bar, all of Bex's customers had full drinks and big smiles, including Henny and Walker.

But down at the other end of the bar, Bex's least favorite customer was trying desperately to snag her attention. Logan Jennings leaned forward on his elbows, waving a twenty at her and flashing a look he probably thought was sexy.

Ugh.

"The usual?" she asked flatly, but she was already reaching for the whiskey sour mix. Logan never deviated.

"You know it. How's my pretty girl tonight?" he purred, also part of his script. As was the shaggy hair, the dingy white Henley, and the dark vest with way too many pockets.

Sorry, dude. Han Solo wore it better.

Bex made quick work of the drink, setting it on a cocktail napkin and sliding it over to him, ignoring his question. "Four-fifty."

"Run a tab," he said. "I'll be here a while."

Lucky me.

He was about to say something else, but she was rescued from further conversation when Nico called out her burger order for the boys.

"Sorry, Logan. I'm slammed tonight. Holler when you need a refill."

She grabbed the burgers and delivered them to Henny and Walker, who dove in so fast she nearly lost a finger.

"What's up with fanboy down there?" Henny jerked his head toward Logan. "Busting out his A-game?"

Walker grinned, mouth full of fries. "Jealous?"

"Of *that* kid?" Henny huffed. "Please."

"It's just Logan Jennings." Bex popped her elbows on the bar and sighed. "Comes in every few nights, drinks alone, never tips, never stops offering to show me his Camaro."

"Is that a euphemism?" Walker asked.

"Pretty sure, yep." Bex blew out a breath. "Guys like that are all the same. They talk a lot of shit, but when it comes down to it, they need a GPS and a compass just to find my clitoris."

"Who's finding your clitoris?" Roscoe appeared suddenly, his face smudged with lipstick, boa looped around his neck.

"Dude. Seriously?" Henny glowered at him. "Far as you're concerned, she doesn't have a clitoris."

"If that's what you think," Walker said, "maybe you need the GPS, too."

Bex tapped her lips, pretending to be deep in

thought. "Funny, my vibrator never has any trouble finding—"

"Jesus, Bex." Henny was beet red, though from the alcohol or something else, she couldn't tell. All she knew was how much she loved messing with him.

And how crazy he was making those little butterflies in her stomach.

Henny finally cracked a smile, pointing at her with a French fry. "Behave yourself, you trouble maker."

"Aw, you know you love me." Her hand shot across the bar, aiming for his hair, but he saw it coming and grabbed her. He brought her hand to his mouth and blew a wet raspberry against her palm.

"Eww! You filthy little *beast*!" Squealing, she wriggled free of his grip and grabbed a beverage gun from under the bar, pointing it at his crotch. "I have a loaded seltzer gun and I'm not afraid to use it."

Henny shrugged. "If you do, you'll have to get on your knees and clean it up."

Walker rolled his eyes. "You two should probably just—"

"Not go there," Henny said.

Again, Bex thought. *We shouldn't go there again.* But even as the words popped into her mind, she knew they weren't true. She *wanted* to go there again. Seeing him now only intensified the desire that'd been burning through her since that phone call.

She wondered what the chances were of going home with him tonight. She was pretty damn sure Henny did *not* need a map and a GPS to find *any* part of her anatomy…

"Bartender?" Logan again, tapping his empty glass on the mahogany and zapping her right out of a perfectly delicious fantasy.

"God. It's never the cute ones," she grumbled. "Only the creeps."

"Do we need to have words with him?" Henny asked.

"Can't you just kick his ass?" Laughing, she scooted back over to Logan and grabbed the whiskey and sour mix.

Logan shook his head, pulling out his wallet instead.

"All set then?" she asked, relieved.

"Listen, my friend is having a few people over tonight, and I was wondering if you—"

"No."

"My Camaro's right outside, and—"

"No. Can I get you anything else?"

Undeterred, Logan flashed a cheesy grin. "Your digits."

Digits? Who even says *that?*

She grabbed for the money in his hand, but he wouldn't release it. "I've told you before. I'm not on the menu, Logan. Please stop asking me out."

"Come on," he pressed, stroking his thumb over hers. "You're missing out."

"I'll take my chances." She jerked her hand away with the cash, her skin crawling.

"So you're just gonna shoot me down like that?" He looked utterly shocked, despite the fact that they'd had this conversation a dozen times. "You got a boyfriend or something?"

Why did it always come down to that?

"No, Logan. I do not have a *boyfriend*. I—"

"Fiancé, actually," Henny said. She hadn't seen him duck behind the bar, but suddenly there he was, standing right behind her, dark and broody and posessive, strong hands sliding over her shoulders.

Normally Bex hated testosterone games like this. As if having a boyfriend was the only acceptable excuse for rejecting the advances of a creep. But with Henny looming behind her, heat radiating off his body, his thumb caressing the bare skin of her neck, Bex forgot every last objection she had.

Turning to face him, she placed her hands on his chest, his heart thudding strong and steady beneath her touch. Henny tightened his arms around her and pulled her closer, heat rising between them.

Lacing her fingers behind Henny's neck, she looked up at his face, searching for another clue, anything to let her know he'd felt this, too. Not the confusion of waking up naked after too much booze. Not the dark, secret pleasure of the things they'd whispered on the phone. And definitely not the familiar comforts of their lifelong friendship.

No, this feeling roiling inside her was different. New. And it was as wild, uncontrollable, and utterly real as the curls in her hair.

Bex swallowed. Hard. She wondered if Henny could feel the tremble in her hands. He met her gaze, his blue-green eyes blazing with fire. With possessiveness. And, she realized with a start, something that looked a hell of a lot like love.

Her mouth parted, but all words were lost, burned away by the passion simmering between them.

"Save it," Logan huffed. Bex had just about forgotten he was there, but he was determined to stake his claim. "I've seen that dude in here a hundred times. He's not your fiancé."

Bex blinked, still locked in Henny's impossibly strong embrace. "He's my—"

Henny's mouth was on hers in a flash, so fast she didn't even know what hit her. One second she was standing there wishing Logan would just vanish, and the next she was looping her arms tighter around Henny's neck, rising on her tiptoes to get closer. Closer. Closer still.

Henny made a low, gravelly noise in the back of his

throat that nearly liquefied her. His kiss was—God, it was everything, all at once. Soft and slow, hot, breathy, desperate. Beyond the cinnamon heat of the Jägermeister, she tasted his hunger, a burning desire she was more than ready to satisfy.

Bex deepened their kiss, her heart banging wildly, her entire body erupting in goose bumps. Henny slid his hands down her back, down over the mounds of her ass, his fingers grazing her bare thighs as they skimmed the hem of her miniskirt. His touch was electrifying, sending sparks all the way down to her toes.

She was dimly aware of Logan yammering on, but she couldn't make out the words, couldn't process anything but Henny—his hands on her bare skin, his tongue and fingers stoking a fire that had started low in her belly and was now spreading throughout her body. All around her the sounds of the pub faded away until there was nothing but lips and tongue and breath and a desperate, white-hot need that seemed to grow deeper and more feverish the longer they kissed.

It was no longer a question, no longer a what-if game she played in front of her bedroom mirror, cheeks flushed from touching herself at his command. She wanted him in the flesh—naked and hard, thrusting inside her. Filling her completely. Commanding her. Making her his.

And she knew—by the sharp nip of his teeth, by the

hot press of his mouth, by the rock-hard bulge of his cock against her stomach—that he wanted her just as badly.

When they finally broke away, Bex's body was tingling head to toe, her lips raw and puffy, her knees wobbly. It took her a few seconds to get her bearings, and when she finally opened her eyes, the sight kicked her heart rate up a few more notches.

The pub was packed with a wave of newcomers. The pool table area had erupted in happy chaos. Logan was finally gone, but Fee and Walker stood at the end of the bar, staring at Bex and Henny with open mouths.

"Sorry to interrupt," Fee said, shooting her a look that could only be translated as, *You* will *tell me everything the moment we close those doors tonight!* "Roscoe and Kooz just bought the entire bar a round, so I need about five million drinks made in the next two minutes."

"No problem," Bex said, smoothing out her hair and plastering on a smile. "Give me one second to get... organized."

Fee winked. "You might want to organize that skirt back down over your ass."

Cheeks burning, Bex turned toward the bottles stacked up behind her and tugged her skirt back into place. Henny hadn't moved. He touched her shoulder, thumb caressing her collarbone. They locked eyes, flushed and breathless, and a new understanding passed between them. Primal. Raw. Powerful. And sexier than waking up naked together. Sexier even than that phone call.

Because the kiss had unlocked something between them that Bex was beginning to suspect had been there all along, lingering just below the best-friend surface, biding its time until one of them finally figured out how to set it free.

Henny leaned in close, his lips leaving a feather-light kiss on her neck.

"Tomorrow," he said. It wasn't a question.

Bex gave her skirt another firm tug, then nodded. "Tomorrow."

CHAPTER TWELVE

Judging from the ache in Henny's thigh muscles, the seven a.m. practice was the most grueling workout Gallagher and Eva had ever concocted for the Tempest boys. But whatever Henny had endured on the ice, he'd forgotten it the moment he'd hit the shower.

Ever since that kiss, trying to remember anything else was damn near useless. His brain just didn't have the capacity—all thoughts, all fantasies, all hopes were trained on one thing: Bex.

He'd gone to Big Laurie's last night to prove to Dunn —and yeah, maybe to himself—that the stuff going on with Bex wasn't anything to worry about. But the moment he'd stepped into the pub, Henny knew the truth. Hard and fast as a body check, it hit him. Damn near knocked the wind out of him, too.

Now, heading back into Big Laurie's to meet his girl

for lunch, it hit him all over again. Despite the icy winds outside, he was too warm, his insides buzzing like he'd had way too much coffee and not enough food. His hands itched to hold her again, to tangle up in those soft, silky curls. To pull her mouth to his and devour her, one kiss at a time.

Whether he'd wanted it to happen or not, Bex was no longer his friend. He couldn't pinpoint when it'd started, how long he'd been feeling that weird tug from friendship into the realm of something more, but denying the feelings now was pointless.

And that fucking kiss? Hell. All that had proved was that Henny wasn't the only one toppling headfirst out of the friend zone. He may have started things, may have caught her by surprise, but she damn well kissed him back, wrapping her arms around him, pressing her luscious breasts against his chest, moaning into his mouth as he kissed her breathless…

"Hey!" Bex popped up from behind the pool table with a measuring tape in one hand, notepad in the other. She had on one of those off-the-shoulder cut up sweatshirt things and a pair of leggings, her hair piled on her head in a messy bun.

God, she was fucking adorable.

"You're, like, two hours early," she said.

"Yeah?" He smiled like a fool. Like some chump who'd forgotten how to make words. How to breathe.

His heart was beating harder than it did on the ice, and he couldn't stop staring at her mouth.

All this after one kiss? Sex would probably put me in the E.R.

"Hen?"

"What?" Henny blinked, then shook his head. "I'm... yeah. Just wrapped up at the arena. Figured I'd stop by, see if you needed help with anything."

"I was just taking some measurements," she said, finally coming out from around the table to stand in front of him. He got a whiff of her tropical scent, and it took every ounce of self-control not to push her back on that pool table and—

"People have been complaining about the table," she said, nudging it with her hip.

Henny blinked away his fantasy. "What's the problem?"

"This." She grabbed the cue ball and rolled it down the center. It veered off to the left just after it passed the side pockets. "Actually, it might be the floor that's crooked, not the table. We probably need to replace it."

"The floor or the table?"

"Both, honestly. But Mom doesn't want to sink any more money into this place, and I've got other stuff to deal with first." She scooped up the cue ball, spun it against the felt. "No one wants to play pool if the place is flooded and the lights don't work, right?"

"Hey." He stepped in front of her, tilted her chin up to meet his eyes. "This is not a big deal. We'll rig up a temporary fix for the table. And once you talk to Bluepoint, you'll be able to do whatever you want in here."

"Henny, I don't think a business loan is…" Bex let out an exasperated sigh, her breath warm on his chest. "I need to figure something else out."

"Even if it means losing this place?"

"Maybe that's for the best." She tried to shrug it off, but Henny could tell her heart wasn't in it.

"Look," he said, "I'm not saying running a pub was your life's dream, okay? But you're here now. You're taking what could've been a suck-ass situation and making the best of it. That's kind of what you do."

Bex laughed, but there was no warmth in it. "If this is the best of things, I'd hate to see the worst."

"So sell the place and find another job. One with better hours, more money. Put all this in the rearview." He took the cue ball from her hands and rolled it into the corner pocket. "A few phone calls, an hour with a realtor, we could have this place listed by the end of the day. Is that what you want?"

Bex crossed her arms over her chest and shot him a glare.

"No, it isn't," he answered for her. "You took the job here to help out your mom, maybe lie low for a while, figure out your next move. But that's not what happened. You fell for this place. You saw the potential, and you made it yours. All that time you've spent on marketing plans, all your big ideas? You aren't walking away from that. Hell, you probably have a new name picked out and everything."

That got a tiny smile. She flipped back a few pages in her notebook and showed Henny the drawing there—a phoenix, rising from a fire. "I was thinking of calling it The Silver Phoenix. I even sketched up a logo concept."

"Of course you did." Henny beamed at her work. Stepping closer, he tucked a loose curl behind her ear. "You have this way of taking something everyone else has given up on and turning it into something amazing. Do you know how rare that is? You're a goddamn visionary, Bex."

Another smile, a little bigger this time. "Going a little overboard on the compliments, aren't we?"

"I speak from experience. You saved my ass in high school, and look how fucking awesome I turned out."

"Now you're going a *lot* overboard."

"Is it working?"

"Maybe." Bex smiled up at him, but he couldn't get a read on where she was going with this. On what she wanted. Henny's gaze lowered to her mouth, to those lush, rosy lips, remembering the sweet and seductive taste of her kiss.

Fuck, he wished he could read her thoughts.

"Thanks, Hen." She stood up on her tiptoes and pressed a kiss to his cheek. All too brief. All too chaste. Her smile was gone, the heat between them dissipating. And then she was on her knees again, scoping out those table legs. "Any ideas?"

Yeah. One. He wanted to haul her back up on her feet, pull her close again. He wanted to brush the hair out of her face and smooth away those worry lines, kiss her until every last fear and stress and disappointment evaporated. For so many years he'd looked out for her, protecting her from bullies when they were kids, watching out for her through all those stupid high school parties and pranks. But he couldn't protect her from life itself, from all the ways things could just go sideways on you, no matter how hard you worked, no matter how badly you wanted something.

"I think we can jam something under the legs on this side," she said now, interrupting his thoughts. "Can you find me some cardboard? There should be some empty wine boxes in the store room."

Grateful for the distraction of a job to do, Henny shrugged out of his jacket and dropped it onto a chair. After a few minutes of searching, he located the boxes and tore them into thick, small squares, then lifted the table so Bex could shove the cardboard under the legs.

"That should do it," she said, standing up and dusting off her hands.

Henny fished out the cue ball and rolled it down the threadbare green table, straight as an arrow, and that damn smile of hers lit up the whole room again.

"See?" he said. "A goddamn visionary."

"Thanks again for your help." Bex leaned in to press another soft kiss to his cheek. This one lasted a little longer, though. Drifted a little closer to his mouth. Lingered as she ran her hand up his back.

"If that's what happens when I help," he said softly, "consider me permanently at your service."

Bex grinned. Sweet. Mischievous. "Maybe I will."

She was close enough to taste, but it wasn't enough. It was never enough anymore, always just out of his grasp.

Fuck it.

He grabbed her hips and dropped to his knees, nudging the hem of her sweatshirt with his nose, inhaling the scent of her skin.

"Henny, what are you *doing*?" The warning in her voice was clear, but he ignored it, pressing his face to her bare belly, desperate to be close. To feel her.

He gripped her harder, waiting for her to push him away. To tell him to fuck off. All she had to say was one little word—*stop*—and that would be it. He'd back off completely.

But she didn't say stop.

She hesitated just for a second longer, then slid her hands into his hair, dragging her nails over his scalp and pulling him closer. He shivered. God, she felt so fucking good. So fucking perfect.

Slowly, he pushed up the hem of her shirt, fingers grazing her soft skin, his touch leaving a trail of goose bumps. She was trembling now, her breath quickening.

He kissed her belly, sliding his tongue along the waistband of her leggings, making her gasp with pleasure. Rising to his feet, he kissed his way up to her luscious breasts, peeling off her sweatshirt as he went. He flicked his tongue against her nipple, teasing and biting her through the fabric of her zebra print bra, his cock pulsing in time with his heartbeat, and when she fisted his hair and begged for his kiss, nothing—not an interruption, not a buzzing phone, not even an earthquake could've stopped him from granting her wish.

She tasted like apples as she melted into his kiss, soft and warm in his arms, her sweet little moans sending ripples of pleasure right down to his dick.

Holy fuck. If last night's kiss was stellar, this one was fucking fireworks.

With his hands full of Bex's perfect ass, Henny backed her up toward the pool table, lifting her up onto it and guiding her legs around his waist. His cock ached, throbbing against his zipper, begging for release, begging to be inside her.

But as hard as he was, he wasn't ready for that. Not yet. He wanted to taste her first. To savor every kiss, every touch, every delicious moan he could coax out of her body.

Sliding his hand down the front of her leggings, he brushed his fingers against the damp silk of her panties. She was so damn hot for him, so wet and ready.

"Henny!" Bex gasped. "I... I don't..." She closed her eyes, head lolling back on her shoulders. Henny slid his hand in further, palming her clit as his fingers sought her soft, wet heat. She was absolute perfection. Tight and slippery, her body pulsing with need.

"Tell me to stop and I'll stop," Henny said. "But don't you fucking lie to me and say this isn't what you want."

"It's not that, it's... Oh, God. That feels...."

"Tell me," he said, sliding two fingers inside. Thrusting deeper, slower. Dragging out every excruciating second.

"Henny," she whispered. She gripped his arms, her blue eyes searching his, full of something he'd never seen there before.

There was a time when he could read her thoughts, know exactly what she was feeling, whether she was scared or happy or confused. There was so much damn history between them, so many memories and moments and a million tiny things that made up their story. Despite all that, this time he *didn't* know what she was thinking. All he knew was the warmth of her skin, the tremble in her body as he touched her, the sweet honey scent of her breath as it ghosted across his lips.

"God, you're beautiful," he said, and her eyelids fluttered closed.

"What's happening?" she whispered.

"No idea. All I know is I *really* want to keep touching you. Making you tremble like this."

She was warm and slick as he stroked her, faster now, deeper with every thrust.

She bit her bottom lip, opening her eyes to meet his gaze again. She still wore the same unreadable expression. In a small voice threaded with uncertainty, she said, "Are we... is this a... a friends-with-benefits thing?"

Friends with benefits?

The thought was a sucker-punch to the gut. Henny couldn't imagine something like that with Bex. No matter what was going on between them, no matter how badly he wanted to tear off her clothes and bury himself inside her, he had zero interest in a no-strings, girl-on-the-side deal with her.

"Is that what you want?" he asked.

Say no. Please say the fuck no.

"I asked you first," Bex said.

Henny pulled back, searching her eyes for a fucking clue. If she wanted friends with benefits, he'd have to walk. Now. Wouldn't be easy to put everything behind them—that first drunken night, the phone sex, the kissing and touching—but the pendulum hadn't swung so far that they couldn't go back to being friends.

But if he put his heart on the line, told her what he *really* wanted, everything would change. There'd be no going back. Only going forward, for better or for worse.

She might send him packing.

Or this could be the start of the best fucking thing in his life. In *both* their lives.

"No, Bex," Henny said. "It's not a friends-with-benefits thing. It's a friend-that-can't-stop-thinking-about-you thing. A friend who's been tied up in knots since that kiss last night, knowing it was just the tip of the damn iceberg. A friend that would do anything to keep touching you. To taste you. To make you shatter."

Her eyes widened, a shy smile curving the sexy edge of her mouth.

"I haven't had a good night's sleep since I woke up in your bed last weekend," he said, "wishing like hell I could remember how it felt to be inside you. Wishing like hell *you* could remember."

"Same." Bex looped her arms around his neck.

"And if you don't kick me out in the next five seconds," he warned, "we won't have to worry about forgetting what happened between us. Because I promise you, Rebecca Canfield. After what I have in mind? You won't remember anyone *but* me."

Bex whimpered, her thighs tightening around his

hips. Even through his jeans, he could feel her wet heat, his dick growing harder by the second. He was so fucking ready for her. So desperate to tear off her panties and slide between those creamy thighs. To mark her. To make her his.

"So do I stay?" He pressed a kiss to her jaw. Her neck. Her ear. She was melting at his touch, her hips already rolling toward him, her back arched. "Or do I go?"

Fisting the back of his hair, Bex forced him to meet her gaze. The haziness was gone from her eyes, their once unreadable depths replaced with something dangerous and intense and clear as a fucking bell.

Hunger.

"You stay," she said. Then, with a wicked grin, "And you make good on that promise, Kyle Henderson."

CHAPTER THIRTEEN

Don't think. Don't think. Don't think.

Bex repeated the mantra in her head, hoping it was enough to keep her brain from taking over. Because if she stopped and let those thoughts in, if she stopped for even one second to consider what was about to happen with her best friend—what was already *happening*—she'd talk herself right out of it.

No matter how good his lips looked. No matter how amazing that kiss had tasted. No matter how tightly her thighs clenched now, her core flooding with desire at his touch and the savage look in his eyes...

Don't think. Just kiss him.

Henny lowered his mouth to hers, and she closed the rest of the distance, parting her lips to let him in. He kissed her gently at first, then deeper, nipping and sucking her bottom lip as she moaned softly.

Everything about his kiss was exquisite. Soft and slow, teasing, then commanding. Hungry. Her core was on fire, desperate for his touch again, his hands, his mouth, the stroke of that perfect cock. Still, they were all alone in the pub, not a soul watching, hours before anyone else would arrive, and Bex intended to take her time. She wanted to savor every touch, every caress.

Their kiss unbroken, she slid her hands up inside his shirt, exploring the hot, rock-hard ridges of his abs and chest. He shuddered at her touch, and as the butterflies inside her took flight, she felt dizzy and sexy and so, so powerful.

She wanted him. All of him.

Henny pulled away just long enough for them to tug his shirt off and toss it onto the table. She reached for his belt buckle, but he stopped her, shaking his head. "You first, beautiful."

Leaning back on her hands, she lifted her backside up from the table as Henny tugged her leggings off, kissing every inch of her exposed skin on the way down.

She sat on the pool table in her pink floral panties and a zebra bra that had no business being on the same body at the same time, trying to hold in her stomach, trying not to think about her thighs, but Henny seemed oblivious to her flaws. His gaze swept her from head to toe, taking in every inch, every curve, every feature.

When he finally met her eyes again, Bex saw only desire. Only appreciation.

She unhooked her bra, let it fall to the table, her breasts heavy, her nipples stiff and aching with need.

"You're amazing," he said, brushing his knuckles along her collarbone. "Everything about you is beautiful."

He leaned in again, kissing her throat, her jaw, his hand skimming over her breasts, sliding down between her thighs. She parted for him easily, arching her body toward his touch as he teased her through the damp silk of her panties. But this time, when he dipped his fingers beneath the lacy edge and pushed through her soft hair, her breath caught, and the thin barrier holding back her thoughts threatened to crumble.

This is it. We're really doing this. What does it mean? Is this the beginning of something uncharted and wild and incredible, or the end of something real and familiar and solid? Can it be both? Do these things ever work out? Is it too soon for me? Too late for him? What if—

"Bex," Henny whispered, his hands going still. "You're a million miles away."

"I'm... sorry." She smiled, curling her fingers around his biceps. "It's okay. I'm here."

"No, you're here." He traced a line across her forehead with his thumb, offering a small smile. "Trust me, I know the look. I see it on the ice every night."

Bex smirked and crossed her arms over her chest, covering herself. "The look of half-naked women who can't keep their hands off you?"

"That'd be a game-changer, wouldn't it?" Henny laughed. "I'm talking about the players. You start over-thinking it, analyzing everything, plotting out your next move, trying to predict how the other guy is going to react. You know what happens next? You lose the puck or crash into the boards."

"Except in this case, the other guy is my super hot best friend that I'm about to get naked for. The puck is our friendship... or maybe that's the boards? And I'm worried about everything crashing and... I don't know. This is all so... wow. Also, my bra and panties don't match. Like, at all. Okay. Clearly I need to stop talking."

Henny shook his head, a seductive smile edging across his face. "You think I'm super hot?"

"I think if missing the point were an Olympic event, you'd get a medal."

"I got the point, Bex. And trust me when I say I don't give a single fuck about your undergarments. They're not part of the naked equation. In fact, I'm trying to figure out why you're still wearing them."

Bex raised her arms like a champ. "And he takes the gold, ladies and gents!"

"Hey." Henny swept the curls from her face, his eyes

filling with concern. "Are you sure this is what you want?"

Bex nodded. That was a question she could answer without thinking.

"Okay," Henny whispered. "Do you trust me?"

"Absolutely." That answer hadn't required thought, either. Henny was making this easier on her by the second.

"Close your eyes," he said, kissing her temple. "No peeking."

Bex did as asked, fighting off the chill he left in his wake as he rustled around for something on the other side of the room. His jacket, maybe?

"Hen?"

"Right here." He returned quickly, flooding her senses with his clean, spicy scent. His hands brushed her shoulders, then her ears. "Earbuds. Okay?"

She nodded as he fitted them inside.

"Lean back," he said. "Keep your eyes closed. Sink into the music. Focus only on the feel of my mouth."

Her heartbeat kicked up a notch. "Your mouth?"

"Remember what I told you on the phone that night?"

A fresh wave of heat swept her body. "Which part?"

"No more touching," he said, and Bex knew without looking at him that he was smirking. "Only my mouth. I want to know what you taste like when I make you come."

Breathless, Bex scooted back on the pool table, lying back on top of their shirts and the threadbare green felt. Seconds later, music drifted from the earbuds. Slow, sexy, wordless beats eased the tension in her muscles even as her body heated with anticipation.

Stripped of sight, lost in the pulse of the seductive music, Bex was blissfully disoriented. When Henny's lips brushed her shoulder, she gasped; her sense of touch was magnified by a thousand, compensating for the senses she'd temporary blocked.

The next kiss fell on her hip bone, lingering only a moment before drifting down the front of her thigh. He kissed the inside of her knee, trailing up her inner thigh, and then he was gone.

Another kiss breezed along her collarbone. Her neck. Teeth nipped playfully at her earlobe. She felt a soft kiss on her chin. On her wrist. A flutter of lips and tongue and breath around her belly button.

Bex arched her hips, desperate for friction, her core aching.

The music slowed, the bass deepening, throbbing in time with her heartbeat. She raised her arms over her head and gripped the edge of the table, afraid she'd lose control, afraid she'd slide her fingers between her legs and give herself the sweet release Henny was denying her with every torturous kiss.

She felt him shift closer, his arms braced on the table around her shoulders, heat radiating from his skin. Silky hair tickled the tops of her breasts as his mouth closed over her nipple, his tongue hot and velvety, his expert caress bringing her so close to the edge she was certain she'd explode. Just when she thought she couldn't take another moment, he moved to her other breast, teasing and sucking, and when he grazed the stiff point with his teeth, Bex cried out in ecstasy, her thighs clenching tight, everything in her cranked up from simmer to boil.

No longer able to resist touching him, Bex lowered her arms and threaded her fingers into his hair, pulling him close, arching up off the table, urging his mouth lower. Henny kissed her belly, blazing a trail from one hip bone to the other as he slid the panties down her legs. She kicked them free, and then she was bare, the air on her damp flesh a reminder that she was utterly exposed to him.

But there was nothing to be embarrassed about. Nothing to fear or regret or analyze or debate. Because this was Henny. The boy who'd always looked out for her. The man she trusted with her life. With her body. With her heart.

"I'm here," she whispered, more to herself than to

Henny, and in that moment she knew it was true. There was nothing left between them now but a promise.

The music in her ears was liquid and endless, her skin tingling as she anticipated his next kiss. Without warning, Henny's mouth closed over her naked flesh, tongue teasing the sensitive bud as heat gathered between her thighs, rushing outward like a river threatening to burst through the dam.

Bex's thighs began to tremble, and Henny pressed closer, tasting her, dipping his tongue into her wet heat, stroking her slow, then fast. Plunging in deep, then pulling back, his hot breath teasing her as he slid inside again, faster now, faster, harder...

Bex cried out in sudden, shocking ecstasy, her thighs clenching around him, hips thrusting as wave after wave of pure pleasure rushed through her body. She had no idea whether her voice was a scream or a whisper, whether she was still on the table or even in the pub. She felt like she was hurtling through space, tumbling, spinning. All that existed for her now was Henny, his perfect mouth, the soft glide of his tongue, the heat of his breath as he soothed her through the final aftershocks.

Bex lay there, lost in pleasure, floating on a current of bliss for two more songs before she finally opened her eyes. She found Henny standing at the edge of the pool table, bare-chested but still in his jeans, watching her intently. The desire in his eyes was vicious.

Bex yanked out the earbuds. She didn't need any more tricks, any more sensory deprivation. She was fully present now, here in this sinfully seductive moment with her closest friend, and she wanted all of him—the sight of his rumpled hair and swollen lips, the warmth of his touch, the taste of her arousal on his tongue, the sound of his ecstasy reverberating through her bones as he plunged inside her, again and again.

She sat up and reached for him, pulling him close, kissing him desperately as she hooked her fingers around his belt.

"I want you inside me," she breathed, unhooking and unbuttoning and unzipping and reaching into his pants, fisting him, stroking him. He was hard and ready, shuddering at her touch, his kiss ferocious.

He brushed his fingers over her clit, teasing her with soft circles that wound her tight once again.

"No… fair," she breathed. "You said you weren't using your hands."

"Fuck that. If I can make you scream like that again, I'm using everything I've got."

"Please," she moaned, her head falling forward as the heat crested between her thighs. "I don't… I don't want to come again until you're inside me."

Henny moaned softly, brushing her lips with a gentle kiss. His eyes were kind and reassuring as he searched her face, a fiercely tender moment in the middle of a raging storm. "You're sure?"

"Don't make me say it again," she breathed.

Nodding, he fisted his cock, teasing her slick folds. "I brought condoms this time, if you want me to—"

"Have you been with anyone else since that night?"

"Fuck no."

"Neither have I," she said, then giggled. Of course she hadn't been. "It's okay," she said, urging him closer.

Lowering his mouth to her breast, Henny sucked her nipple as he finally, blissfully, perfectly slid inside her.

Oh, God...

Bex cried out again as her body stretched to accommodate him. He pulled back slowly, then slammed into her, a deep delicious plunge that filled her completely. Sitting up again, she wrapped her legs around his waist, pulling him closer. Deeper.

The rough denim of his jeans scraped the back of her thighs, but she didn't want to stop, not even to finish undressing him. Instead she rode him, slowly at first, then faster, harder, gripping his shoulders as the two of them found their rhythm together.

Everything about it was crazy. Intense. Insane. Henny? *Oh my God. Henny.* A week ago, Bex would've rolled her eyes and scoffed at anyone who suggested something like this could happen. She'd been deflecting jokes and assumptions like that for their entire relationship.

Yet as crazy and bizarre as it seemed, it also felt inevitable, as if the long and winding road of their friendship had always been leading them here, right to this moment, this beautiful explosion of passion and heat and a feeling deep down in her bones that Bex wasn't ready to name.

Still gripping Henny's shoulders, Bex kissed his jaw, his neck, his throat, relishing in the salty taste of him, the strong pulse of his heartbeat throbbing beneath his skin. He whispered her name, rolling his hips, fingers digging into the flesh of her ass, both of them quickly losing control.

With a resounding cry, Bex finally shattered, tightening around him as he rode her hard and fast. Seconds later, Henny's muscles went rigid, his orgasm rampaging through his body, spilling into her as he shuddered and growled with pleasure, leaving them both breathless.

Henny nuzzled the space between her shoulder and neck and pulled her close, his bare flesh warm and slick. They stayed like that until their heartbeats finally slowed, two bodies happily spent, holding each other up as they always had.

When she was certain she could stand on her own two legs, Bex disentangled from his embrace and hopped off the table, smiling as she wordlessly gathered up her clothes. She stared at Henny openly, wanting to hold on to this image, to remember it always.

"You okay?" he asked, his voice scratchy and sexy. His hair was sticking up everywhere, his lips puffy, pants still hanging off his hips. His goofy grin lit her up inside.

For the first time since she'd moved back to Buffalo, Henny looked truly happy.

Bex pressed a soft kiss to his mouth, then grinned right back at him. "More than okay."

CHAPTER FOURTEEN

Despite multiple attempts at the bathroom sink, Bex had no luck washing the smile off her face. Fee would figure it out the minute she saw that grin, but Bex was too blissed out to care.

Back in the main room, Henny waited for her at the bar, his clothes rumpled, hair still adorably disheveled. Bex took a moment to admire the view before joining him. No matter how real it had felt in his arms, on that pool table, under the hot press of his body, she still couldn't believe it had actually happened.

I just had the most incredible sex of my life—with my best friend.

She pressed her fingers to her lips, puffy but still smiling, and headed over to the bar, perching on the stool next to him. His eyes were dark and intense, his breath quickening as he reached for her face and he leaned in close, brushing her lips with a kiss as soft as a whisper. She parted her lips, welcoming the soft stroke of his tongue.

He pulled back entirely too soon, his eyes suddenly serious. "Is this really happening?"

Bex cupped his face, bringing his mouth back to hers. He didn't pull away this time, just threaded his hands into her hair and kissed her, teased her, traced her lips with his tongue until her whole body felt like it was on fire.

Holy hell, that man could kiss.

Unfortunately, Bex had to work. And Henny had to rest before his game. And whatever was supposed to happen after that, when the clock struck midnight and Bex turned back into a pumpkin and their fairytale finally ended... No, she wasn't ready to think that far ahead. Not while the ghost of his touch still lingered on her flesh.

Breaking off the kiss, she hopped off her stool and slid behind the bar, filling up two glasses with the water gun. Playtime was officially over.

For now.

"Gallagher called a meeting before tonight's game," Henny said ominously, pushing his phone across the bar. "PR's involved."

"PR?" Bex narrowed her eyes. "Please tell me there wasn't another fight."

"Believe it or not, this one ain't my mess." He tapped the phone screen. It was open to a YouTube video—Bex recognized the location immediately.

"That's the pub," Bex said, tapping the play button. The video was chaotic and loud, Bon Jovi's "I'll Be There For You" competing with laughter and wolf whistles from the crowd, and it took her a minute to figure out what she was looking at. "That's... oh my God."

"Yep."

The video was uploaded late last night, but it already had half a million views. In it, two of the bridesmaids from the bachelorette party were stretched out on their backs on the pool table, giggling their asses off while Kooz, Jarlsberg, and Kenton took turns doing belly shots and... *wow*. Other not-so-family-friendly things involving whipped cream and body parts.

And how did Roscoe end up shirtless in a red lace bra?

And more importantly, where the hell had Bex been during all this?

Oh. Right. Making out with my best friend.

"Who knew my rickety old pool table saw so much action?" Laughing, Bex handed back the phone. "Okay, the video's a little obnoxious, but what's the issue? They're all consenting adults. And the guys didn't miss practice this morning, right?"

"No, but with PR involved? I'm guessing it's an

image thing. Far as management's concerned, it's not just a couple of consenting adults blowing off steam. It's Team Tempest showing the world that off the ice, we're nothing but a pack of drunk-ass frat boys."

"Well, you kind of are," she teased.

"No, *those* guys are the frat boys. *I'm* the bad boy. Remember?" Henny arched a brow, the glint in his eyes wicked. "Or do you need a reminder?"

"Pretty sure my aching thighs are reminder enough."

He grabbed her hand and leaned across the bar, kissing her neck. In a gravely voice that made her shiver, he said, "Have I told you that I love being the reason for your aching thighs?"

She tried to answer, but Henny was working his way up to that spot behind her ear, and she forgot how to speak.

"If you keep making that sound," he warned, "I'm never leaving this bar."

"Then we'd better stop," she breathed. Her thighs clenched, her core flooding with a fresh wave of desire.

"Probably." Another kiss, another low growl vibrating across her skin.

Bex gripped the edge of the bar, her knees weak. "If I make you late," she panted, "PR will kill me."

"Only if you put this on YouTube."

"Don't even joke about that!" Bex laughed, finally

breaking away from his addictive kiss. "We are *not* making a video."

"Roscoe ruins everything." Henny settled back down on his stool and grabbed his water, chugging down half the glass before he finally came up for air. "Bright side? Tempest PR might hate it, but this shit's publicity gold for Big Laurie's."

"I can see it now," she said, coming out from behind the bar. "Happy hour specials: half price drinks, all-you-can-eat wings, get licked by your favorite hockey star!"

"Speaking of getting licked by your favorite hockey star..." He pulled her into his lap, brushing the hair back from her face, staring intently at her mouth. The look in his eyes said it all: If she said the word, he'd have her on that pool table again, his face between her thighs, his hot mouth on her flesh...

Bex couldn't believe how wet she was again. One look from Henny, and she went from zero to throw-me-down-and-fuck-my-brains-out in three seconds flat.

But at the moment, she needed those brains. It really was getting late. Nico would be there soon to start prepping the kitchen, and Bex had a lot of work to do before they opened for the night.

"Henny," she protested, feeling like a traitor to her own body, "I've got things to do here, and you need to get your ass into bed. You need to rest before you hit the ice again."

"Sorry. All I heard was *ass* and *bed*, and my mind went somewhere else. Like back to *your* bed. Where we can go right now and spend the rest of the afternoon discovering all the ways I can make you come."

Bex closed her eyes, her mouth watering. God, how she'd love to take him up on that offer, take him home where they could strip each other bare, take their time exploring every naked inch. "You are *such* a cheater, Kyle Henderson."

"Don't hate the player, hate the—"

"Hey frat boy?" She slid out of his lap and stood before him, looping her arms around his neck. "Let me stop you right there, cheese ball. You sound like Logan Jennings."

"Don't diss Logan. I owe that guy a drink. He's the reason I ended up with such a hot fiancée." Henny hooked his fingers in the waistband of her leggings, his knuckles brushing her belly.

"Oh, yes. He's a real prince among men."

"Long as he's not *your* prince, I don't give a fuck what you call him." Henny dipped his fingers lower, brushing over the lace edge of her panties. "On second thought, forget the bedroom. I think we need another round on that table. I forgot to call my shots last time—doesn't count."

"That's convenient."

"My mouth, your belly." He lifted the hem of her

sweatshirt, then kissed her stomach, his tongue swirling around her bellybutton, turning her legs into jelly again. She ached with pleasure, her hips arching toward him, seeking the delicious friction of his touch as he slid his hand down the front of her panties. "My fingers," Henny said, "your gorgeous pus—"

"Game over, lover boy." Bex grabbed his hand and backed away, saving herself from what was bound to be another marathon session. As much as she wanted to give in, she really couldn't. Too much work, not enough time. "Nico's coming in, and I've got citrus to prep, and you are *not* heading back to the ice without getting some sleep first."

"Fine." Henny sighed, pressing a kiss to her palm. "You owe me a rematch."

Bex looped her arms around his neck again. "You're not pouting, are you?"

"This is not a pout."

"Pretty sure it is." She kissed him, nibbling playfully on his bottom lip. "A nice one at that."

"*Nice*? What happened to super hot?"

"Time to go, super hot." She pulled him up to his feet, lingering a few extra moments in his embrace. She wouldn't be able to make the game tonight, but she loved the idea of sleeping in the same bed together, waking up naked in each other's arms, and actually *remembering* what happened.

"I have to do the liquor inventory tonight," she said. "Fee's closing, but if you want to stop by after the game, I'll wait for you. Sound like a plan?"

"I've got a better one. Here's how it's gonna go." He reached into his pocket for his keys, pulled the house key off the ring, and handed it over. "I get home from the game and find you in my bed." He kissed her mouth. "Naked." Her neck. "Wet." Her ear. "And ready for that rematch."

CHAPTER FIFTEEN

"God, I love your morning face." Henny leaned against his bedroom doorframe in a pair of sweats, a mug of fresh-brewed coffee in each hand, unable to tear his eyes from the beautiful woman waking up in his bed.

They'd survived their first night together—*really* together. After yesterday's insanely hot pool table adventure, Henny kept waiting for the awkwardness to kick in. The regrets on both sides. The "what have we done" wrecking ball to crash through their perfect little bubble.

But it never did, and when he raced home after the game last night, he'd found her as he'd hoped—naked, in his bed, more than ready to pick up where they'd left off in the bar.

Bex yawned and stretched, sitting up against the headboard and tucking the sheet under her arms, offering a bright smile. Her eyes were still half-closed, her curls fucking *everywhere.*

He could not stop staring at her.

"You've seen it before," she said.

"Let me rephrase: God, I love your post-sex-with-me morning face."

Bex laughed. "You've seen that before, too."

"No, I've seen your post-sex, hungover, totally-freaked-the-fuck-out morning face. As well as your post-sex, I-can't-believe-this-pool-table-didn't-collapse-underneath-us afternoon face. Completely different categories of sex face." He handed over her coffee—no sugar, just a splash of milk —and sat down next to her, pressing a kiss to the corner of her mouth. "This face? I could get used to this face. In fact, this whole scenario is looking pretty damn good to me."

Bex took a sip from the mug, her eyes fluttering closed as she savored the coffee. He realized now she'd always done that—at home, at his place, in a café, even on road trips with the shittiest gas station coffee—wrapping her hands around the cup, inhaling the scent, that first sip lingering in her mouth a few seconds. For Henny, coffee was a kick start. For Bex, a whole fucking experience.

Just like everything she did. Bex didn't know the meaning of half-assed.

Add that to the list of things he loved about this girl.

Why had it taken him so long to make a move? To even consider it? Now that she was here in his bed, naked, sharing this tiny everyday moment with him, Henny wondered how he could've missed it before.

She was fucking breathtaking. And the best part? No small talk, no fakery, no masks. Thanks to their friendship, they could skip all the bullshit of trying to impress each other. Henny and Bex already knew each other, heart and soul.

Not to mention body…

Henny grinned. He couldn't believe what a lucky bastard he was.

"Promise me breakfast in bed next time," she said, "and I'll sleep over every night. Also, you need some new mugs." She held up the plain white mug, one of a set of four he'd picked up at some big box store when he moved in. They were the only mugs he owned. "These things have zero personality."

"Done and done." He kissed her shoulder, her neck, drinking her in. She was damn lucky, too—lucky he was giving her a chance to enjoy the coffee before his dick started calling the shots. "Hurry up with that coffee, though. Can't promise I'll keep my hands off you much longer."

"If I'm going to be waking up in your bed on a regular basis, we need to get something straight. No rushing coffee." Raising the mug to her lips again, Bex closed her eyes and sipped.

Henny was mesmerized, taking in every detail, all the little things he'd noticed but hadn't given much thought to in the past. The blush in her cheeks, the sweep of her dark lashes, the arch of her eyebrows, the tangle of auburn hair floating around her face, the spray of California freckles on her shoulders that hadn't quite faded.

He wished he didn't have practice today. He'd much rather spend the afternoon mapping those freckles with his tongue...

"Hey, what happened with the PR meeting?" Bex asked, the interruption keeping his rapidly-hardening cock in check. "I didn't get a chance to ask last night."

"Nothing that couldn't have been handled with a five-minute phone call." Henny set his mug on the night table. "Management wants us to start making ourselves quote unquote 'more accessible' to the fans. They think it'll make us seem more like upstanding citizens and less like drunken meatheads."

Bex raised a brow. "Define accessible."

"Fundraisers, hockey clinics for kids, shit like that." Henny winked, sliding his hand under the sheet, brushing his fingers along her upper thigh. "Nothing to be jealous about."

"Jealous? Ha! I just don't want them wearing you out before I've had my—*stop*!" Squealing, she did her best to balance the coffee mug as Henny squeezed the top of her thigh. "I'm ticklish!"

"How did I not find this spot before now?" Henny relaxed his grip, but kept his hand in place. He wasn't ready to stop touching her. He still wasn't convinced all of this wasn't some elaborate hallucination. Had he hit his head on the ice last night?

"A woman has *many* secrets, Hen. Even after all these years, you're still only scratching the surface."

"Okay, coffee time is over." Henny took her mug, setting it on the night table next to his. "I've got a burning question, and I'm gonna need an answer right now."

Bex rolled her pretty blue eyes. "I can't *wait* to hear this."

"Morning sex: Hot or not?"

"Hmm." Grinning, Bex lowered her gaze to his cock, straining hard now against his sweats. "I can't answer that until I've got all the facts."

"You want facts? I've got facts for days, baby." Henny stripped off his sweatpants, then tore that damn sheet right off her body, climbing on top of her. Her warm, supple curves melded against his bare flesh, their bodies fitting together perfectly. Heat radiated from between her thighs, making him even harder.

She was wet and ready for him again, legs parting easily as he slid inside her. "Deep," he said, rolling his hips, sliding out, then plunging back in. "Penetrating." Another thrust. "*Hard*-hitting." *God, yes. Right there.* "Facts."

"Kyle..." She whispered his real name—the only woman who'd ever done that, and it drove him fucking wild—already losing herself to the pleasure. Henny could not believe what was happening between them. One drunken night, one kiss, and suddenly two-and-a-half decades of solid, steady friendship ignited into a blaze that made him hot and dizzy.

Yeah, until you fuck it up and she bails...

Henny closed his eyes, driving away the thought with another deep thrust, his hands tangling in her soft curls. Bex was the best thing in his life—hell, she always had been. He may have been losing his footing on the ice, pissing off his friends, doubting whether he even belonged in Buffalo anymore. But if there was one thing in his pathetic, screwed-up life he'd always protect and cherish, it was her. It was this.

Opening his eyes, he found Bex looking up at him through those feathery lashes, her lower lids smudged with yesterday's eyeliner, her gaze both serene and intense, completely open to him. Trusting. She whispered his name again, pressing her fingertips to his lips, her gaze unwavering. Both of them stilled, their bodies pressed together, breath mingling, hearts banging like drums. Something passed between them, fiery and fragile. Henny didn't have the words to describe it, but he knew she was sharing something with him then—a soft, vulnerable hope flickering back to life inside her.

He wanted to fall into those eyes, get lost there forever. It made his heart hurt, his throat tight with emotion he couldn't explain.

Holy shit…

The moment was too much, too raw, too everything-all-at-once. Henny had never experienced anything so intimate. He couldn't take it. One more second, and his heart would fucking burst.

Breaking their gaze, he pulled out and flipped her over on the bed, positioning her on her hands and knees. He grabbed the soft flesh around her hips, sliding back into her from behind, burying himself to the hilt. Bex arched her back and moaned, pushing against his thrusts, curls bouncing down her back as Henny lost himself in the feel of her slick, hot flesh.

Leaning forward, he ran his palm up the curve of her back, kissing the soft skin between her shoulder blades, the nape of her neck, her hair. The sweet taste of her made his mouth water, desperate for more.

"That's… right there," she breathed, her body tightening around his shaft. She was close to the edge now, her legs trembling, skin glowing with a thin sheen of sweat as he straightened up and rocked forward again, plunging back inside, deep and hot and oh-so-fucking-perfect. Everything about this was so damn right.

They'd side-stepped it for decades. Now, they'd crossed into brand new territory. One night with Bex, and he was just about ready to carve out his heart and surrender.

Hell yeah, he'd make her breakfast in bed. If she let him, he'd spend every day dreaming up new ways to make her laugh. To make her happy. To keep that flame inside her burning bright.

He didn't have the words to tell her all that, though. Not yet. So when he felt the last of his control slipping, felt the hot, familiar tightening in his balls, he took the easy way out, sliding his hand between her thighs, rubbing her clit as he slammed into her from behind, harder, faster, sending them both into blissful fucking overdrive before he spent himself in a final shudder and collapsed on top of her, panting and exhausted, happier than he'd been in years.

Happier than he'd been *ever*.

CHAPTER SIXTEEN

Eva grabbed the bottle of Malbec and topped off their glasses, grinning at Bex across the table. They'd met up after Eva's Tempest practice at Chop's Grill, a new pub in Buffalo's Allentown district that Bex had been eager to check out. The place did not disappoint. It was more upscale than Bex's cozy neighborhood pub, but the vibe was unpretentious, the food delicious, and the wine selection unique and affordable. Bex found herself taking lots of mental notes for her marketing plan, dreaming up new ideas for Big Laurie's. By the end of the meal, she was so wrapped up in her thoughts that she hadn't realized Eva was talking until she heard her friend's warm, jovial laughter.

"Sorry," Bex said, blinking away the daze. "I've got work on the brain. What were you saying?"

"Oh, nothing much." Eva smirked, reaching for her

glass. "Just that Henny's been playing like a rock star lately, smiling like an idiot, and walking around like a man who's *really* making the most of his free time. Don't suppose you know anything about the sudden improvement in his mood?"

"Wow," Bex said, scooping up a forkful of the peanut butter cheesecake they'd decided to share. "We made it all the way to dessert before you started the third degree."

"Don't keep me in suspense."

Bex swallowed the velvety-smooth cheesecake, wondering why her mother had never considered chocolate peanut-butter menu items for Big Laurie's. *Add that to the list of things to fix when the place is finally mine...*

"Fess up," Eva said. "This is a safe space."

Laughing, Bex gave a playful shrug. "Why are you asking *me* about Henny's game?"

"Hmm. Maybe because you're wearing the same guilty, wanton look he's been wearing lately?" Eva cracked up, clearly enjoying this. "You two are *so* busted. Spill it."

"A lady never kisses and tells."

"Good thing we're not ladies."

Bex laughed again, stealing another bite of cheesecake. Since they'd started hanging out, Eva had been the one with all the red-hot stories; Walker's athletic prowess apparently extended well beyond the rink. Now that Bex had a few stories of her own, she was more than a little out of her element.

It'd only been a few weeks since she and Henny had "leveled up" on the pool table, but she'd already lost count of all the places they'd done it since then. In his bed. In her bed. In her car. In the tiny office behind the bar. In the even tinier store room behind the tiny office. In the press box at the practice arena. Two more rounds on the pool table before they finally decided to give that rickety old thing a break.

To say Henny was insatiable was like saying Buffalo winters were a little on the cool side. Bex's body had been in a constant state of beautiful exhaustion for weeks, and she'd never felt so damn good.

"Things are definitely heating up between us." Bex sipped her wine, trying to hide her smile. "Maybe it's helping his stamina."

"It's the enhanced personal training program." Eva winked. "I've got Walker on it, too."

"Do you think those boys have any idea we control their destiny?" Bex teased.

"It's way more fun to let them think they have free will."

Bex poured herself a little more wine, enjoying the oaky aroma as it swirled into her glass. She really needed to broaden Big Laurie's wine list. "Long story short, after the whole drunk nachos thing, we just kind of went for it. And now it keeps happening. Like, everywhere. We can't keep our hands off each other."

Eva placed a hand over her heart, lashes fluttering. "Young love in a kid-free, dog-free home. I can't even remember what that's like."

Bex nearly choked on her wine. "Slow down there, hotpants. It's only been a few weeks."

"Plus or minus twenty-some years."

"As *friends*. No one's talking about the L-word here."

Eva shrugged. "Maybe you're not talking about it, but it's pretty obvious you guys are crazy for each other."

Bex opened her mouth to deny it, but she couldn't. Her feelings for Henny were complex, growing deeper and less defined by the day. Unspoken or not, the L-word had always been part of the package. But now, that love was evolving so quickly, she couldn't keep up.

The friendship was as solid as ever. All the inside jokes, the secrets, memories of a thousand heartaches and triumphs and everyday moments they'd shared over the years—none of that had gone away. And the passion between them? The new path they'd been forging together as they spent their nights touching, kissing, bringing each other to the edge and back again? Epic. Bex had never felt so desired. So alive.

She sighed. It should've been perfection.

"Hey," Eva said gently. "What's wrong?"

Bex met her eyes across the table, trying to find the words to explain the uneasiness in her heart.

It wasn't that she didn't trust Henny—total opposite, actually. He was the only man she *did* trust, and she could easily see herself falling for him. Hard. But she was still reeling from her past mistakes. From rushing in, not seeing the signs, losing herself. And as much as she cared for Henny, she couldn't deny that he was unpredictable, moody as hell, and saddled with his own baggage. There was a lot he hadn't dealt with in his life, and it manifested in all sorts of ways he'd never admit; if she wanted proof, she didn't have to look any deeper than his NHL discipline record or his reputation with the media. The so-called "Bad-Boy Bachelor of Buffalo" might not see the connection, but Bex knew his troubles hadn't appeared out of nowhere.

Sure, Eva had said he'd been playing well lately, joking around with the team, hamming it up for the media. Bex had noticed it, too. He seemed to be playing with a purpose now, skating away from fights, keeping things cool with his coach and management.

But no one knew better than Bex that big changes could throw Henny completely off balance, and nothing was a bigger change in his world right now than his relationship with her.

"Henny's a little... all over the place," Bex said. "You've seen it. These past few weeks aside, his game has been off for months. I wish I knew what was going on with him, but that's the one thing he won't talk about."

Eva's eyes softened. "Honestly, I think he's just adjusting to having you back in his life again. I wouldn't be surprised if he feels responsible for you, especially after everything you went through in California."

"I know he does," she said. "He thinks he could've saved me from all that, which is ridiculous. I'm a grown woman. He's always been like that, though. You should've seen him in high school."

Eva smiled, shaking her head. "Scared off all your boyfriends, right?"

"What boyfriends? He basically threatened all the guys long before they worked up the nerve to ask me out." Bex rolled her eyes. "Everyone thought we were together anyway. Henny never bothered correcting them."

"Some things never change." Eva sipped her wine. "When he first told us about you, one of the guys joked about asking you out. Henny almost bludgeoned him with a water bottle."

Bex laughed. "Such a charmer, my boy."

"And now you're in the same city with that boy. Same *bedroom*. It's bound to cause some upheaval for both of you—good and bad. It will level out."

"That's the thing, Eva. I'm not sure I can wait for it to

level out. And I definitely can't handle the bad. Not right now."

"Come on, hon. Women are a lot tougher than we give ourselves credit for."

"Still doesn't mean a relationship is a good idea." Bex and Henny hadn't even talked about what was happening between them. Hadn't tried to define it or think too hard about the future. So far, they'd just been rolling with it, enjoying every moment as it came. "I'm not sure I'm even staying in Buffalo long-term, and Henny's never been one to pin himself down. Not for anything."

"I'm pretty sure there's nothing that man wouldn't do for you."

"That's not the issue." Bex's eyes glazed with tears. Henny was the most loyal man she knew, and he'd never *not* shown up when she'd needed him. "He's always looked out for me."

"Oh, it's *so* much more than that, Bex. Looking out? He does that for Walker and the rest of the boys. Heck, he looks out for me and Gracie. You should've seen him on family skate night last year. Someone brought their kid's friend—this smug little ten-year-old asshole who thought he owned the place. He nailed Gracie so hard she nearly face-planted, but Uncle Henny got to her quick, scooped her up just before she hit the ice. Then he and Walker chased the kid down and put the fear of God in him."

Bex cracked up. "I would've loved to see that."

"It was pretty amazing." Eva smiled. "Gracie wouldn't leave Henny's side after that. And I may be biased, but I think my seven-year-old is an excellent judge of character."

"Well, she gave Walker the seal of approval, so she *must* be good." Bex lowered her eyes, staring at the last bite of cheesecake. "Everything you're saying... I get it. Henny is amazing. And yes, maybe there's more than friendship here—a lot more. But there's still so much we... I mean, he's... and I'm..." Bex trailed off. How could she explain it to Eva when she hadn't even been able to explain it to herself? With a sigh, she met Eva's eyes again. "I just don't think the timing is right."

"If you wait around for the perfect time, you're liable to miss it altogether." Eva grabbed her fork and speared the last bite of cheesecake, popping it into her mouth. "Case in point."

"How long have you been planning that?" Bex asked, laughing.

"That was all improv, baby. Live in the now."

With dessert and wine finally finished, they settled the bill and headed outside to say their goodbyes. Eva would be heading down to South Carolina with the team in a few hours, and Bex needed to take care of some admin at the pub before she could see Henny off to the airport.

"Thank you." Bex hugged her friend. "I know it's not easy trying to talk some sense into this thick head of mine."

"Takes one to know one." Eva kissed Bex's cheek, her eyes serious. "Listen, Bex. No one is telling you to rush into something you're not ready for. And you and Henny certainly don't need to define your relationship for me or anyone else. I just... I know what it feels like to be afraid, and I don't want you to miss out on something that could change your life just because you're a little scared."

Eva was right—Bex *was* scared, and that fear was holding her back. It was a typical response to her brain's hyperloop of constant analysis, picking apart every good thing in her life and trying to predict all the possible ways it could implode.

For once, maybe she could set all that aside. Stop waiting for the floor to drop out from beneath her and just let herself truly *feel*. Truly fall.

After walking Eva to her car, Bex spotted a little souvenir shop across the street, one of those chintzy tourist traps that sold T-shirts and collectable plates painted with pictures of Niagara Falls and Buffalo-themed puzzles. She headed inside, curiosity getting the better of her.

She hadn't known what she was looking for until she saw it there, stacked on the half-price shelf with the other misfit gifts. The oversized mug was shaped like a bison —the city's unofficial mascot—its tail curved into the handle, horns painted on the sides. It was the goofiest, cheesiest thing she'd ever seen—in other words, perfect. She picked out two of them, and when the clerk asked if she'd like them gift-wrapped, she accepted the offer with a smile.

Nothing but the best for my man.

CHAPTER SEVENTEEN

"Fee?" Bex stepped inside the pub, blinking as her eyes adjusted from the bright afternoon light outside. The front door had been unlocked, but the place was dark and lifeless, not even a sappy rock ballad to greet her. "Fee, you here?"

"Bathroom!" Fee shouted. "Get me the toolbox and as many towels as you can. Hurry!"

Bex dropped her stuff inside the door and sprinted for the back office, grabbing the requested supplies. She found Fee on her knees in the bathroom, her upper body buried inside the cupboard under the sink, trying to hold back a deluge.

A quarter inch of water already covered the bathroom floor, quickly seeping out toward the pool table. From the looks of things, Fee's quick thinking and a few rags were all that separated a big mess from a total freaking disaster.

"Holy shit!" Bex handed over the tools and some of the towels, then chased the rapidly-spreading puddle into the pool table room, dropping towels as she went. Fee had already cut the power, but Bex unplugged the jukebox and electronic dart game just in case, tucking the cords up away from the floor.

Back in the bathroom, Fee was getting to her feet. Black makeup streaked down her face, her dark hair plastered to her forehead. She looked like a drowned rat, poor girl.

"Good timing," Fee said, finally cracking a smile. "Any later and I might've been swept out to sea."

"No kidding! What happened?"

"I was running late—just got here a few minutes ago. Not the warm welcome I've come to expect from my place of employ." Fee grabbed the toolbox from the countertop and plodded out of the bathroom, her feet kicking a small wave over the threshold. "I think I stopped the bleeding for now, but that pipe is shot. I give it a week, maybe two before it goes again."

"I thought your uncle replaced the pipes. Twice."

"That was the toilet. This is the sink." Fee wrung out her hair, adding a few more drops to the lake at their feet. "Pipes are all original in this place. We really need to gut the whole bathroom and start from scratch."

"Don't remind me." Bex pressed her fingers to her temples. She'd managed to save a little cash since moving back, and there was some emergency money in the bar account, but not enough for a remodel. Best they could afford was a patch job on the pipes and some new linoleum.

"We can't open like this," Fee said.

"Nope." She grabbed her phone and sent a quick text to Nico, then one to Henny, swallowing her disappointment. There was no way she'd be able to get over there now. She'd have to wait until he got back tomorrow to give him his present.

Until then, it was time to put on her big girl galoshes and get to work.

"You get the mops," Fee said, twisting her hair up into a knot. "I'll get that jukebox hooked up again and pick our music montage."

"Montage?"

"Every epic cleanup needs one, babe."

Ten minutes later, Bex was on her hands and knees in the bathroom with Fee, scrubbing to the beat of Missy Elliot's "Work It."

"This is disgusting." Fee plunged her rag back into the bucket of murky gray water.

"Understatement." Bex reached behind the toilet to mop up another puddle. Cleaning the bathroom on a Friday night wasn't exactly her idea of a rocking good time, but she found herself smiling anyway. There was something deeply satisfying about investing elbow grease into a place she one day hoped to own.

She still had to figure out the finances, and a bathroom remodel was definitely going to set her back. But her brain loved a challenge, loved puzzling out all the possible solutions. It reminded her that she was still a smart, capable, creative woman, even after all the dumb mistakes she'd made with her last business. Her last relationship. Her last... just about everything.

But those mistakes were all in the past.

Maybe she was crazy, but for the first time in months, when she imagined Big Laurie's a year from now—bigger, a new name, a full menu, and yes, a new bathroom—she felt hopeful. Excited. Despite the impossible odds, maybe she'd find a way to make it happen anyway.

And if moving on from the past was possible, and buying and rebooting the pub was possible, then maybe the idea of a real relationship with Henny wasn't so farfetched, either.

"What are you grinning about, Swamp Thing?" Fee tossed her rag into the bucket, cringing as it hit the edge with a wet slap.

"Nothing," Bex said, still smiling. "Just... this is actually kind of fun, no?"

"If this is your idea of fun, Henny is definitely *not*

doing his job between the sheets." Fee slid her hands down over her hips, doing a little shimmy. "Maybe I should take him off your hands, teach him a few things about how to handle a woman. Well, not in *this* outfit, of course."

Bex cracked up. "He doesn't need any more lessons in that department, thanks." She leaned over the bucket to wring out her rag, then knelt down again for another pass behind the toilet. "I'm talking about you and me. Here. Two smart, sexy, kickass ladies working together for a common goal. We're getting shit *done*, girl."

"Is that a bathroom pun, or—"

"Don't harsh my girl-power vibe."

As if on cue, the opening verse of Gloria Gaynor's "I Will Survive" floated in from the pool table room, sending them both into a fit of raucous giggles.

"If that's not a message from the universe," Bex said, "I don't know what is."

"The cheese factor is high with you today. I like it." Fee hopped up on her feet, pulling Bex up with her. They grabbed the mops that'd been propped against the wall, holding them like microphone stands as they danced out into the pool table room, singing along with Gloria at the top of their lungs.

Bex could not stop laughing. She felt like she was in high school again, happy and free and silly and just... glad. It was one of those rare moments where everything felt okay, all of her stress temporarily melted away, and hope reigned supreme.

She *would* survive. In so many ways, she already had.

The song ended, but the girls were still cracking up, winded from their sudden outburst.

"Drinks. That's what this dance party needs." Bex turned toward the bar, only to spot Henny sitting on one of the stools, his eyes sparkling with amusement.

"Um." She tucked her hair behind her ears, unable to hold his gaze. "How long have you been here?"

"Long enough to see your sweet, sweet dance moves. Was that the cabbage patch?"

Funny how she had no reservations about Henny seeing her naked, with bedhead and morning breath and sheet marks on her face, but knowing he'd caught her rocking out like a goofball? That made her cheeks burn. "Not all of us can be graceful athletes, Henderson."

"Oh, you're totally graceful. In a 1980s kind of way."

"What are you even doing here? Your flight—"

"Can wait." Henny rose from the stool and scooped her up into a hug, ignoring the dampness of her clothes. "I'm not leaving town without a good-luck kiss."

"You wouldn't feel so lucky if you knew what I'd been kneeling in for the last hour."

"Does this look like the face of a man who cares?" Without waiting for her reply, Henny lowered his mouth to hers, capturing her in a delicious kiss that melted away the chill.

"You just made my whole night better," she said.

"Not mine," Fee said. "Next time, bring your hot friends."

"Last time I brought them, they ended up on YouTube. We're still dealing with the fallout." Looking around the bar, he asked, "What's the damage, anyway?"

"Bathroom floor and cabinet are a little warped," Bex said, following him into the pool table room. "The water came all the way out here, but Fee stopped the leak before it hit the jukebox."

"Thank God." Henny pressed his hand to his chest. "Losing all those Whitesnake CDs would set this town back decades."

Bex punched him in the shoulder. "I was more concerned about electrocuting everyone, jerkface, but you make a valid point."

Henny crouched down to inspect the pool table legs. The cardboard they'd shoved under there to stabilize it had disintegrated into mush. "Life has not been kind to this poor pool table."

"Neither have we," she teased.

"Wait. Did you guys... on the *pool* table?" Fee's eyes went wide. "And you were worried about health code violations and Yelp reviews?" In a mocking voice, she said, "Big Laurie's: Awesome service, great food, but the pool balls are a little on the sticky side. One star."

"No one likes to play with sticky balls," Henny said.

Fee wrinkled her nose. "You guys are so gross. Adorable, but gross. Remind me never to touch the pool table again."

"If that's how you feel," Henny said, "better steer clear of the office, the store room, and the—"

"This guy!" Bex patted him on the chest. "What a comedian. Too bad he can't stay."

"I've got—"

"A flight to catch." Bex ushered him to the front door, looping her arms around his neck and stretching up on her tiptoes for another kiss. Taking advantage of the privacy, she pressed herself against his muscled chest and parted her lips, savoring the deep stroke of his tongue, the soft scratch of his stubble against her chin, the warmth of his strong, protective embrace.

"I hate that I have to get on that plane." Henny moaned softly, kissing her cheek, her jaw, the shell of her ear, his breath hot and inviting on her skin. "Any chance I can talk you into coming with me?"

"Probably, but Mom's counting on me to keep this place running. Don't be a bad influence, Kyle Henderson."

"Excuse me, but *you're* the bad influence in this operation. Always have been."

"I'm the angel. You're the Bad-Boy Bachelor of Buffalo. Says so right in the newspaper, so you know it must be true."

"You love it when I'm bad."

"In bed, yes. When I've got work to do? Not so much."

Henny finally relented, pulling away to zip up his coat. "How's Mom doing, anyway? Any news from Florida?"

"Aunt Sharon is doing great, but Mom wants to stick around a few more weeks, just to be sure she gets back into her routine okay."

"Did you tell her about...?"

Bex waited for him to finish his thought, but he left it hanging there, and she wasn't sure how to fill in the blank. What was there to tell? That they'd been sleeping together? That his kisses left her breathless and weak? That she still had no idea where this thing was going, or whether Henny even wanted it to go anywhere?

Bex lowered her eyes. It was probably time for them to have an actual conversation about things, to figure out just what each of them wanted out of this arrangement. But not at the bar, and certainly not when Henny had twenty minutes to catch a flight before they left him behind.

After a beat, she finally looked up at him again and

smiled. "And confirm her age-old suspicions about that night at the lake? No way. We're never telling her."

If Henny was bothered by her obvious deflection, he didn't show it. He only laughed, his smile making the skin around his eyes crinkle. "Remind me again why we didn't take full advantage of that situation?"

"Let's just be glad we're making up for lost time now." She pressed another quick kiss to his mouth, then pointed at the door. "Airport. You. Go."

"To be continued," he said with a wink. Then, "Listen, don't worry about the pool table. I have a feeling things will start looking up again real soon."

Bex smiled, tucking her hair behind her ears. *Things already are.*

CHAPTER EIGHTEEN

The following weekend, Bex headed to Big Laurie's with a light step and an even lighter heart, more optimistic than she'd felt in months.

The Tempest was on a hot streak, winning four of their last five games, and she and Henny had started a new post-game tradition Bex had coined "naughty naked nacho night."

Unless he was traveling, they spent their mornings together before his practices, catching up over coffee in their matching bison mugs, a gift that had amused Henny to no end.

Business at the pub was picking up, too—after closing last Friday to deal with the water damage, they'd offered all-night happy hour specials for the rest of the weekend, and word-of-mouth had been fueling a small but steady surge of new patrons, keeping Bex and Fee on their toes even during the typically slow Monday to Wednesday shifts. If things kept going like this, soon Bex would be able to hire another waitress and cook.

After seven months back in her hometown, she was finally hitting her stride. Henny had been right—things were looking up.

So when she headed into the pub Friday morning to do the payroll and prep for a busy night ahead, the last thing she expected to find was another disaster.

Oh, no. This can't be happening again…

"Fee?" Trying to cool her simmering panic, Bex picked her way through the entrance, stepping over an explosion of plastic sheeting, ropes, foam, and cardboard. Raising her voice to be heard over the sounds of Pat Benatar's "Love is a Battlefield," she shouted, "Please don't tell me the pipes exploded again!"

"Hey!" Fee ducked out from the kitchen, calm and happy. "No worries. I'm supervising them *very* closely. Especially that one in the Zeppelin tee. Do you see those forearms?"

"You and your arm porn." Relieved, Bex turned toward the pool room to check out the guys Fee was talking about. The bar didn't technically open for five more hours. Still, she couldn't complain. She'd take a few day-drinkers over another bathroom flood any day. "I saw the plastic and thought for sure I'd be walking into a river."

"Nope. Just the delivery guys, who I'd be very happy to walk into. Horizontally."

"Delivery?" They weren't due for another liquor order until next week, and Bex hadn't even put in the glassware order yet—the catalog was sitting on her desk, buried under all the other administrative stuff she needed to catch up on.

She dropped her bag on the bar and headed into the pool table room for a closer look. Four men crowded around the center, not shooting pool as she'd initially thought, but… setting up? They grunted as they nudged what looked like a massive piece of furniture into the spot where her old table used to be.

"Where's my pool table?" she asked.

Arm Porn turned around, smiling. "You the owner?"

"Bex Canfield," she said. "What's going on?"

"We're just about done. Come check 'er out if you'd like."

The guys yanked away the last of the plastic sheeting from the base and stepped aside, revealing a brand new table that made her old one look like something from a frat house garage sale. In all the bars and pubs she'd visited, all the places she'd scoped out for ideas and research on the competition, she'd never seen such a gorgeous pool table.

It was a stunning piece, rich mahogany wood covered with deep burgundy felt that looked so much better than the green, classing up the room by a factor of a thousand. On the far wall, they'd mounted matching mahogany cue racks loaded with more than a dozen new cues and bridges, all different lengths. Scanning the room, she also spotted new racks, balls, felt brushes, and chalk.

It was a setup fit for a pro tournament, and it must've cost a small fortune.

"Everything look okay?" Arm Porn asked. The other guys had already begun cleaning up the mess of cardboard and foam. The old table was long gone. It may as well never have existed.

"It's... beautiful," she said. "But I didn't... where did it come from?"

"Queen City Custom Billiards," he said.

"Who sent it?"

"Can't help you there, ma'am. Boss doesn't tell us anything but where to deliver the goods." He handed over a proof-of-delivery slip. Hers was the only name on the paperwork.

"I take it you didn't order it?" Fee asked, running her hands over the felt.

"Nope." Bex signed the paperwork, fishing out a few bills from her wallet to tip the guy. "But I'll give you one guess who did."

CHAPTER NINETEEN

"Are you crazy?"

"Um…" Henny stood in his doorway in a pair of basketball shorts and sneakers, a towel draped over his shoulder, ripped torso gleaming with sweat. "I'm gonna need a little more context here."

"It's going to take me *years* to pay you back." Clearly Bex had interrupted his workout, but she didn't care. She pushed her way into the house, determined not to be distracted by the sight of him, all hot and sweaty and one stupid pair of shorts away from being naked. Her entire body shook, though from anger or lust, she couldn't quite decide.

"Ah. I see you got my present." Henny shut the door, a dopey grin plastered across his face.

Why does he have to be so infuriatingly sexy?

"Call Queen City Big Balls and tell them to take it back," she demanded.

Henny laughed. He actually laughed. "Keyword, Bex. Present. There's no taking it back."

"Flowers. Flowers are an appropriate gift, remember? Chocolate. A pair of earrings. A nice, hand-knitted scarf. Matching bison mugs. Not a pool table that cost more than everything else in that bar put together."

A bead of sweat tricked down his neck, his chest, his abs. Bex was T-minus three seconds from pouncing on him like a happy dog and licking him senseless, when he rudely patted himself with the towel, cutting off her view.

"You said it yourself," he said. "The place needs some upgrades."

"I also said I'd figure something out." She poked his firm, hot chest. "Listen, Mr. Muscles. You can't just swoop in and save the day whenever you—"

"Wrong." He grabbed her hand, pressed a kiss to her fingertip. "I can swoop in whenever and however I want. I swoop for you and you alone."

"I'm about five seconds away from swooping my... from the..." Bex sighed, snatching her hand out of his grip. "I have no idea where I was going with that."

"Let me help you." Henny reached for her hand again, looping her arm around his neck, pulling her close. The hard press of his cock against her stomach made her weak with desire. "Take off your clothes."

Bex squirmed out of his enticing embrace, desperately trying to hold on to her anger. "Why did you do that? We were managing just fine with that old table."

Wisely, he didn't respond.

Bex sighed. Some part of her understood his need to take care of her, to do things for her that she couldn't afford to do herself. Hadn't she done the same thing for her ex? Picking up the check when he was short, paying their shared expenses while he was out of work, loaning him money?

Yes. And in the end he'd taken her for all she was worth, financially and emotionally.

It may not have been the same situation with Henny—not even close. But the whole money dynamic was another callback to the darkest days of Bex's life, a big neon sign reminding her that her bad decisions had caused a serious ripple effect, one that had left her dependent and ashamed in ways she couldn't even begin to articulate.

After feeling optimistic all week, Bex was filled with uncertainty again. Moving back here, working at her mother's pub, spending time with her best friend... it was supposed to be stable. Familiar. Predictable.

None of this stuff with Henny was supposed to happen. Not the extravagant gift. Not the sex. Not even the bison mugs, which currently mocked her from their honorary spot on Henny's kitchen counter.

Bex closed her eyes, all the old doubts rushing back in, squeezing her heart.

"You wanna tell me what's really going on here, Bex?" Henny crowded in close again, running his hands up and down her arms, soothing and warm.

I'm scared that I can't take care of myself, and I'm scared that I'm falling for you, and one day you're going to realize you don't want this....

She opened her mouth, took a deep breath. But the only words that came out were, "You can't just buy me a pool table. That's a little crazy, even for you."

Henny was smiling again, the light in his eyes melting a little more of her resolve. "Don't think of it as a pool table. Think of it as another flat surface for me to throw you down on and—"

"Henny! Is everything about sex with you?"

"No. It's about sex with *you*." He kissed her neck, inching his way up to her earlobe. "If you don't like it, I'll tell them to bring your old one back. It does have a special place in my heart."

"I didn't say I didn't like it," she breathed, losing herself in the feel of his lips, his teeth, his tongue. "Just that it's... Oh, God. That feels... It's..."

"What is it?" he teased, nipping her earlobe again. "I didn't quite catch that last part."

"Totally inappropriate." She finally managed to pull herself together, putting a hand on his chest and gently pushing him away.

Why couldn't he understand what a big deal this was to her?

"Extravagant, maybe," he said. "I'll give you that. But inappropriate?" Henny shoved a hand through his damp hair, frustration finally breaking through. "Come on, Bex. It's not like I'm just some rich asshole trying to get into your pants. It's *me*. How the hell long have we known each other?"

"I know. It's just... I appreciate the gesture. I really, really do. It's sweet and thoughtful and the table looks amazing in there. But for me, it's kind of the same thing as you loaning me money to buy the place. When it comes to the bar, that's just something I need to do on my own."

"But why? I'm part of your life. It's no different than when we were kids and your mom helped me get my shit together for college. She found out about those scholarships—"

"Yes, she found out about them. Got all the paperwork, helped you with the applications. But in the end, you had to earn it yourself. You had to skate your ass off and show up for all those five a.m. practices and prove you had the balls to go all the way."

"I care about your dreams, and if I have the means to help you get there, I can—"

"You can respect my wishes on this." She folded her arms over her chest. "That's not negotiable. I need to do this my way. It doesn't mean I don't want you by my side—just that I don't want you leading the charge."

After a beat, Henny finally nodded, blowing out a breath. "What about the pool table? You really want me to send it back? I doubt they still have the old one."

Bex smiled, sliding her hands up his chest, hooking her fingers over his broad shoulders. "If you promise to behave yourself, and stop being so crazy, I will accept your amazing, generous, completely over-the-top gift. But next time you get the urge to spoil me, do it with chocolate. Or a massage. Or—"

"This?" Lowering his mouth, he kissed her chin, her throat, blazing a trail down to her collarbone, his fingers working at the buttons on her shirt.

Bex laughed. Two minutes in his presence, and she was completely disarmed. "You're impossible. You know that, right?"

He'd gotten three buttons open so far, just enough to reveal her lacy black bra. Skimming his fingers over the top, he said, "I think you mean irresistible."

"No way." She faltered, her heart rate kicking up a notch as he teased her nipples with his palms. "I can... totally... resist you."

"Yeah?"

"Watch me." With great effort, she pulled out of his embrace and went to the fridge, pretending to look for something to eat. There wasn't much inside—a bag of carrots, leftover sour cream from their last batch of naughty nachos, some thawed chicken breast, takeout containers that probably needed to be tossed. "You need to go shopping, Henny. Without my input, your snack game is pathetic."

"Make a list. We'll get whatever you want." Henny tossed his towel over the back of one of the kitchen barstools. "In the mean time, I need to get ready. Gallagher set up a meet-and-greet with one of the high school teams before tonight's game." He kicked off his sneakers, then peeled off his shorts.

Naked. The man was standing before her in all his beautiful, muscular, sweat-glistened glory.

Her gaze trailed over his muscled chest, the firm ridges of his abs, the line of dark hair that led down from his belly button, the v-shaped muscles that pointed to her most favorite places. He was hard, and made no attempts to hide it.

Damn, he was beautiful.

Damn, she was horny.

"Was that eye-fucking good for you?" he teased. "Because it was *great* for me."

"I'm not... I wasn't..." Bex yanked open the refrigerator again, but she wasn't fooling anyone; she couldn't tear her gaze away from him.

"I need a shower," he said, his hand wrapping around his cock, his eyes full of mischief. "Care to join me, or are you too busy resisting?"

"I don't know yet. I'm thinking about it."

"You're gawking."

"I'm considering."

"Consider this." Still fisting himself, Henny began to stroke, slow and steady, turning her bones into Jell-O. "The longer you take to make up your mind, the less time this cock will spend between your thighs."

"Or between my lips," she countered.

Henny gaped at her, but recovered quickly, turning and walking down the hall toward the master bath. "You know where to find me when you're done considering."

Bex held out as long as she could, but as soon as she heard the water turn on, she was toast. No way could she stand there unaffected while her man was in the shower, wet, soaping himself up, stroking that smooth, perfect shaft…

"I'm coming!" By the time she reached the bathroom, Bex was already naked, her clothes disappearing so fast she didn't even remember tearing them off. "You win, Kyle Henderson."

"I always do." Henny opened the shower door, inviting her to step inside the huge, stand-up shower.

She sighed happily, grateful as always for the dual shower heads.

Water streamed down over his pecs and abs, and she traced its path with her fingers, his skin slick and warm and inviting. His cock pressed urgently against her belly.

She wrapped her hand around it, stroking him slowly as hot water slid deliciously down her back.

Henny whispered her name, his head tipping back, his chest rising and falling as his breathing quickened.

Suddenly, Bex didn't want to touch him. She wanted him in her mouth. All of him. And she wanted him to remember this moment. To think of it every time he took a shower. Hell, any time someone turned on the hot water, she wanted him to get hard.

Without warning she dropped to her knees, ignoring the hard press of the tile as she took him between her lips, her tongue seducing him deeper and deeper into her mouth.

"Fuck," he breathed, sliding his fingers into her wet hair.

She sucked him, then pulled back, stroking him with her hand, guiding him in and out, deeper and harder. He was hot and smooth and perfect in her mouth, filling her completely as she licked and teased, bringing him right to the precipice, then backing off, building and building until she was afraid he might collapse from her exquisite torture.

"I want to taste you," she whispered, licking the end of his cock, his flesh hot and salty.

"Bex," he warned, "I can't hold back much longer."

She looked up at him through her lashes, hungry and needy and so, so desperate to make him come.

That was all it took. Henny growled her name, his fist tightening in her hair as he took over and fucked her mouth, faster and deeper, harder, water pelting her bare back, tiles digging into her knees, his orgasm exploding in a final, perfect thrust that left him shuddering and gasping for air.

Certain he was more than satisfied, Bex took her time easing his cock out of her mouth, teasing the tip with her tongue before finally releasing him. He slumped back against the shower wall, barely able to stand.

He watched her rise from the floor, his mouth parted, water sluicing down his body as he fought to catch his breath. The look he gave her was one of amazement. Like he'd never seen her before. Like every time with her was a brand new adventure, full of surprise and intrigue.

"I should probably let you get ready," Bex said softly. She grabbed the shower door, but before she could step out, Henny's mouth was on the back of her neck, his hand snaking around her belly, fingers dipping lower, lower... *Oh, God.*

"Sorry, beautiful," he breathed. "We're not even *close* to done here."

CHAPTER TWENTY

Leaving Henny to finish getting ready after their marathon shower session, Bex put on his Radiohead T-shirt and headed into the kitchen to refuel. She didn't have much to work with, but she managed to throw together a salad and a half-decent stir-fry with the chicken breast and leftover Chinese. She was pretty sure the wok she'd found had never been used.

Like the rest of the house, the kitchen was showroom gorgeous, all granite and stainless steel, with gleaming oak floors and cabinets and enough high-end appliances to delight even a pro chef. But it wasn't Henny. *Nothing* in the house was Henny.

He'd bought the place online sight unseen before moving back to Buffalo years ago, paid a decorator to get it all set up for him, bought whatever else he needed without much thought or care. It was beautiful, yes. Functional, too. But cold. Even after all this time in Buffalo, Henny still hadn't made it his home. No photos. No knickknacks or books or plants or magazines. No mess, other than the shorts and towel he'd left out earlier. Just a bunch of high-end decor, dusted and polished to a spotless gleam once a week by his cleaning service.

It was a stark reminder that for Henny, Buffalo wasn't really *home*.

Would it ever be?

Bex returned her attention to the stir-fry, refusing to chase those thoughts down the rabbit hole.

"Smells good." Henny came around behind her, pressing a kiss to the back of her neck, nuzzling the still-damp hair at her nape. Peeking over her shoulder, he asked, "Where did that pan come from?"

"It's a wok, and I found it in the cupboard with the rice cooker and the crockpot you've probably never plugged in."

"What the fuck is a crockpot?"

"You should charge admission to this place," she teased, dishing their meal into two white bowls that'd probably come with the mugs he'd been using before she'd given him the bison set. "It's like an art exhibit in here."

"You don't like the house?"

"I didn't say that." Bex smiled as they sat down across from each other at the table, digging into their food. She hadn't realized how famished she was until that first bite. "Just needs a woman's touch."

"You're right. Move in with me."

She swallowed her chicken, eyes wide. "Henny, that's not what I meant! Woman's touch? It's just a stupid saying."

"But not such a stupid idea, right?" He shrugged and shoveled in a forkful of veggies, so casually she couldn't tell whether his invitation was serious. "Dude. This is fucking *good*."

Bex's head was spinning. Had he really just asked her to move in with him?

She reached for her water, gulped down half the glass. Insane. That's what this was. Totally insane. Wordlessly, she watched him wolf down the rest of his food, barely able to touch her own.

Henny pointed at her bowl with his fork. "You gonna eat that?"

She handed it over, finally finding her words. "You *were* joking, right?"

"I don't joke about food."

"*Henny.*"

Abandoning his efforts to inhale everything in sight,

he set down his fork and slid over to the chair next to her, his sudden closeness both comforting and suffocating. "I want you to move in with me. No joke."

"But..." Bex blew out a breath. Where did she even start with this?

Glancing around, she tried to imagine herself roaming the house, waiting for Henny to get back from the airport, from the ice, from his meetings, from all the places his job took him.

And then she tried to imagine doing all of that waiting in another big empty house in another city, far away from the pub and her mom and the friends she'd made here. Away from everything and everyone she knew. Totally alone, one hundred percent dependent on Henny.

If he got traded off the Tempest, that's what would happen. And what if it didn't work out between them?

"We've already lived together once," Henny said. "This should be easy. You know I rock as a roommate."

"Oh, right. Because sleeping in separate beds as teenagers with my mom down the hall is totally the same thing. Plus, as I recall, sharing a bathroom with you was not the most sanitary experience of my life."

"I have a cleaning service now. Problem solved."

Bex tried to laugh, but it came out shaky. Move in together? Last month, they were best friends who'd never so much as made out during a game of spin the bottle. Bex still wasn't even sure whether they were officially seeing each other, whether it was going anywhere beyond the amazing sex.

Now he wanted to share his home with her?

The room tipped sideways again, her heart hammering in her chest. It was all happening so fast. Words like *dangerous* and *obsession* floated behind her eyes.

But no, those weren't the right words, she realized. This wasn't some insta-love infatuation with a stranger that would come crashing down the minute they discovered each other's flaws. This was Henny. A man she'd known for almost her entire life. They'd spent all those years, all those moments large and small building the foundation of an awesome, unbreakable friendship.

Maybe it was time to build something else now. Something even more incredible.

And what if it fails? What if I lose him?

"What is it, beautiful?" Henny's voice was laced with concern, his knuckles brushing softly against her cheek. "Where are you?"

Bex hated thinking about her final days in California, but now the memories crept back in unbidden, stabbing her behind the chest. She'd been so, so lost. Everything inside her had ached so badly, it was as if her seams had come undone. Fear, anger, and shame had twisted around her heart, reminding her every time she took a breath how stupid she'd been. How careless.

She was over the man who'd done that to her. But she wasn't over herself. All the mistakes she'd made. The signs she'd ignored. The parts of herself she'd given up, all for the wrong guy.

"I'm terrified," she finally admitted, closing her eyes. It was too painful to look at him when she felt this raw and exposed. "I don't want to get hurt again. I don't trust myself to... to... I just can't, Henny. I can't go through that again."

"Hey. You're the most important person in my life. Always have been." He slid his fingers under her chin, and she opened her eyes, leaning into his touch. In a voice so tender it nearly melted her heart, he said, "Do you honestly think I would hurt you? That I'd do anything to put our friendship at risk?"

A tear slid down her cheek. "Not on purpose."

"Fuck that, Bex. The answer is no, I wouldn't. Not ever."

"You can't make a promise like that."

"For you I can. I will." His brow furrowed, his eyes turning fiery and intense. "There's nothing I wouldn't do for you. You have to know that. I look at you sitting here at my table, in my house, wearing my T-shirt, and I can't believe how fucking lucky I am. How lucky I've always been, long as I've known you."

"Don't," she whispered, lowering her eyes, blinking away the rest of her tears.

"Why not?"

"If you keep looking at me like that... If you keep saying things like that... I might just..." Her breath hitched, heart pounding as she struggled to reign herself in. She'd said too much, exposed herself in ways she just wasn't ready for.

But when she looked at Henny again, he was smiling shyly, nothing like the cocky, confident man she knew.

"I might just, too," he said. Then, without breaking their intense gaze, "Pretty sure I already did."

Did he just... is he falling in love with me?

"This wasn't supposed to happen between us," she whispered.

"But it did." Henny swiped a tear from her cheek, caressing her skin with his thumb. "Are you saying you regret it? That this isn't what you want?"

"No." Bex pulled back, reaching for her water glass. "I don't regret it at all. I'm just... I'm all over the place. And you..." She glanced around the catalog-perfect kitchen, her earlier thoughts poking out of the rabbit hole again. "You've got a few things to figure out, too."

"Sounds like we're a pretty good match."

"Great." She laughed, some of the tension easing. "So who's actually driving this bus to crazy town?"

"As long as we're both on it and going to the same place, I don't give a fuck."

"But that's the thing, Hen. Are we? I feel like I'm still picking up the pieces from my old life. My career is..." Bex sighed. "Half the time I don't know what I want anymore. And what about you? What's going on with the Tempest? You want me to move in, but are you even planning on staying in Buffalo?"

"You'll figure out your stuff, Bex. You always do. And me? Hell, the NHL is a crap shoot no matter what. You know that. I could get traded, or injured, or—"

"Fired?"

"Not likely."

Bex shook her head, all the old worries rushing back in. She wasn't sure what had changed for him this season, but after her arrival in town, he'd gone from top-ranked pro to back-alley brawler in a matter of weeks. His recent improvements felt more like a temporary bubble than a real change.

Great sex could be an elixir for all sorts of ills. But eventually, it would wear off. And then what?

"You're going to be late for your meet-and-greet," she said, rising from the table and picking up their dishes.

"Screw it. I hate that dog-and-pony shit anyway. The other guys will handle it."

"Yeah? Do you really think Gallagher's going to keep you on the roster if you keep acting like this?"

"Fuck him. I've got a backup plan."

"Let me guess: stand-up comic? Investor in local dive bars? Underwear model?"

Seemingly oblivious to her sarcasm, he followed her into the kitchen, wrapping his arms around her from behind as she rinsed off the dishes. "Still working out the details, but it involves you and me on some secluded little island where clothing is optional. And by optional I mean banned." He bit her shoulder through the T-shirt, his hard length pressing against her backside.

Bex shook her head. He wasn't taking any of this seriously, and she didn't know how to make him.

Yes, you do. You're just avoiding it.

Bex turned around in his arms, grabbing his shoulders. She was his best friend, and he'd always counted on her to call him out on his bullshit. Now more than ever she needed to push him hard, to challenge him to face his demons before he lost control of the one thing he'd loved and depended on his entire life—hockey.

But for the first time in their long history, she felt herself backing down.

The truth hit her hard and fast: She didn't want him to be mad at her. She didn't want to push him so hard he'd walk away.

She didn't want to lose him—not even to help him save his career.

They'd both jumped into this thing unexpectedly, and maybe they stayed in it assuming their friendship would automatically smooth out the bumps along the way. Seemed logical, but it wasn't really working out like that. Not at all.

They needed to slow down, start again at a much slower pace. Bex had meant what she'd said to him—she didn't regret any of this, and she definitely didn't want it to end. But she was starting to miss him—the Henny she'd known as a friend. She missed *them*. Their easy banter, their Netflix nights at her place, chatting about work over a couple of beers at Big Laurie's, always saying exactly what was on their minds without fear of repercussions—it was starting to fade, dimming behind the bright light of their intense affair.

"Come on, Bex. You're overthinking it." Henny traced a line across her eyebrows. "I can practically smell your brain melting."

"Maybe you're *under*-thinking it." She looked around the kitchen again, biting her lower lip. "Henny, you don't even have magnets on your fridge."

"Seriously?" He grunted out a laugh, totally missing the point. "Because I can get you magnets, beautiful. Hundreds of them. I'll get magnets from every damn city and tourist trap I visit for the rest of my life. Two magnets from every store. How's that?"

Still laughing, he kissed her forehead as if that settled the matter.

Bex untangled herself from his embrace and went back to the dishes in the sink.

"Come on, Bex. You know you can do whatever you want with the place." He rested his hands on her shoulders, his tone softening. "And I don't want you worrying about rent or bills anymore."

His words were like ice water.

After everything she'd told him, he was still trying to save her, still trying to write a check to cover her past mistakes.

Is that what he saw when he looked at her? Some helpless little girl in need of a sugar daddy?

"I made a few bad calls, Hen. I'm not incompetent. And I certainly don't need you to fix my money problems." Bex yanked open the cupboard above the stove, looking for something to put the leftovers in. "Don't you have any Tupperware? What is *wrong* with you?"

"You think I want you here so I can fix your money problems?" Henny reached for her arm, forcing her to face him again. Anger flashed in his eyes, then disappointment, the weight of it pressing down on her shoulders.

"I want you here because waking up with you in my

arms is the best part of my day," he said. "Because I want to drink coffee with you in those stupid bison mugs every morning and make love to you before I go to practice. Because when I hear you humming in the shower, my fucking heart explodes. Because I want your damn basil plants on my windowsills and your toothbrush next to mine in the cup. Because when I get off the plane after a week on the road, playing my ass off every night in a different city, sleeping in hotel rooms and smiling for bullshit interviews, I want to know it was all worth it, because at the end of it all, I get to come home to you."

Bex's chest hurt, Henny's words wrapping her up like a thick blanket in the summertime. She wanted to be comforted by them, but all she felt was hot and sweaty and breathless.

"I just... I need some time to think," she finally managed. "This all happened so fast, and maybe we—"

"You're not into it, Bex. I got it. Message received." He grabbed a banana from a bunch on the counter, totally shutting down. "I should head out. Meeting starts in ten minutes."

"I thought you were blowing it off?"

Henny shrugged. "Guess I'm not in the mood to get fired after all."

Defeated, Bex closed her eyes, blowing out a breath. She hated fighting with him, hated the tension creeping in, exploiting all the cracks—cracks that hadn't even existed until they started sleeping together.

"Play hard tonight," she said, following him to the foyer. Her smile was a peace offering. "I'll be watching from the pub."

Henny nodded and offered a quick smile in return, but it was gone before he turned to reach for his coat. He didn't ask for his usual good luck kiss, just headed out, leaving her all alone in that big empty house, the leftover stir-fry congealing in the pan.

CHAPTER TWENTY-ONE

"Fuck with me tonight, asshole. I dare you." Henny pushed away from the boards, shaking off a body check from Spence Merkle, captain of the Quebec Phantom. Yeah, the hit was fair play, but Henny was not in the mood for any bullshit. Two periods in, and he'd already served time in the box twice for high-sticking. He was sucking ass tonight—hadn't scored a single goal or assist. On top of that, he'd blown off the meet-and-greet after all, driving around before practice to cool off after that whole shitstorm with Bex.

Didn't work. All he'd managed to do was dig himself into a deeper hole with Gallagher.

"Work it out, one-nine." Dunn popped him on the shoulder as he skated past. "We need you sharp out here."

Henny saluted. "As a motherfucking tack."

They charged back toward center ice, where Roscoe was duking it out with Quebec's right winger for control of the puck. He finally broke away, then passed to Henny, who shot it over to Dunn. Dunn wound up and took the shot—*damn it*. Goalie stopped it easily, knocking the puck back into play.

They chased it around the ice a few more times, keeping control but not putting any points on the board. Seconds before the buzzer, Roscoe snuck in a sweet slapshot, first goal of the night.

By the end of the second, they were still down two-one. Quebec wasn't even playing a tight game. Their defense was sloppy, their offense weak—their long-time starting center had been out all month on the injured list, and the new guy just wasn't hacking it.

Salt in the wound, far as Henny was concerned. Should've been an easy night. Would've been, if Henny could get his fat head in the game and off his personal problems. He was surprised Gallagher hadn't yanked him yet.

Start of the third, the boys lined up for the face-off. The ref dropped the puck. In the blink of an eye, Dunn lunged forward, tying up the other center so Jarlsberg could swoop in from behind and grab the puck. Jarlsberg nabbed it, passed it over to Roscoe, and the front line was off, charging down into Quebec's goal zone. Roscoe slapped it over to Dunn while Henny followed at a good clip, running interference as the other guys wove in and out between them, everyone gunning for the puck.

Somehow he managed to keep his focus, buying Dunn the time he needed to slap that bitch into the net.

Two-two, and team Tempest was back in business. Henny shook out his arms and gripped his stick, ready to send these motherfuckers packing. Dunn lost the face-off, but Roscoe dug in and stole the puck back, sliding it to Henny. It hit the blade of his stick with a familiar thunk.

Keeping it right in the sweet spot, Henny skated it down to the goal zone, but Quebec was riding him hard. Dunn and Roscoe were totally covered, too—those Phantom bastards weren't giving them an inch of air to breathe, and Tempest defense was too far away to help. Henny couldn't risk a pass. His only option was to send it home himself.

Henny pushed harder, breaking out of the knot and speeding toward the net. The goalie was totally exposed, pivoting on his skates as he tried to anticipate Henny's move.

This one's going bar down, no doubt.

Henny's muscles tensed for the shot. He could see it happening in his mind—the puck hitting the bottom of the crossbar and shooting right into the net, the crowd roaring, his boys raising their fists...

Henny stumbled. The puck slid out of his control,

straight into enemy hands. He righted himself before he fell, recovering just in time to catch Merkle's twisted little grin. The douche bag captain who'd nailed him to the boards last period had clipped Henny's skate with his stick, right under the ref's nose.

No way was that an accident. And no way was Henny letting it slide.

Merkle tried to pass, but Dunn swooped in and stole the puck, shooting it over to Roscoe. With the Tempest on top of the game again, Henny turned his attention back to Merkle, tracking him like a fucking shadow. That asshole wasn't getting anywhere *near* his boys again.

Let him fucking try it.

Dude must've been psychic, because suddenly he pivoted sharply, breaking away from Henny and heading right for Dunn. Right for the puck.

Oh, fuck this guy.

Henny charged after him, adrenaline taking over, pushing him harder and faster, beyond all reason. Soon as he got in range, he lunged, reaching out for something —anything—to slow the guy down.

Bad idea. He'd grabbed Merkle's stick without even thinking. Even before the ref blew the whistle, Henny knew he'd just fucked himself.

Sonofabitch.

"Buffalo penalty, nineteen," the ref announced. "Kyle Henderson. Holding the stick. Two minutes."

Henny hopped into the penalty box and grabbed a bottle of water, ignoring the boos of the crowd and the burn of shame in his gut. It was his third penalty of the night, and a stupid-ass one at that. He was playing like a fucking amateur. Gallagher's hair was turning grayer by the minute.

He was in it up to his eyeballs.

The only saving grace was that Bex wasn't here to see this shit. Of course, that fact was also eating Henny alive. Every time he looked at her regular seat behind the glass, all he saw was the empty space where his girl was supposed to be.

The girl who'd said no.

The girl who was slipping away before he'd even had a chance to really hold on to her. To make it count.

Henny's gut twisted. He hated the way they'd left things today. Hated that he'd made her feel bad, as if he thought she couldn't handle her own finances. Hated even more that she'd tried to poke holes in all his bullshit excuses, shined the light right through them.

No wonder she said no.

What was she supposed to think? That he was a strong man? That he'd always be there for her? Henny couldn't even be there for himself. His career was falling apart right before his eyes, but it was like a damn out-of-body experience: he could see it happening, feel it slipping away with every bad game, every shitty practice, every fight he got drawn into. Yet he felt absolutely powerless to do anything about it.

Maybe he really was broken. Fucked up beyond repair. Maybe that's why his parents had bailed on him as a kid, leaving Bex and her mom to pick up the pieces.

And maybe Bex had finally figured out his big secret —that for all his jokes, all his money, all his kisses, all the ways he'd tried to love her as a friend and beyond, maybe Henny just wasn't worth the risk.

He gripped his stick and sucked in an icy breath, fighting back the doubts that threatened to suck him under. He had a game to finish. A team to support. A Phantom to fucking nail to the wall.

The clock ran out on his penalty, and Henny was out of the box like a shot fired, zooming right into the action, right for his man.

Don't. He's not worth it, you dumb fuck.

At the last possible second, Henny pulled back, reigning himself in. Blowing up right now would only put the guys at risk, and it certainly wasn't going to fix his issues with Bex. He needed to keep a cool head, buy Dunn and Roscoe some more time to make the goal.

The move paid off. With Henny keeping the heat on Merkle, Roscoe broke away, skating right into the zone and tapping that baby into the net like he was born to do it. Three-two. Tempest was finally ahead.

Henny raised his arm to cheer for his man, but before

he could even make eye contact with Roscoe, he was on his back, right on the ice.

Merkle had taken him down, late as fuck, hard as hell, and in no way was it even remotely kosher. The two of them were tangled up on the ice, Merkle on top, pinning him down, his stick pressed across Henny's chest.

"Fuck's your problem?" Henny shoved him off and jumped back up to his feet, gripping his stick hard, panting like a cornered animal.

Merkle was up again, too, already tearing off his gloves. "Douche bag," he spat. "Your old lady fucking someone else? You sure look like a guy who's only getting leftovers."

Henny dropped his stick, yanked off his gloves and helmet. Grabbing a fistful of jersey, he got right in Merkle's face, so close he could practically smell what the asshole ate for dinner. "You wanna say that again, dickless?"

"Fuck you."

"Newsflash." He shoved Merkle into the boards, forearm pressed against the guy's throat. "I'm not the one getting fucked tonight, pal."

His vision swam with red, all that "keep a cool head" shit zipping right out the window. Henny was ready to throw the first punch. Ready to sign his own walking papers. He was done. Done with this bullshit league, working his ass off, taking shit from guys like this, getting spanked by management any time he tried to defend himself or his boys.

If playing by the rules meant bending over and taking it in the ass any time the refs fell asleep on the job, then Henny was done with this entire fucking game.

But this time, he didn't have to throw down first. Merkle did the honors.

Henny took the hit hard, Merkle's fist like a bat to the face. His head snapped back, mouth filling with blood. Roscoe and Dunn were at his side in a heartbeat, but not before Merkle picked up his stick, stuck it right in Henny's grill.

Everything else was a blur, a series of flashes Henny barely had time to register: Dunn coming down on Merkle like white on ice, punching the guy square in the mouth. Roscoe hauling Henny out of Merkle's clutches. A sea of Phantom white-and-silver surging forward, the other Tempest guys piling in after them.

Henny couldn't even tell who was doing the punching, who was trying to break it up, who was shouting—only that the whole mess had turned into a fucking gong show of epic proportions.

Couldn't have been more than a minute or two before the refs and team docs finally made it through the knot, trying to separate the teams while Roscoe dragged Henny toward the net, out of the fray.

"Dude. You okay?" Roscoe took Henny's head in his hands, looking over his face. "You hit your head?"

"No. Just ate a little stick." Henny spit out a mouthful of blood, checking that he still had all his teeth. One in the back was loose, but he'd live. More blood trickled down from a gash over his eyebrow, warm and sticky, and he was pretty sure he'd fucked up his hand, too. But he was beyond feeling pain. "Thanks for the backup. I'm good."

Roscoe clapped him on the shoulder. "Wasn't your fault."

"Debatable."

"Sounds like the refs are calling Quebec for roughing and unsportsmanlike conduct."

"And Gallagher's calling for a line change." Henny nodded at the bench, where Gallagher fumed. Quebec may have taken the penalty call, but Henny was in for a world-class reaming.

"Don't sweat it. We're up by one. Fahey and the boys'll bring it home." Roscoe put his arm around Henny's shoulders, leading him off the ice.

"You guys good?" Dunn asked, falling in next to them. Narrowing his eyes at Henny, he said, "That rock-hard bucket of yours okay?"

Henny knocked on his head. "Fan-fucking-tastic."

"Jesus fuck, we need a group hug," Roscoe said.

"More like group therapy." Dunn glared at Henny, but then looked away, hopping up into the box.

Sitting down on the players' bench, Henny almost wished Dunn would take a swing at him. Beat some sense into his stupid ass. He had every right to do it, but of course he wouldn't. End of the day, Dunn was a good fucking guy, and he cared about his team.

It was a hell of a lot more than Henny could say about himself.

Six minutes left on the clock. Tempest was up by one. Phantom was getting tired. Roscoe was right—Fahey and the boys could wrap this up, no problem. Far as the team was concerned, yeah, they were good.

But the message in Gallagher's eyes was clear. Henny should've walked away from that fight long before it even started. They got fucking lucky with the penalty call—it was that simple. And he'd played a shit game tonight, totally distracted, totally unprofessional, letting his team do all the heavy lifting while he skated around with his head up his ass.

What happened to the stone-cold pro who could play his way through any personal tragedy? Who could find a way to channel all the bad shit into raw, unadulterated power on the ice? Who could find his purpose out there, no matter who came at him?

"Henderson." Gallagher glanced at his face, the

disgust clear in his eyes. "Go have Doctor Langford take a look at that cut."

Henny swiped the back of his hand across his brow. He was still bleeding. "You want me back here after, or should—"

"No." Gallagher turned his attention back to the game, watching Fahey and the second-line guys take their positions on the ice. "I want you the fuck out of my sight."

CHAPTER TWENTY-TWO

Henny couldn't fucking breathe.

He sat on the toilet lid in the bathroom at Big Laurie's, trying not to flinch while Bex cleaned his cuts.

The pain had returned full force, but he could deal with that. Hell, over the course of his career he'd probably left his body weight in blood out on the ice. But being this close to Bex without touching her—close enough that the fine hairs on her arms tickled his face, the scent of her skin making him ache? It was killing him, and he couldn't do a damn thing about it. One move, and she'd probably deck him.

"I can't believe you didn't let the team doc patch you up," she said.

"I needed to get out of there, Bex."

"Yeah? Smart call on your part." She poured half a

bottle of alcohol onto a fresh cotton ball and jammed it into the gash.

"Damn it, woman!" He jolted at the sting, his eyes watering. "Take it easy!"

"Hold *still*."

Henny closed his eyes, dizzy and overwhelmed in a way that had nothing to do with his messed up face. It was Bex, all Bex. Ever since he'd left her at his house today, all he'd wanted to do was come back to her, take her into his arms, fix what he'd fucked up.

But now that he was here with her, close enough to touch, to taste, he didn't know what the fuck to say to make it okay between them.

"You are a red-hot mess," she said, exasperated. Her breath was soft and warm on his cheeks as she finished taping up the cuts. "Are you even *capable* of behaving yourself anymore?"

"Not where you're concerned."

He hadn't meant to say it out loud, but fuck it. He was already in a world of shit with his team and managers. Why not pile it on a little thicker? It was the truth, anyway.

For so many years, their friendship had cruised along without so much as a hiccup. Now, no matter how hard he tried, Henny kept saying the wrong thing. Doing the wrong thing. *Being* the wrong thing.

But instead of scolding him again, Bex only frowned.

She cupped his chin in her palm, running her thumb over his lower lip, her touch so soft and gentle he shivered. The anger vanished suddenly from her eyes, replaced by worry. By sadness. By something else he thought he recognized but didn't want to name, because he was too fucking scared to be wrong again.

"Oh, Hen. This isn't about me," she said softly. "You have to know that."

Henny grabbed her wrist, wrapping his fingers around it, bringing her palm to his lips. "I don't know anything anymore."

Ignoring this, she pulled her hand away and reached up to put the Band-Aids back in the cabinet above the toilet. Her shirt rode up, exposing her taut belly, the bottom edge of her rib cage, all the curves he'd mapped with his tongue a hundred times since they'd started down this road. All he had to do was lean forward, press his lips to her perfect flesh…

She stood before him again, crossing her arms over her chest, all the anger and disappointment rushing back into her eyes. "So are we going to talk about what happened out there tonight, or just keep pretending that everything's even remotely okay with you?"

Henny leaned his head back against the wall and closed his eyes. "You saw what happened. Quebec started some shit. I finished it. Lucky for me, Merkle got nailed for starting the fight, so even though Gallagher's gonna rake me over the coals tomorrow, I'm in the clear with the league. And now I'm sitting on your toilet getting a lecture I really don't need while you torture me with alcohol and Band-Aids."

"Were you always such a man-baby, or is this some kind of midlife crisis? Because if that's what's going on here, go get yourself a convertible and a younger woman and get over it."

"Did you forget what happened earlier? What you said to me?" Henny sat up straight again, shoving his hand through his hair like a total fucking idiot—he snagged the bandage, tearing it clean off. "Sonofa—"

"Jesus, Henny." She reached for the box of bandages again. "Hold still. You're bleeding. Again."

"Forget it. It's fine."

"It's not fine. You probably need stitches."

"Just use more Band-Aids."

Bex clenched her jaw, but did as he asked, blotting away the blood and then shaking out a few extra bandages from the box. Henny closed his eyes, losing himself in a memory... tenth grade, maybe? Some schoolyard bullshit, couple of dude-bro assholes trying to intimidate Bex and her friend outside the art room. Henny rolled up on the scene, saw the fear in Bex's eyes as one of the guys cornered her. Three minutes later, dudes were on the ground. Henny got a black eye, a gash on his chin, and two weeks of detention, but he told the teacher he'd do it again in a heartbeat if it meant keeping his girl safe.

They'd walked home together, back to Laurie's house. Henny sat on the toilet seat in the upstairs bathroom, Bex doing her best to patch him up, just like now.

He still had the scar on his chin.

"Are you… is that a smile?" Bex asked. "What is so funny, Kyle Henderson?"

Henny opened his eyes, relieved to see her smiling back at him. "Just thinking about the time I beat down those two guys outside the art room."

Bex laughed. "Oh, boy. Well, not that I wasn't grateful, but there was only one guy. And I'm pretty sure he wasn't the one who got beat."

"What? I laid those dickholes *out*. I remember them curled up on the pavement, crying like little bitches. Kellerman gave me detention."

"Um, sorry to burst your little man-bubble, but you were the one curled up on the pavement. Brock Lipowicz took off right after he kicked your ass."

"Okay, that is *so* not how it went down. But… Damn. We got bested by a dude named Brock Lipowicz?" Henny shook his head in disgust. "We should Facebook that motherfucker and see what he's up to now."

"I can probably guess." Bex blew out a breath. "That was what, fifteen years ago? Sixteen?"

Henny smiled, bigger this time. So big it hurt his

aching jaw. "Guess you've been fixing me up a long time."

"We've been fixing each *other* up a long time." Bex's smile faded, her shoulders slumping, the lightness gone once again. "You can't throw off your whole game every time we have an argument, Hen. And technically, that was just a misunderstanding."

"I asked you to move in with me like a total tool, and you shot me down. Not much room for interpre—*ouch!*"

"Sorry." Bex winced. "I need to tape this tighter. Hang on." She finished up, smoothing her fingers over the bandages to make sure it would hold. "I didn't shoot you down. I said I needed time. Or at least I *tried* to say it. You left before we could finish the conversation. You know, like adults."

Henny sighed. She was right. That's exactly what he'd done. It's what he always did when someone hurt him—even if it wasn't her fault. Thing was, he hadn't been hurt in years. He'd made damn sure of that, keeping himself at arm's length, never letting anyone too close. Other than Bex, Dunn and Roscoe were the only ones who'd even gotten in at all. It'd been so long since he'd put his heart out there, he'd damn near forgotten what rejection felt like.

He didn't like it. Didn't know how to deal with it. And he certainly didn't know how to talk about it. He didn't *do* talks—he'd never had to.

But now, seeing that look in her eyes, knowing he was the one who'd put it there... Hell. Henny might be a brawler on the ice these days, but he really didn't like hurting people.

Especially not his best friend.

He looked up into her angel face again, trying to anchor himself. Hoping like hell it wasn't too late to fix things. His head ached like a bitch, but when she ran her fingers through his hair and sighed, he found another reason to smile.

"What's the prognosis, doc?" he asked. "Will I live?"

"Unfortunately, yes." Bex rolled her eyes, grabbing a fistful of his hair and giving it a gentle tug. "But we might have to amputate your face." She put away the bandages for a second time, then sighed. "What am I going to do with—"

An angry fist pounded on the other side of the door. "You two baking cookies in there? Wrap it up already."

"Sorry!" Bex called out. "Just a minute." Then, to Henny, "We should probably—"

"Stay," he whispered, reaching for her hand.

"Someone's waiting for the bathroom."

"You know that's not what I mean." He pulled her close in front of him again, sliding his hands up her thighs, her hips. Pressing his mouth to her belly, he said, "Stop fighting this."

"I... I can't."

"You can."

She pulled away again, but Henny stood up, his hands on her hips, backing her up against the sink. Her eyes were wide and glassy as she looked up at him, her lashes wet with tears.

"I can't lose you, Henny—and that's what it feels like." She lowered her gaze, shaking her head like she was having an entire argument in there, all by herself. "Being with you like this… It means losing you in all the other ways. The *friend* ways. Every day we're together, more and more it's like I'm holding my breath, waiting for the bubble to burst. Waiting for you to tell me you don't want to be friends anymore."

"But I don't, Bex." Henny shook his head. They couldn't go back. Not when all he wanted to do was go forward. Give this thing a real shot. Try his best to make her happy, to put a smile back on her beautiful face. "What we have now… Everything is different. *Good* different."

"It isn't, though. That's what I'm saying." Bex swallowed hard, still not meeting his eyes. "For weeks, I watched you play like a rock star. Weeks that we've been having the most amazing sex. And then—"

"So? You telling me that you don't have a little more spring in your step lately?"

"And *then*," she continued, "we have one fight, and you just…" She finally looked up at him, her eyes full of genuine fear. In a voice so small he had to lean in to hear it, she said, "What if you're just using sex—*me*—as a distraction?"

"Hey!" Another knock on the door, another angry grunt on the other side. "What the fuck?"

"Five minutes, asshole," Henny snapped. Then, to Bex, "I can't believe you'd ever think that."

"What am I supposed to think? Look at yourself right now. Look at tonight's game. Do the math, Henny." She tried to duck out from under his arms, but he wouldn't let her go. Not like this. He moved in closer, pressing out the last of the space between them, caging her against the sink.

Abandoning her useless escape plans, she said, "This isn't working. I don't know why your game is off this season, what's going on in that head of yours, whether you even want to play hockey anymore. All I know is that you need to figure out your shit, and I need to figure out mine, and we don't need more complications getting in the way."

"So this is what? Your version of tough love? Hard pass."

Henny might've been able to handle tough love when they were just friends. It was the kind of things friends were supposed to do, right? Keep each other on the level. Kick each other's asses once in a while.

But tough love wasn't what he wanted from the

woman he was falling for. He didn't want to make her worry. To upset her. To give her a reason to doubt for even a minute that he could be the kind of man she could count on. The kind who had his shit together, who could take care of her and give her the world, support her in her own dreams. The kind who could back her up without crowding her out. The kind who'd never put that fear in her eyes, never make her doubt that being with her was the best damn thing in his life.

Well, asshole, maybe she has every right to doubt you. Maybe you're not *that guy.*

"You don't get a hard pass on this, Hen," she said. "Sorry."

"What are you saying? You don't want this? Us?"

"You're too important to me. Our *friendship* is too important to me. I'm not willing to risk it for just sex. Not anymore."

"*Just* sex?" Henny cracked a smile he wasn't really feeling, but if he didn't do something to turn this tide, he might explode. He leaned in close, brushing his lips over her neck, over that spot behind her ear that always drove her wild. "I don't think a woman having *just* sex is capable of making sounds like the ones you made in the shower when—"

"*Kyle.* I'm serious."

Kyle? She hadn't said his name in that tone since middle school. She was *beyond* serious. Which was exactly why he'd been trying to avoid this conversation ever since they'd woken up together that morning, hungover as shit. Hell, he'd probably been avoiding this conversation since they were in high school and he first realized she was a woman. A very hot, crazy, amazing woman that for some reason kept putting up with his bullshit, no matter how much he threw at her.

But this was it. She was already turning away. She was standing right in front of him, the heat from her body radiating against his chest, the sweet smell of her hair reminding him of home, the taste of her skin fresh on his lips, yet he could already feel her disappearing. Could hear all the words she wasn't saying, right there under the words she was.

The thought stabbed him behind the ribs. He didn't have the strength to listen to those words from her, to face the possibility of losing her.

So he did what he did best.

He cupped her face, brought her mouth to his, and kissed her.

Bex resisted for less than a heartbeat before she finally parted those sweet, pillowy lips, releasing a soft little moan as his tongue slid into her mouth. God, she tasted amazing. Felt amazing. Every sound she made, every hot breath ghosting across his lips, every beat of her wild heart made his head swim. His cock ached for her, straining hard against his jeans as he devoured her mouth, desperate to get closer. Deeper.

Grabbing her hips, he lifted her onto the countertop, hands running up her bare legs, pushing her skirt up around her waist. She fumbled with his belt, his button, his zipper, her small, warm hand sliding into his boxers and fisting him, stroking him just right.

But it wasn't enough. It would never be enough. He wanted more of her, all of her.

Henny ran his hand up the inside of her leg, seeking the warmth between her thighs. Her panties were already damp, and when he pressed his fingers against the silky fabric, Bex arched her hips, digging her nails into his shoulders.

Jesus fuck…

He hooked his fingers inside the top edge of her panties, knuckles brushing her soft hair. She was so warm, so wet, so fucking ready for him. Sliding two fingers inside her, he stroked, slow and soft, his thumb teasing her clit as he plunged his fingers in deeper, making her writhe.

"How bad do you want this?" he whispered, grazing the sensitive flesh of her earlobe with his teeth. "How hard do you want to come?"

Bex whimpered, her body tightening around his fingers as he slid in deeper, faster. She was slippery and hot, so needy for his touch. The thought drove him wild. God, they were so fucking good together.

Bex kissed him hard, biting his lower lip, barely breaking for air. She tightened her grip on his cock, rubbing her thumb over the tip, her touch sending shockwaves of pleasure up and down his spine.

"I want you inside me." She kissed him again. His lips. His jaw. His throat. "Fucking me. *Owning* me."

Henny nearly came at her words, the scent of her arousal flooding his senses. But before he could tear off those panties and plunge inside her, the door rattled on its hinges, the cheap sliding lock straining as the dude outside tried to force his way in.

"Got a line out here, assholes!" the guy shouted.

"Fuck off," Henny grumbled. Then, to Bex, "This joint really needs another bathroom."

Bex didn't laugh. Didn't even smile. She looked at him with the wild, desperate eyes of a succubus ready to feed.

"Office," she demanded, hopping off the sink and yanking the skirt down over her luscious ass. "Now."

CHAPTER TWENTY-THREE

Bex perched on the edge of her desk, watching Henny pace the closet-sized office.

"You're not saying anything," he said, but he wasn't looking at her. Wasn't touching her. The flames he'd stoked to life only minutes ago had been snuffed out by the interruption.

Bex didn't know whether to be disappointed or relieved. Everything inside her still ached for his touch, the hot pulse between her thighs an inescapable reminder of his effect on her. Despite the sudden chill between them, she still longed for him.

"Neither are you," she said.

"Don't know what else to tell you."

Bex's eyes glazed with tears. The gulf between them had never felt so wide.

Somewhere along the twisty path of friends to lovers,

they'd taken a wrong turn. The more she tried to get back on course, the more confused she felt. Now she was alone in the woods, no map, no gear, no compass. Totally lost.

And for the first time in her life, her best friend wasn't there to help her find her way again.

"What are we doing, Hen?" she asked.

"Fuck if I know." He still hadn't looked at her, not since they'd left the bathroom.

Hope leaked out of her body, one breath at a time.

Henny turned toward the door, his back to her, his hand reaching for the doorknob, and in that moment she knew exactly what he was thinking. Henny was the most loyal friend she knew, but he didn't do drama. Didn't do entanglements or messy, confusing, friends-with-whatever-the-hell-they'd-become disasters.

Bex didn't blame him. In his own way, he needed stability, too.

Just as he'd been her beacon, she'd been his rock. But she was unmoored, his light had gone dim, and neither of them seemed to have a clue how to fix it.

"Henny, wait," she said, hoping the right words would come. The magic answer that would make all of this okay again.

They didn't.

Henny stopped anyway. Turned around. Crossed the small space between them in a heartbeat. His hands were on her face, in her hair, his mouth devouring hers, hungry and demanding, raw and passionate. Angry, too. Afraid. It was like he poured every last emotion into that kiss, a punishment and a promise all in one.

"Leave with me," he demanded. He was breathless now, his eyes wild and desperate and intense and oh *God*, she wanted it to be real. So, so badly.

"Where?" she breathed.

"Does it matter?" He fingered one of her curls, tucking it behind her ear as he brushed his lips along her jawline. "We can travel around, see the country. Camp at every national park, just like we used to talk about."

She smiled, remembering their summer after junior year. Henny had saved up money from odd jobs to buy her a telescope and a star map for her birthday, and while the rest of their friends were out partying and hooking up and trying to get into skeezy dive bars with fake IDs, she and Henny had spent the summer learning the constellations, falling asleep under the stars almost every night. She used to dream about taking an epic road trip with him, visiting the parks in every state, wondering if the stars looked the same at the Grand Canyon, in Death Valley, in Yellowstone as they did in Buffalo.

Decades later, she still hadn't taken that trip. She'd never wanted to do it with anyone but Henny.

"I haven't camped since an earth science overnighter

in college," she said. "I don't even own a sleeping bag anymore."

"Fine, we'll stay in five-star hotels. I don't care, Bex. Let's just… let's just go. Right now. Tonight."

"What about the league?" she asked. "The bar? Everything? We can't just leave. We have—"

"Forget the NHL. Forget the bar. Forget Buffalo and the guys and all the bullshit. That ends now, Bex. Let your mom sell the place like she'd planned. Walk out that door with me and start over. You and me against the world, just like always."

Hell, he was serious. One word from her, and they'd be out of there. On the road to some faraway fantasy.

But that's all it was. A fantasy. They weren't children camped out in the backyard anymore, fenced in from danger, ten steps away from her mother's safe embrace. And no matter how simple and fun he'd made it sound, Bex knew bailing on Buffalo wouldn't solve anything. Not for either of them.

"Where's my wild girl?" he whispered, his lips brushing hers. Slowly, his hands drifted to her thighs, hiking her skirt up again, his fingers stroking the bare skin of her legs. "The one who made a hundred bucks on a dare to drink hot sauce. The one who jumped off the waterfall at Letchworth when none of the boys would."

"You gave me hell for that after," she reminded him.

"Only because I was completely intimidated by you."

He palmed her ass, fingers dipping beneath the fabric of her panties. His touch was warm, melting her inside and out. "You were so wild, then. Reckless," he whispered. "I know that girl is still in there, beautiful."

He kissed her full on, testing the last of her resolve. His touch was electric, her whole body shivering, trembling, aching for it. She was losing herself again, drifting away into the now-familiar comforts of his kiss, his breath, his promises that seemed to transport her to another world.

But they lived in this world. Reality. And now it came crashing between them once again, cold and unforgiving.

She pushed away. They were going in circles.

"You can't keep kissing away every argument," she said, trying to catch her breath. "Earlier today you wanted me to move in with you. Now you want to leave Buffalo, see the country? You're making me dizzy."

"Think of the possibilities for your magnet collection." Henny grinned, but it didn't reach his eyes, and soon his smile vanished entirely. "Jesus, Bex. I can't make you happy tonight."

"You need to make *yourself* happy. That's the problem."

"You think?" He met her gaze again, all the tenderness and excitement gone from his eyes. He was shutting down, pushing her away bit by bit, but as much as she wanted to comfort him, to give him what he wanted, to fix this for him, she couldn't. Not anymore.

"Got any tips?" he snapped. "Secret formula? Twelve steps? Maybe an audiobook?"

Taking a deep breath, she said, "Maybe start by figuring out what you want to do with your career. You can't keep jerking your team around like—"

"My career." He laughed, but in it was a bitterness that chilled her to the core. "That's pretty good advice coming from someone who keeps dropping the ball on her own business plans."

"By dropping the ball, I assume you mean not taking your money?"

"For one thing, yeah."

"I told you it was super important to me that I handle the bar on my own terms, no matter how long it took me, no matter what the outcome. Remember?"

"Even if you lose the whole thing? Do you think I can stand by and watch you do that to yourself? All because you're too damn stubborn to—"

"It's not your call. And we're talking about you and the Tempest, not me. Stop changing the subject."

"Oh, I'm changing it, baby. You think you can criticize my career fuck-ups and not take it on the chin yourself? Wrong." He pulled out his cell, his thumbs flying across the screen. Seconds later, her phone buzzed with a text. "That's contact info for Miguel, my guy at Blue-point. Call him. He's been expecting you."

"What?"

"I told him about you weeks ago," he said. "First time you showed me that little bird sketch."

"You had no—"

"The minute I saw that sketch, I could picture it on the new sign. I could picture all of it, every last idea you ever told me about, all the stuff I saw on your spread-sheets. But I also knew you wouldn't call him on your own. You're stubborn and too damn proud for your own good. You needed the push. Still do."

"Yet two minutes ago you were ready to whisk me away from this place."

"Now who's changing the subject?"

Bex pinched the bridge of her nose, her head throbbing. "I told you I'd *think* about Bluepoint. Not that you should call your man and tell him my life story"

"But you *didn't* think about it, did you?"

"No," she admitted.

"It's not like I told him all your secrets, Bex. Just that you were a friend with a small business and some kickass ideas that just needed a little startup cash."

"And?"

"And what? He said he'd look forward to your call. But obviously he never got it." Henny sighed. "Look, I know you want to do everything on your own, but sometimes you gotta set aside your pride and—"

"Oh, it's that simple?" Rage bubbled up inside, making her tremble in ways that had nothing to do with his earlier kisses. "I set aside my so-called pride, call your buddy Miguel, drop your name, and the bank magically sends me a check? What, as a favor to their star customer?"

"You worked your ass off." Henny grabbed the stack of papers on her desk, the ever-expanding folder of ideas and research she'd been wasting her time on for months. "Once they see all these plans, I know they'll—"

"They'll run my credit and show me the door."

He tossed the folder back onto the desk, papers spilling across it, colored pie charts catching her eye and making her insides hurt. She really had done a lot of work. Put her whole heart into it, actually.

"You've already figured it out, huh?" he asked. "Already ruled out your options before you've even given yourself a fair shot?" Henny shoved a hand through his hair, narrowly missing his bandage. "What the hell, Bex? What *happened* to you out there?"

She knew at once he was talking about California. Her ex. Her personal shame.

And this time, he wasn't backing down.

CHAPTER TWENTY-FOUR

"Are we really going there?" Bex asked. "Now?"

Henny sat down on her desk, folding his arms across his chest. There was no more dodging her gaze. He glared at her intently, unflinchingly, demanding a response. "I got all night."

Leaning back against the wall, Bex sucked in a shaky breath, trying to gather her thoughts. She'd never told anyone the whole ugly truth—not her mom, not any of her friends back in California, not Eva and Fee, and definitely not Henny.

The official story was that things had crashed and burned in a big way—a life-altering, career-ending, run-back-home-to-mama kind of way. But she'd been intentionally hazy on the details, and whether it was because her friends had finally started respecting her privacy, or just didn't want to see her crying anymore, they eventually stopped asking.

The truth wasn't anything crazy. It's not like Bex was on the run from the law or had to change her identity. She hadn't harmed anyone. As far as most people's stories went, hers felt tame by comparison.

But for Bex, it was mortifying. The lowest moment of her life, the biggest mistake. She'd never planned on talking about it. Not like this.

Maybe it was the anger loosening her tongue. Maybe it was Henny, big and strong and impossible, demanding answers she'd been holding back for months.

Or maybe she was just too tired of carrying around this shame.

"He destroyed me, Hen," she said, not mentioning her ex's name. That name would never pass her lips again.

"You think I don't know that? That I could ever forget walking into your place in San Francisco, finding you like that? Not eating, barely moving, not..." His voice cracked, shocking her with its raw pain. "Your heart was shattered, Bex. I know what that looks like. And I'd never—"

"I'm not just talking about a broken heart, Henny." She moved away from the wall, sitting on the desk next to him, her leg brushing against the cool fabric of his jeans. For the first time, she felt the full weight of the responsibility he'd always carried for her. The pain. The love. No matter what else happened between them, she loved him for it. Fiercely.

And she owed him the whole truth.

"He took everything from me," she said. "Money. My business. My credit. Literally all of it."

Henny's brow creased with confusion.

"We were supposed to get engaged," she continued, hanging her head. "We'd already picked out the ring, the wedding date, all of it. We were just waiting until he found a good job."

Henny cleared his throat, his hands clenching into fists on his lap. "You never said anything."

"I wanted to wait until it was official. Never got the chance." She found a loose thread in her skirt, wrapped it around her finger until the tip turned red. "He had a lot of student loan debt. I knew that going in. But my catering business had taken off, I was debt-free, so when we moved in together, I paid all our bills. I even opened a credit card for him on my account, just to hold him over." She unwound the thread, watching the color drain from her fingertip. "I was an idiot."

"You're not the idiot in this scenario, Bex. You loved the guy."

"You won't think so highly of me when you hear the

rest." She wound the thread around her finger again, tighter this time. "Even with me taking care of things, he couldn't seem to get ahead. Couldn't hold a job, always had an excuse for why he was short that month. Things came to a head one night and he finally broke down, confessing that his loans weren't from school. He'd never even gone to college. It was all gambling debt."

"Holy shit." Henny shifted on the desk beside her, his voice low in the small space of the office. "So you left?"

"A smart girl would've. But no, I actually felt bad for him. I actually believed we'd had some kind of break-through. Like, no more secrets! We can get through this together!" Bex yanked the thread from her skirt, forcing back tears. She would *not* cry over that asshole. "Two weeks later, I came home after a twelve-hour catering stint, totally fried. All I wanted to do was take a hot bath and go to sleep. He was supposed to be out of town on a roofing job with his brother, but there he was in our kitchen, playing cards and drinking with five of his buddies, big pile of money on the table. He freaked out, said I'd lied about my hours. He turned the whole thing around on me. And you know what? *Still* I didn't bail. I felt sorry for him, Hen. I actually thought I could save him. That I could fix his money problems and get him back on track. Get *us* back on track."

"Still doesn't make you an idiot," Henny said.

"There's more." Bex closed her eyes. "I'd built up equity in my business, so I used part of it as collateral for a consolidation loan to pay off his debts. The loan had to be in my name because his credit was shot, but he'd found steady work with his brother, and he was making the monthly payments. I trusted him, even after everything."

She blew out a breath, her stomach twisting with shame. In so many ways, the story still didn't feel like hers. Maybe she'd seen it in a movie, or maybe one of the patrons at Big Laurie's had told it to her, crying into a vodka cranberry while Don Henley extolled the virtues of forgiveness on the jukebox.

"Things got better for a while," she said. "He took me out for dinner, made all the usual promises. I thought we'd finally moved past it. Then one afternoon I answered a knock on the door—a messenger service with important information from the bank. They were foreclosing on my business assets. That asshole had stopped making payments after just one month. He'd been hiding the bank statements from me, shredding their notices."

Blood simmered in her veins, but Bex forced herself to keep going. "That was the breaking point. I threw his ass out that night, but the damage was done. My business was on the chopping block, and there was no way I could afford a lawyer to help me fight for it. I was out of cash, maxing out my credit cards, still paying off the card I'd opened for him. Thanks to that and the loan default, my credit was ruined."

The worst part wasn't even the financial loss. Things like that happened all the time to people. No, the worst part was that she'd let herself believe he actually loved her. Even at the very end, after she'd tossed his ass out, she still kept waiting for him to call and explain. To talk her into giving him one more chance.

"He robbed me blind, Hen. One drop at a time. I should've seen the signs, but I didn't. I went from a successful business owner with money in the bank and impeccable credit to a woman who wouldn't even qualify for a used car loan. The only reason I got the lease on my house in Buffalo was that the landlady thought I was dating a famous hockey player. Thanks to you, she let me skip the credit check."

Henny was silent for so long, Bex worried he'd tuned out. She lifted her head, surprised to find him watching her. His eyes were full of rage, dark as night.

Through clenched teeth, he finally said, "You realize the only reason that motherfucker's still walking on both legs is that I don't know where he lives?"

"I don't know where he lives, either," she said. It was probably for the best. Last thing she needed was Henny getting arrested for maiming her dirtbag ex.

"Why didn't you take his ass to court?"

Bex shrugged. "Why didn't I do a lot of things? By the time the shock wore off and the shame set in, I didn't have anything left. He took *everything* from me—my money, my self-confidence, my faith in myself as a smart, independent woman. Now I'm dealing with the fallout." She looked up at him again, finally managing a weak smile. "So when I tell you I need to handle this bar on my own, it's not about being proud and stubborn. It's about finding my way back to myself. It's about making sure I still know *how* to find it."

Henny cupped her face, tracing her cheek with his thumb. When he spoke again, his voice was pained. "I should've been there."

"There was nothing you could've done. And you have your own life, Hen. You can't drop it every time I fall apart."

"Yeah. I can. You want me to stop meddling in the bar business? Fine. But sit back and watch you fall, knowing there's something I can do to stop it? Knowing I can protect you? Take care of you?" He shook his head. "Draw that line in the sand all you want. That's one I'm *always* gonna cross, every fucking time." He looked at her with so much compassion, so much love it made her ache. "You're everything to me, Rebecca Canfield. Maybe I made a mess of things between us, but I won't sit on the sidelines while you're in pain."

She leaned into his touch, taking comfort in his strong embrace as he stroked her hair, kissing the top of her head, whispering that everything would somehow be okay, as long as they stuck together.

It would've been so easy to fall back into it. To wrap herself up in all those promises, fasten them across her chest like armor. But for all his words, all his kisses, all the ways his touch had made her scream out in ecstasy, Henny could not fix this for her any more than she could fix his messes for him.

"What can I do?" he asked. "What do you need? Anything. Just name it."

"I need... I..." Bex lost her words, heart hammering in her chest as she realized the truth. Right now, what she needed most from Henny wasn't passionate kisses and runaway road trips. It wasn't the man who'd rage against the storm to save her from crashing onto the shore, but the one who'd shine a light for her to follow on her own. It was the man who'd always stood by her as a friend. A best friend.

Pulling out of his embrace, she reached for his hands, holding them tight, hoping this wouldn't be the last time she got the chance.

"I thought I could handle this," she admitted. "Go along for this crazy ride with you, see where we ended up. But I was wrong. I need stable. I need predictable.

And you—no matter how incredible these past few weeks have been—are anything but those things."

"Because those things are boring as fuck." Henny squeezed her hands, his eyes wild again. "Come away with me. Tonight. We'll just… we'll wing it."

Bex lowered her eyes.

Maybe there was a time when she would've gone along on his whirlwind adventure. Packed up a suitcase and followed him right out that door.

But the Bex who would've done that was gone.

"I'm sorry, Henny. I just want… I want my friend back."

"You've got me. I'm not going anywhere without you." He tried to kiss her again, but she pulled back.

"I can't," she said, watching the hope drain from his eyes.

"Can't?" he asked. "Or won't?"

"I want our friendship back," she said firmly. "Back the way it was."

"Not happening." Henny released her hands and stood up from the desk, pacing the room once again. "I can't go back. I want you in my life. In my bed. In here." He pressed a fist to his heart. "It's all or nothing for me."

"So that's it? I run away with you tonight, or you walk away from me? From us?"

"Something like that."

"Don't you think that's a little extreme? Not to mention childish?"

"You don't do anything in your life halfway, Bex. I'm not letting you start with me."

Bex gasped, her heart constricting, the walls closing in on her. "You don't even want to be my friend anymore? After all this?"

Henny glared at her, the coldness in his eyes all the answer Bex needed.

All she could manage was a whisper, the words nearly tearing her in two. "I really hope you change your mind about that someday."

"And if I can't?"

"Can't or won't?"

Henny didn't respond. His eyes were shuttered, his stance rigid. That was it. He'd finally shut down completely, kicking Bex out of his heart and changing all the locks.

Anger and sadness wrapped around her chest, squeezing tight, and she knew in that moment it was truly over. Not because they didn't care about each other. But because they'd never be able to find a way to do it on each other's terms.

Bex rose from the desk and opened her office door, the familiar sounds of the bar rushing in: the clack of the new pool balls, a group of girls laughing, Fee's voice floating above the opening chords to "Stairway to Heaven."

Stepping aside to let Henny pass, she squared her shoulders, sucked in a deep breath, and called upon the last of her reserves to whisper the words that sealed their fate.

"Then I guess this is goodbye, Kyle Henderson."

CHAPTER TWENTY-FIVE

Bex was in a tailspin.

It'd been nearly two weeks since she'd told Henny goodbye, and he hadn't tried to contact her. No texts, no calls, no showing up at the bar after his games. She didn't know whether to appreciate that he'd finally decided to respect her boundaries, or to call him up and tear him a new one for letting her push him away so easily. But despite all the confrontations she played out in her mind, re-imagining all the right things to do and say, ultimately she'd done nothing. Nothing but let him walk out that door, right out of her life.

And now, in the smallest, stickiest booth in the darkest corner of the bar, Bex sat nursing a glass of whiskey, trying not to notice the mahogany pool table that gleamed at the center of the room. Trying not to notice the fact that everything good in her life had evaporated.

Henny was gone. Her mom would be back from Florida soon, ready to put the pub on the market. She'd be out a job, out everything she'd come to love and cherish here in Buffalo.

Where do I go from here?

She reached into her pocket, pulled out the folded paper where so many weeks ago she'd sketched out her logo ideas—the powerful phoenix reborn in the fires of an old life, rising out of the ashes of tragedy. What better imagery to symbolize all she'd endured, right? She'd survived a horrible breakup. She'd seen her life savings, her business, all of her plans burn to ash, forcing her to move back home to Buffalo, yet somehow she'd found the strength to rise up and start over. Stronger. Better.

Before now, the days following her breakup had been the most painful of her life. She'd thought that if she could survive them, she could survive anything.

But now she knew that was bullshit.

Her ex? Hell, that guy had simply messed up her plans. Losing Henny, though... *that* was a broken heart. Now that he was gone, how could anything ever be okay again?

Bex sipped her whiskey, blinking back tears. She could hear the voices of her friends echoing, Eva and Fee encouraging her to give this thing with Henny a shot, give it time, give him space, give herself space. She thought about all those romance novels and movies where she'd wanted to scream at the couple to just sit down and talk things through—how it was so obvious they were meant for each other, that they could have a beautiful life together if only they'd wake up and get over themselves.

How many times had she rolled her eyes at that stuff?

Now, she was living it. She got it. Maybe this rift between her and Henny could've been repaired with a heartfelt conversation, but when she'd looked in his eyes that night in her office, when she saw the coldness there, all of her words vanished. She didn't know how to make him understand how deeply she cared for him, and how simultaneously scared shitless she was to admit it. How embarrassed she was about all of the mistakes she'd made in the past.

For as strong as Henny thought she was, most days she was terrified she'd fall apart again. How could she admit that? How could she tell him that she didn't want him to be there when it happened?

That she really *did* want him to be there, just like he'd been there in California?

That she really was falling for him?

That she was beginning to suspect it'd started years

ago, maybe decades. A spark working its way into the foundations of their friendship, slowly igniting into the flames of something so much more.

I am in love with my best friend.

The loss hit her all over again, fresh as the night he'd walked out. The emptiness inside her was so vast, so endless, she didn't know if she could ever crawl out of it.

How did it come to this?

Bex tucked the sketches back into her pocket. She was no phoenix, and what'd happened with Henny wasn't some mystery, some great, unsolved vanishing in the night. The simple fact was she'd lost him because their relationship had changed, and she'd refused to change along with it. She'd wanted all the benefits of something new while keeping everything else *exactly* the same, especially the easy parts—the good times, the shared history, the jokes.

Maybe that was enough for a friendship—even a friendship with benefits. But when it came to someone you loved, someone you wanted to make a life with, there was so much more to it.

You had to be willing to fight the hard battles, to show your ugly parts and help him feel safe enough to show his. You had to strip yourself bare, to take the kind of big, impossible risks that shook you up and wrung you out. No matter the outcome, with a true partner by your side, all those difficulties would only be half as painful. And the joys? They'd be doubly beautiful. Always.

That's what Bex could've had with Henny, but instead she'd let it slip right through her fingers. Why? Because she was afraid of showing him her soft underbelly? Of letting him see all those scary, insecure parts? Because she was too wrapped up in her own fears to truly see and understand his?

Oh, Hen…

No, it couldn't end like this. They'd been friends for too many years to let this all fade away. Maybe she'd blown her chance at love—something she'd live to regret for the rest of her days. But there was still one thing she could do for him, one thing to show him that she'd truly heard him. That she appreciated everything he'd tried to do for her, even though she'd been too damn scared to take the risk.

Bex downed the last of her whiskey, shaking off the desolation. She could take that risk now. For Henny. For herself. And maybe someday—a month from now, a year, a decade—someday when that anonymous stranger bumped into her at Wegmans while she was picking out tomatoes, instead of looking into the pleasant eyes of a man she used to know but didn't quite remember, she'd smile at him warmly, grab his hands, kiss his cheek, and ask if maybe, just maybe, they could find their way back to being friends.

Bex fished the phone from her pocket, checking her calendar for next week. Then, steeling herself for the biggest leap of her life, she pulled up the contact details and hit the call button.

CHAPTER TWENTY-SIX

"Someone here to see you, one-nine." Dunn sat down on the locker room bench next to Henny and mussed his hair, an all-too-fatherly gesture that told Henny everything he needed to know about who was waiting for him on the other side of the doors.

Bex.

"We got time?" Henny asked.

Dunn nodded. "Ten minutes. Get it done."

Henny pulled off his skates and rose from the bench, half-dressed for the last game of the regular season, heart in his fucking throat. He hadn't seen her in weeks. Drove by the pub and her house without going inside. Picked up the phone a hundred times, only to chicken out before he hit the call button. Looked for her in the stands at all of his games, but her absence carved a fresh gash in his heart every time.

Now she was here, right outside those doors, and he didn't know what the fuck to say.

Maybe he never would.

"Clock's ticking," Dunn said.

"No shit." Henny wrenched open the doors and headed out into the hallway. There she was, pacing at the end of it, her back to him.

Damn, he'd missed her.

She was dressed in a jet-black suit and white blouse, her skirt and heels showing off her toned legs. Her hair was tamed into some kind of complicated twisty thing at the nape of her neck, and all Henny could think about was how it would feel to slide his fingers into that hair, untie the knot, kiss her until they both ran out of air.

She looked good. Real good.

If Henny wasn't so damned heartbroken, he might've been intimidated.

"Hey," he said. "Dunn said you wanted to see me?" *Real smooth, dickhead.*

Bex turned to face him, her smile tentative. Forget kissing—she was so fucking beautiful, just looking at her knocked the wind out of him.

"Is this awkward?" She approached him slowly, fidgeting with her purse strap, not quite meeting his eyes. "It's awkward. I know. I just... I was so excited to tell you, and I wanted to call, but then I remembered you had a game tonight, and then I didn't know if I should come in, so I called Eva from the parking lot and—"

"I'm—"

"She said if I hurried, I might catch you before the game, but now I see I'm totally interrupting and—"

"Bex." He reached out to touch her, but then pulled back. He had no right. Not anymore. In the uncomfortable silence that followed, he said, "What's with the suit?"

Bex lowered her eyes, her smile still so damn shy. "I finally took your advice. Met with your friend at Bluepoint today."

"You serious? How'd it go?"

"My credit isn't doing me any favors, but Miguel told me about a new investment program for local women business owners." She met his eyes, her whole face coming to life as she spoke. "They pair up individual investors with women whose businesses directly benefit the community, either through job creation or business-to-business spending. They don't always find a match, but given my circumstances and my presentation, he thought it was worth a shot. He was pretty impressed with the expansion and marketing plans."

"Are you surprised?" Henny flashed a proud grin. Couldn't help it. "You've got this one in the bag."

"You think so?"

"I wouldn't say no to you." *Not even now. Whatever*

you want, just fucking say it. The answer is yes. Friends? Not friends? A kidney? It's yours.

A lifetime passed between them, neither of them speaking, the only sound coming from the locker room behind him: Kooz teaching the boys the latest Russian insults, Roscoe and Fahey kicking around a hacky sack, Kenton butchering a Men at Work song. All the familiar pre-game stuff Henny had come to know and depend on.

He adjusted his jersey over the pads again, not sure what else to say. What else she wanted from him. When she didn't fill in the gaps, he said, "I should probably get back."

"Oh, right. Okay." She smiled again. Then, softly, "Henny, I just... Thank you. For always having my back. For encouraging me. For pushing me when I was too stubborn to push myself."

"With Bluepoint?" He waited for her to say no, or better yet, to say nothing at all and simply throw herself into his arms, kiss away the arguments and all the bull-shit that had come between them.

But Bex only nodded. "I feel like whatever happens now, at least I took action. If it wasn't for you, I'd still be doodling logos and obsessing over Yelp reviews."

"No way. You would've made a move eventually." Henny shook his head. "Jesus, Bex. You're the smartest, most capable, most kickass woman I've ever known. I didn't push you on Bluepoint because I thought you couldn't handle the bar on your own. I did it because you were having a hard time after California, and I thought I could help. That will *always* be my first instinct when it comes to you."

"I'm... I know."

He waited for her to open up a vein, to tell him how she was truly feeling, to call him out on the things he'd said to her that night in her office. But all she said instead was, "I've been watching your games. You're playing pretty tight lately."

Henny nodded. "Had a little heart-to-heart with Gallagher and the suits. I fucked up a lot this season, but I'm done with that schoolyard bullshit. Time to get back to business, focus on the playoffs."

"Good for you."

"Yeah, well. *Someone* suggested I stop acting like— what was the term? Man-baby, I think?"

Bex laughed. She actually laughed. Henny had never wanted to hit the rewind button so hard in his life.

How the fuck did I screw this up so bad?

How was it possible that weeks ago he had his face between this woman's gorgeous thighs, making love to her in every possible way, waking up with his hands in her hair, his cock pressing against her backside, his mouth on the soft skin of her neck, and now they were standing here afraid to touch each other, afraid to say any of the things that really mattered?

"You, ah, sticking around for the show?" he asked.

"Fee and I are double-teaming it at the pub tonight—trying out a mock pool tournament on that table of yours. Oh!" Her eyes widened. "I made something for you. Almost forgot."

She picked up a poster board that'd been leaning against the wall behind her, flipping it so Henny could read it.

It was a big-ass sign covered in glitter stars and stickers shaped like hockey sticks. In the center she'd written a message in Tempest blue.

You GOT this, 19!

God, his fucking heart hurt.

"Maybe one of the wives can wave it around for you," she said, handing it over.

After another long and punishing silence, she finally leaned in close, standing on her toes to kiss his cheek. Henny closed his eyes as her lips lingered, warm and soft, the haze of her sweet scent making him dizzy, his damn heart betraying him with every thud.

When she finally pulled away, her eyes were wet with tears. "Play your ass off tonight, jerkface. Okay?"

———

Henny took Bex's advice. He played his ass off, pushing himself harder and faster with each play, taking no fucking prisoners as the front line dominated the ice. There was nothing violent or dirty about it—the whole team was simply on point tonight, like they'd all taken a shot of adrenaline in the collective ass. Their passing game was flawless. Kooz and his defense shut down every single goal attempt. By the start of the third, it was clear that the Nashville Tomcats had already given up.

In the end, they mopped the floor with those boys, shutting them out seven to zero. Henny'd even nailed a hat trick, and when the crowd roared their appreciation, Henny waved at them. Acknowledged it. Thanked them. For a minute there, he started to remember why he loved this game so damn much. Not because of the screaming fans, but because of how he and the boys had come together as a team, playing their tightest game of the season, playing hard, playing clean. They'd had a job to do, and they'd gone out there and gotten it done.

He'd actually had fun.

But when Henny scanned the crowd, his gaze settled on an empty seat. Bex wasn't in the stands, banging on the glass with her glittery sign. He'd left the sign in the locker room. She wouldn't be waiting for him in the hallway tonight to give him a congratulatory hug, or pouring him a beer at Laurie's, or making her cure-all nachos, or waiting for him in his bed, as eager to hear about the game as she was to feel him inside her. She wouldn't be cheering for him during the playoffs, or watching the boys dig in and fight for the cup.

Sure, maybe they could try to talk it out. Get back to paling around again. But even if they managed to salvage their friendship, it would never be the same. There would always be this awkward space in the middle of everything, the black mark on their otherwise unblemished history that they just didn't talk about anymore.

Henny skated off the ice, heading into the locker room ahead of the team, staring at that sign until the sparkly letters all blurred together.

In all the ways that counted, he'd fucking lost her.

CHAPTER TWENTY-SEVEN

Considering the intense night on the ice and an equally grueling post-game workout, Henny should've been exhausted. But hours after he'd showered and gone home for the night, he still couldn't sleep. Couldn't unwind. Couldn't forget.

Standing in the middle of his kitchen with a bison mug full of whiskey, he looked around at... absolutely nothing.

What the hell am I doing in this place?

Bex had been right—his house needed her touch. Without her, it felt cold, fake, like one of those model homes with cardboard appliances and plastic food in the fridge. A decorator had picked out his furniture, set it all up like something out of a magazine. He'd hardly touched any of it. The only time he'd ever really noticed anything in this place was when Bex pointed it out.

When she touched it.

When she made the coffee, he noticed the high-end digital coffee maker, the way she ground the beans and measured it just so. When she cooked dinner, he noticed the way she shook the veggies in the pan he never used, humming as she brought everything to the perfect sizzle. And when she whispered his name in bed, wrapping her legs around his hips, begging him to touch her, to kiss her, he noticed his pillow, the way her hair fanned out, the warmth of her skin seeping into the sheets.

He'd paid for this place in cash. Paid that decorator to make it look nice. Paid a housekeeper to clean it up once a week.

But it had never *once* been his home. Not until Bex showed up.

She was everywhere now, inescapable. In his head. In his heart. In the damn mug in his hand. Her game signs were all tacked up in the workout room in the basement, her scent still filled his bedroom, her shampoo still sat on the shower ledge. He should've tossed it all out, but he couldn't. He wasn't ready to let her go.

I'm completely fucked.

Ever since he was a kid, Henny had been telling himself the same thing, over and over and over: when shit starts to go south—with women, with friends, with work—it's better to walk away unscathed than to stay in the fight and risk getting hurt. For decades he'd convinced himself he'd been doing just that—living life on his own terms, keeping people at a distance, avoiding drama, walking away before anyone got a chance to walk out on him.

But that was some bullshit, right there. All those walls he'd put up, all that attitude—none of that had ever saved him from getting hurt. All it had done was prevent him from being loved.

But Bex? She saw through it. Didn't care how hard he pushed, how cold he got, how stupid he was acting. All the macho bullshit talk in the world, and that woman still loved him. He knew it now. He'd seen it in her eyes a thousand times since that tequila-induced wakeup call.

He'd seen it in her eyes even tonight. Even when he'd been doing his damnedest to hold back. To keep her at that safe, untouchable distance.

Now, he picked up the sign she'd given him, propped it against the wall.

You GOT this, 19!

He'd given her an ultimatum—all or nothing—and she'd said goodbye. But she hadn't really bailed after all. Hadn't stopped loving him. Even after everything Henny had said, everything he'd done, all the mistakes he'd made, Bex had left the door open.

So now?

He could kick that door closed for good, walk away

before he bled out completely. Spend the rest of his life trying to forget her.

You GOT this, 19!

Or he could tear that damn door off the hinges, march across the threshold, and surrender his heart.

CHAPTER TWENTY-EIGHT

Fifteen minutes till closing.

Close enough.

"Wrap it up, Logan." Bex clicked off the neon Big Laurie's sign over the bar. "Last call was an hour ago."

"Need any help cleaning up?"

"Just need you to get on home so I can do the same."

He tossed back the last of his whiskey sour, then pulled out his wallet, counting out exact change. "Four bucks, right?"

"Four-fifty." *I should charge him double.* Bex sighed. "You know what? Never mind. On the house."

"Yeah? Cool." Scooping up all of his dollar bills and shoving them back into his wallet—*of course*—he said, "For the record? I wouldn't let *my* fiancée close a bar by herself."

"Then don't propose to a bartender. Problem solved."

"Bex, that guy—what's his name? Henry? He's no good for you. You need a man who—"

"The only thing I need right now is for *this* man—a.k.a. *you*—to turn around and walk out *that* door." She jerked her head toward the exit. "Good night, Logan."

"I could wait for—"

"Good *night*, Logan."

God. Were all men seriously that dense?

Finally, the lunkhead zipped up his coat and scooted out of there, leaving her alone for the first time all day.

She washed out his glass by hand, then set it in the drying rack with the others, checking that she hadn't left any stray glassware or dishes around. She moved on to the beer taps, wiping them down with care, then the liquor bottles, checking the nozzles and turning them all face-forward. The floor had already been mopped, the grill turned off and cleaned, all the water rings polished from the bar.

Closing had always been Bex's favorite part of the night. There was something cathartic and deeply satisfying about working alone in the quiet pub, restoring order from chaos.

Keeping thoughts of Henny at bay.

Seeing him tonight before the game had been one of the hardest moments of her life. She'd gone in there wanting to say so many things—I'm sorry. I'm in love with you. Can we hit the reset button on this?—but in the end, all of her carefully rehearsed speeches had abandoned her.

No, there would be no second chance at love for Bex and Henny. Best she could do now was accept it and move forward, hoping that eventually they'd be able to rebuild some semblance of friendship.

Her throat tightened, but she swallowed her sadness. She had work to do. Then she'd head home for the night, slip into her bed, and drift off to dreamland.

Alone.

Bex shut off the main lights over the bar area, then moved on to the pool table room, picking up a couple of cues the players had left on the table. She was about to slide them back into the wall rack when she heard the front door whoosh open.

"Logan, you are seriously pissing me off." Brandishing a pool cue, she spun around on her heel. "I swear I'm going to call the cops if—"

"Tell me something, beautiful." He stepped out of the shadows, offering a familiar smile that melted her heart, his ocean-blue eyes warm and soft and utterly, completely home. "What's a guy gotta do to get a beer in this place?"

"Henny," she gasped. Her mouth went dry, heart leaping up into her throat. "I thought... what are you doing here?"

"I was in the neighborhood. And I'm thirsty."

"You... oh. Right. Well, last call was—"

"Bex." Henny sighed. "I don't give a fuck about the beer." He tilted his head, his gaze sweeping her face, his smile faltering. "I, uh... I couldn't... Seeing you today... And then you were gone, and I didn't..." He shook his head, blowing out a breath, then held up a gift bag stuffed with tissue paper. "Here. It's a jersey."

"Spoiler alert."

He smiled. "Sorry."

Bex set the cue on the pool table and peeked inside the bag, spotting the Tempest blue and silver. "Let me guess. Your numbers?"

"Better late than never, right?"

She pulled the jersey out of the bag and held it up in front of her chest, blinking back tears. Had it only been a couple of months ago that he'd joked about this? That he'd asked her to burn Kooz's jersey, never to wear another man's numbers again?

"Thank you," she whispered, her throat raw and tight. "It's now officially my favorite jersey."

"*Shit*. It's not about the jersey, either. I'm totally screwing this up. Again." Henny ran a hand through his hair, leaving it sticking up in every direction. She wanted to touch it. To feel it between her thighs. To let it tickle her nose, her lips, her cheeks as he kissed her goodnight. Good morning. And everything in between...

"This is nuts," Henny continued. "Can we get a do-over here? Because I'm pretty sure I just fucked up the best thing in my life. You're my best friend, Bex. I never wanted to hurt you. And I definitely don't want to lose you."

She sucked in a breath, lowering her eyes. Her body trembled. Hope? Fear? Love? It was all there, roiling inside her, urging her to bolt for the door. No more complications. No more overanalyzing. No more painfully awkward conversations or accidental morning-afters. Just freedom. Just Bex.

Just run.

But Bex didn't run. Instead, she took a steadying breath and lifted her chin. Looked him in the eyes.

And then she told the truth.

"I used to know everything about you, Hen. I could predict your moods, read your thoughts, finish your sentences. But I don't know where you're at anymore—not with me or anything else. And that scares the hell out of me."

Nodding, he touched her cheek, tucked a lock of hair behind her ear. After going so long without it, his gentle caress made her shiver. Three or four times he took a breath and opened his mouth to speak, only to clamp it shut again.

Bex didn't push him to explain. She was beginning to understand the difference between backing down out of fear, and simply leaving a little space. Time. Room to breathe.

No matter how hard it was to wait, sometimes that was exactly what love needed in order to grow.

"I fucked up a good thing," he finally said, "and I'm asking for another shot. We're friends, yes. Always will be, no matter what dumb shit comes out of my mouth. But we have a chance to crack this thing open, build something even more amazing on top of it. I don't want to do that with anyone else. Never have. For me, there's only you."

Her heart kicked up again as she remembered that night in her office, all the things he'd said. "All or nothing, right?"

Henny held her gaze a long time before he spoke again. "I was an asshole. It was selfish and stupid of me to say those things."

"But not bullshit, right? I mean, that's how you feel."

Henny sighed. "You coming back to Buffalo... It sent me on this wild trip, but it was like riding a roller coaster in the dark. After all the time we spent apart, having you back again stirred up so much for me, things I didn't understand. Things I didn't want to admit. I was losing my mind, screwing up on the ice, totally spinning. When we woke up in your bed that morning... Hell, I didn't know what the fuck to do. I freaked. I tried to pretend it wasn't happening, to talk myself out of what I was feeling. But no matter what I did, all roads led right back to you. Every single one."

He paced the room, then stopped in front of her again, so close she could smell the fabric softener in his clothes.

"You're my home," he said. "My fucking heart. I'm crazy in love with you, Bex. Not because we got drunk and hooked up, not because I needed a distraction, but because of who you are. Because I fucking admire the fierce girl I knew in high school and the badass woman you've become. Because of who I am when I'm with you —who you *let* me be—even if I don't always show it to you. I love that you know how to make pie charts and nothing in your house matches and you put kale on your nachos. I love that you have so many stupid fucking magnets they fall off the fridge every time I open it. I love that you snore, but only in the mornings. I love that you let me read your diary when we were seventeen, and that even after knowing you for twenty-five years, I'm still learning your secrets."

Henny leaned back against the pool table and closed his eyes, finally taking a breath. When he spoke again, his voice was soft. Resigned. "So yeah, I want it all with you. But if you can't give me that, I get it. I'll take whatever you're offering. Just friends? No, I don't like it. But it's a hell of a lot better than not having you in my life at all."

Bex could hardly breathe. Her body was warm and buzzing, her heart full.

"Say something," he whispered, opening his eyes to look at her once more.

Bex cracked a smile. A small one at first, then it grew, stretching across her face until her cheeks hurt. "First of all, I don't snore, and secondly, I didn't *let* you read my diary. You stole it, and then I found it shoved under your mattress."

Henny raised a brow. "What were you doing under my mattress?"

"Hello? Looking for porn."

"Should've checked my health textbook."

Bex's jaw dropped. "You stashed porn in your health textbook?"

"What else was I supposed to do in that boring-ass class?"

"I don't know... Pay attention? Learn something?"

"From old Mrs. Farnsworth? That woman brought in vegetables to re-enact the entire human reproductive process. I couldn't eat salad until my late twenties."

"You really are a man-baby."

"Hey. Until you've seen a cucumber fuck a grapefruit, don't judge."

Bex cracked up. It felt good to laugh with him again. Her Henny. Her best friend. Blowing out a breath, she said, "These last couple weeks without you have sucked some serious ass."

"You're telling me." Henny's smile finally faded, his eyes turning serious. "I meant what I said, Bex. About us. Whatever you want, just—"

"Turn around," she demanded.

"Excuse me?"

"Turn around. Hands on the pool table."

"Kinky." Raising a brow, he did as she asked. "So we're going with friends with benefits, then? That's your final answer?"

Bex took a deep breath, willing her heartbeat to slow.

Loving Henny was *so* much more than friendship with benefits. It was mutual respect. Admiration. Compromise. Sacrifice. All the things that would bind them close, keep them together when the crazy-hot pool table sex faded and life was doing its damnedest to chip away at their souls. It was a thousand moments, large and small. Words. Convictions. Actions. Apologies. Laughter. Tears. Commitment. Showing up for each other when it really counted. Not being afraid to fight, even when it got messy, even when it hurt like hell. It was everything he'd said, all the reasons he loved her, the same reasons she loved him.

Forever love. That's what they had. It's what they'd always had.

That was her final answer.

"Benefits?" she teased. Silently she wriggled out of her clothes, her skin erupting in goose bumps. "You waltz in here bearing gifts and romantic little speeches, and I'm supposed to drop my panties again, just like that?"

"Joke! It was a joke." Henny started to turn his head. "Bex, I didn't—"

"Turn around or we're done, Kyle Henderson."

He whipped his head back into place, and Bex slipped the jersey over her naked body, loving the feel of his numbers on her chest. She was Henny's, now and always.

"Bex," he said, desperation creeping into his voice, "I said I'd let you make the rules here. I mean it. Just tell me what you want, and I'll accept whatever—"

"All."

"—even if it means—"

"All."

"—that we can't... Wait. What?"

"You said all or nothing. I choose all. Turn around."

Slowly, Henny turned to face her, his eyes wide with surprise.

Standing before him in nothing but the jersey, she said, "I messed up, too. I didn't know how to deal with our friendship changing so quickly, and I panicked. I'm done panicking. Done running from this. From us. You know my brand of crazy, Hen. All my secrets, all my shame, my strengths, my stories, just like I know yours. And guess what? I fell for you too, jerkface. A long time ago. So if you think you can deal with me—all of me— then I say we give this thing a shot. A real one. You in?"

Henny ran his thumb over his lower lip and swallowed hard, his eyes dark with desire.

"Henny. Are you listening to me?"

"I don't... Are you wearing panties?"

Bex rolled her eyes. "Did you even hear a word I said?"

Henny blinked. "You had me at... standing there naked in my jersey."

"See what happens when you look at porn instead of studying? You've conditioned yourself to respond only to naked women."

"No, only to you." He reached for the jersey, tugging it up to reveal the triangle of hair between her thighs.

"See? You never developed critical listening skills." Grinning wickedly, Bex pushed him back onto the pool table and climbed up to straddle him. His jeans were rough against her sensitive skin, the zipper warm from his body heat, radiating to her core.

Henny slid his hands up the front of her jersey, fingers tugging her aching nipples to stiff peaks. "Lucky for you I have lots of other skills."

She was wet in an instant, reaching down between her legs for his button and zipper, freeing his cock from the confines of his clothes. His hard length was hot and velvet-smooth in her hand.

This. This was right. All of it.

Bex wasn't naive enough to think they'd never have another fight, never hit another roadblock. She and Henny still had so many things to work through on their own—her fears and insecurities about her business plans, his frustrations with the league and the mistakes he'd made on the ice, all of the pain and anguish they'd been carrying from their pasts. Those kinds of wounds didn't repair themselves overnight, not even when you fell in love.

Bex and Henny had an uphill road ahead of them, and it wouldn't be an easy hike.

But they wouldn't be walking it alone.

"Now we have a problem." Henny slid his hands down her rib cage, her hips, her thighs, squeezing her tight. "Every time I see my number, I'm gonna think about this moment. You've already ruined pool for me. Now I won't be able to wear my own jersey without getting a raging hard-on. Do you know how fucked up that is?"

"*So* fucked up. Maybe I should help you with that." She arched her hips, slowly sliding down over his shaft, taking him in fully. "Better?"

"This is… not… helping." Henny closed his eyes as she rolled her hips, her body stretching to accommodate him, to learn him all over again. "*Fuck.* You're making a bigger problem, Bex. Emphasis on bigger."

"Bigger isn't a problem for me," she teased, her body shuddering with pleasure. They'd been apart for far too long, and now that they'd found their way back into each other's arms, Bex intended to make up for every lost second, one delicious thrust at a time. "In fact, I'd say everything about this situation is just about—yeah, right there—*perfect*."

CHAPTER TWENTY-NINE

"We've got a problem. A big one."

At the sound of Henny's voice, Bex looked up from the index cards spread across her desk, her breath catching—partly from the note of concern in his voice, but mostly from the charcoal gray suit clinging to his muscular build. Good lord, that man cleaned up well.

Bex crossed her legs, trying to relieve the sudden pressure between her thighs. She needed to finish her speech, not jump his bones. "What's the emergency?"

"We're gonna need more booze," he said. "More food. More... everything." His serious mask slipped, a smile stretching ear to ear. "There's a line down the fucking block, Bex."

Bex hopped out of her chair, knocking half her notes to the floor. "Are you serious? But we're not set to open for another two hours!"

"I've got Roscoe out there keeping everyone entertained. Kooz left to go round up some of the other guys early, see who can help work the door."

"Where are Fee and the girls?" Bex asked. She'd recently hired another bartender, a cook, and two more cocktail servers to help with the weekly pool tournaments—the games had been a huge hit, the crowds getting bigger every weekend. The new staff had jumped in hard and fast, quickly becoming part of the ever-expanding pub family.

"Fee, Gemma, Meg, and Elsie are all out at the bar, dressed to the nines and ready to rock," Henny said. "Your mom's here, too. Nico and Annie are already on the grill—Nico's trying to get his cousin to come in and help. From the looks of that line, two cooks won't cut it today."

"But I..." Bex blinked. None of this seemed real. "How did this happen?"

Henny slipped his arms around her waist. "I'm gonna go out on a limb and say it was your kickass marketing campaign, your tireless spirit, your endless array of spreadsheets, and your super handsome, amazingly helpful, strapping young assistant."

"Not to mention horny," she teased, the hard length of him pressing urgently against her stomach. "You are the poster boy for inappropriate workplace behavior."

"Fire me if you want, but good luck finding an

assistant with my skill set." He kissed her neck, grazing her skin with his teeth.

"Fine, you're not fired. But seriously. Down the block?"

"Pretty sure your investor's here, too."

"Jared?"

"English guy, good hair, suit that cost more than my house?"

"That's him."

Bex smiled, shocked at how it'd all come together. Jared Blackwell owned FierceConnect, a major social gaming company based in New York. He and his wife Ari had recently started investing in bars and restaurants all over the state. When they heard about the women's business program at Bluepoint and Bex's ideas for the pub, they jumped on it, flying up to Buffalo for a meeting. Bex hit it off with them immediately. The papers were signed the next day, and after a few conference calls to fine-tune the plans, they began the renovations.

Bex couldn't have asked for a better arrangement.

The pub looked incredible. She'd kept the original mahogany bar and jukebox, complete with the 80s rock her regulars loved so much. But everything else inside was different, reborn. The investment had allowed her to expand the bar, doubling the interior space and adding an outside patio for summer events. They'd built a stage for bands, remodeled the basement into a wine cellar, gutted and upgraded the kitchen to accommodate the new menu, expanded her office and storeroom, brought in a second pool table, and added three more bathrooms. They'd also commissioned custom-painted signage to show off the new name: The Silver Phoenix.

Today was the official grand opening. She'd promoted it to all the regulars and taken an ad out in the paper, booked a radio spot, spread the word on social media. She figured it would be a fun party—a great way to spend a Saturday night and kick off the next chapter of her life, maybe bring in a few new customers who hadn't yet heard about the place.

But she'd never expected such an amazing turnout.

"This is really happening," she said, gathering up her speech cards. Suddenly, her stomach bubbled with nerves. "Holy shit. I need to rehearse. I need—"

"How's my girl?" Fee stuck her head in the doorway. "You good?"

"I understand we're in for quite a party," Bex said, fanning herself with the cards.

"You have no idea." Fee winked. "But we've got this, babe. Survivors, remember?"

Bex laughed. They'd come a long way from mopping up the leaky bathroom. They *so* had this.

"Alright," Bex said. "Let's open the doors early, get those thirsty people some drinks."

"Go ahead," Henny told Fee. "We'll be out in a few."

Fee flashed a thumbs-up, then headed back out to the bar, closing the door behind her.

"Let them rush in, check the place out, get comfortable," Henny said. "Then you can make your grand entrance."

She slid her hands over his shoulders. "If this is a trick to sneak in a quickie before the mad rush... then I'm all for it. God, you look good in that suit."

"If you think I can see you in that short, sparkly-ass dress and only settle for a quickie, then we've got some serious communication issues."

"They're called sequins, and fine, I'll make it up to you later." Bex flipped through her note cards again, wondering if she'd forgotten anyone. So many people had come together to make this happen, to support her, to cheer her along the way. She wanted them all to know how much it meant to her. "Do you think I should—"

"Bex?" Henny took the cards, slipped them into his back pocket. "I think you should stop worrying. You're fucking awesome. Everyone out there knows it. I know it. And we are all *so* damn proud of you." He kissed her forehead, immediately calming her nerves. "Got something for you. A little gift to mark the occasion."

"You're not going to make me cry, are you?"

"No promises." From a pocket inside his suit jacket, he pulled out a flat velvet box.

"What's this?" she asked, grinning.

"I've been looking for this little beauty for months," he said. "It had to be perfect. Had to be right."

Bex was bouncing on her toes, her heart ready to burst. "You're killing me, Hen. Open it. Open it!"

He popped the lid, revealing a broach so beautiful it took her breath away. Nestled into the black velvet box, a platinum phoenix rose out of a fire made of teardrop-cut garnet and topaz jewels. It looked shockingly similar to the logo she'd drawn all those months ago, the same image that now adorned the sign out front.

She reached into the box and pulled out the phoenix, surprised to find a smooth, black backing without a pin. "Wait, this isn't a broach."

"It was, but I had it modified." Henny traced his fingers over her collarbone. "In all the time I've known you, I've never seen you wear jewelry. But magnets? That's all you."

Her eyes glazed with tears. She couldn't imagine a more perfect gift. "It's... Henny, I don't know what to say. I love it so much."

He stuck it on her metal filing cabinet. "Our first official commemorative magnet."

"*Our* first?" When she looked up at him, she found him searching her face, the question in his eyes clear.

Her heart expanded, fluttering in her chest. She'd said no once before, but she was ready now. Ready to wake up in the same bed every morning, to eagerly await his return from games on the road, to make his house their home. "Henny, are you asking me to move in with you?"

"No." He held her gaze a beat too long, his chest rising and falling rapidly, his breath soft on her lips. Then, "I'm asking you to share your life with me. To let me spend the rest of my days making love to you. Making you laugh that sexy, sequin-covered ass off. Making you happy. Covering our entire damn fridge with magnets from every place we visit, every celebration we have, every day we're on this earth together." Henny dropped down on his knee and reached for her hand. "I'm asking you to marry me, Rebecca Canfield."

Bex gasped.

Sliding a delicate ring on her finger, he kissed her knuckles, then looked up to meet her gaze. "Please say yes."

There was only one thing to say. Pure, true, and twenty-five years in the making.

Dropping to her knees, she took Henny's face in her hands and answered without hesitation. "Yes."

His lips were soft and sweet, a gentle kiss with the promise of so much more to come.

"If you're not into rings," he said, kissing her finger, "we can have that made into a magnet, too."

"Don't you dare!" She held it up, admiring it. It was gorgeous, a simple square-cut diamond in an ornate antique setting, delicate and perfect and totally Bex, just like the magnet.

Together, they rose from the floor. She took his face in her hands again, staring into his ocean-blue eyes, awed by the ferocity of her love for him, by its boundless capacity for growth and change. Henny was her oldest and most cherished friend, and in so many ways it felt as if they'd already shared a lifetime together. Now, they'd be starting a new one, filling it with brand new memories as husband and wife. And maybe someday, as Mom and Dad.

For everything she knew about Henny, there was still so much more to discover. Lifetimes upon lifetimes to share with him.

Bex had never felt so blessed, so complete.

"I'm crazy for you," she whispered. "You know that, right?"

He swept the curls off her forehead, his eyes intense. "You're so beautiful. I can't stop looking at you."

"You never have to." She kissed him again, holding him close, inhaling his clean, masculine scent. The soft thud of his heart was a familiar drumbeat against her own, the sound of love, the sound of home. Glancing at her ring again, she said, "Does everyone already know? Does Mom?"

"Not the details. I asked for her blessing two months ago, though."

"You've been planning this for two *months*?"

"Not so much planning as waiting for the right moment."

"Did Mom bring up the lake again?" When they'd finally told her mother about their relationship a few months ago, she'd smiled knowingly, claiming she'd seen it coming for years, and implored them to come clean about the fact that they'd had sex at the lake in high school. Despite what her mother believed, they hadn't. Of course, they'd since remedied their lakeside oversight with a few recent trips to the beach, but Mom didn't need to know about that.

Henny laughed. "I finally admitted that you threw yourself at me like a common hussy, but being a gentleman of class, I—"

"Hussy? Who *says* that?"

"What she actually said was, 'What the hell took you so long?' Then she proceeded to call your aunt and order her to pay up. Apparently they had a bet going on us. Started the day you moved back to Buffalo."

"Seriously? Those old broads are worse than Walker and Roscoe. They need to mind their own business."

"Good luck with that. Aunt Sharon already put a wager up for our first kid." Henny shrugged. "She's giving us a year, but Mom said eighteen months. I say we split the difference."

"And I say we need more practice. Do you even

know how to *make* babies, Mr. I Looked At Porn Instead of Studying in Health Class?"

"You're a much better teacher than Mrs. Farnsworth and her produce. Way hotter, too." Henny kissed her again, nibbling her lower lip until she went weak in the knees. "With your heartfelt dedication to my studies, we'll figure it out in no time."

"Starting tonight. Right now we've got a party to host." She arched a brow. "To be continued?"

Henny winked. "Holding you to it, my little grapefruit."

"I... wow. You really are disturbed."

"You know you love it." Henny reached for her hand, his eyes sparkling like the ring on her finger. "You ready for this, beautiful?"

Bex glanced at the phoenix magnet on her cabinet, the mythical bird reborn out of the ashes, and knew that whatever waited on the other side of that door—at the Silver Phoenix's grand opening, at the Tempest games, at the place she and Henny would make their home, for all the celebrations and challenges to come—they'd face it together. Not just as lovers, but as true partners and confidants. As co-conspirators. As husband and wife. As friends.

The very best.

Her heart swelled with joy.

Yes, she was ready for this. Ready to rise up, spread

her wings, and take on the world. With Henny by her side, she was ready for anything.

Blinking away the happiest tears, Bex took a deep breath, opened the door, and stepped out into the light.

Thank you for reading DOWN TO PUCK!

Now that you've fallen for Bex and Henny, it's time to give Roscoe his due. Don't miss BIG HARD STICK, a red-hot hockey mom romance with cameos from your favorite Team Tempest lineup!

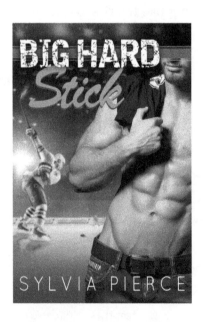

About Big Hard Stick

Roscoe may be a fan favorite at the Tempest summer youth clinic, but when it comes to winning the hockey mom's wounded heart, he's going to need a lot more than a big, hard stick. Does he have what it takes? Find out in BIG HARD STICK! Grab your copy now.

Read on for an excerpt...

EXCERPT: BIG HARD STICK

1

First day of summer, eight in the morning, and one thing had just become abundantly clear: Rob "Roscoe" LeGrand was going to need a bigger set of balls.

"Knock it off, sixty-one," he called out across the rink. "You too, thirty-four! Helmets stay on at all times."

Fuckface. He'd said that last bit in his head, because cursing out kids less than half his age was a surefire way to end up on the wrong end of the publicity train. The Buffalo Tempest had done enough of that already, and as team captain he'd promised Coach Gallagher and the suits he'd help them turn it around, whatever it took.

Make himself available for more interviews and photo shoots than he could stomach? No problem!

Donate a fuck ton of money and signed merchandise to Children's Hospital? Happy to!

Spearhead the team's new youth hockey clinic? Bring it on!

Yeah… He probably should've read the fine print on that last one.

Because now he had less than half an hour before the PR manager—Chief Executive Ball Buster, as the guys affectionately called her—showed up with the photographer, which meant less than half an hour to organize this rabble into some semblance of a team, complete with newspaper-worthy smiles.

"This is a shit idea," Roscoe grumbled, not for the first time that morning.

Henny, his right winger and second-in-command for this community enrichment fiasco, tapped his stick on the ice and shrugged. "No worse than getting caught on camera licking whipped cream off a woman's—"

"Hey. That was a completely consensual licking. Gallagher's overreacting."

"Doesn't matter." This from Alex Kenton, Roscoe's best defensemen and co-whipped-cream-licker. "We did the crime. Unless we want Gallagher up our asses all season, we're doing the time."

Crime? Technically, Roscoe hadn't done *anything*. It was just a bachelorette party at Big Laurie's—the pub Henny's girl Bex owned—a few months back. A bunch of pretty, perky bridesmaids were looking for a few laughs with the hockey players, and Roscoe and company obliged. Despite the whipped cream, a few shared drinks, and autographs on various body parts, Roscoe had gone home alone that night, same as always. Next morning, he'd woken up solo, wearing nothing but a feather boa and red lace bra, phone blowing up with the news that some fanboy had caught the whole thing on video and uploaded it to YouTube. Shit went viral. Gallagher went ballistic.

That video, coupled with the Tempest losing the Cup this spring after last year's big win, was the reason Roscoe had stepped up this summer. He respected his coach, loved his team, and there wasn't much he wouldn't do to boost their sinking rep in the community, including sacrificing his summer vacation to manage Gallagher's latest pet project. Alex Kenton, Sven Jarlsberg, and Dimitri Kuznetzov—his bachelorette party partners in crime—had lined up to help, right along with Henny, whose only crime was being a damn loyal friend.

The boys had spent a few weeks planning their strategy while PR handled the marketing and media crap. It was supposed to be a cakewalk. Neighborhood kids, pro athletes, fun times on the ice? Guaranteed positive press.

"Settle down over there," Roscoe shouted at the kids now, "or you're all going in the box."

Ignoring his lukewarm threat, two kids chased each other around the net while another entertained himself by spitting in the air and catching it on the way down.

Nice photo opp. PR's gonna love this.

"They need to find a way to channel that into the game," Henny said. "I'd kill for that kind of energy."

"Yeah?" Roscoe chuckled. "Pretty sure Bex would kill for you to have that kind of energy too, old man."

That earned him a punch in the arm.

"They're not even human," Roscoe continued. He was certain of it. Twenty minutes into the practice, and he still couldn't get most of them to pay attention. Only one kid—number forty-four—seemed like he wanted to be there. The kid stood a little bit apart from the rest, eyes on Roscoe and Henny, tracking their moves like he was taking notes in his head.

But one decent kid wasn't enough to make up for the rest of the bunch.

Roscoe shook his head. "Have I mentioned this is a shit—"

"Idea? Once or twice." Henny laughed. "Thought you loved kids, Mr. Sunshine."

"Used to. Until about twenty minutes ago." Besides, all of the kids in Roscoe's life were under the age of ten, a whole brood of adorable nieces and nephews still young enough to think he was cool. The punks on the ice today were teenagers, and judging from the scowls on their faces, Roscoe's coolness factor was at an all-time low.

It wasn't supposed to be like this. He was supposed to win them over, inspire them to greatness, all that jazz. But they'd barely paid attention to his intro speech, didn't even cheer when he and Henny showed off some of their best tricks. Roscoe was starting to feel like a glorified babysitter.

"Maybe I should go Russian mafia on them," Kuznetzov deadpanned. He'd spent the morning trying to talk to the kids about the importance of stretching and warming up, but all they wanted to know was whether he'd ever taken a shot to the nuts. "My accent can be pretty scary."

"Your *face* can be pretty scary, Kooz," Jarlsberg said.

Kooz cocked his head and smirked. "Not according to your mother, my friend."

"Knock it off, children," Roscoe told them. "Or you're going in the box, too."

"My offer is still on your table," Kooz said, the accent making him sound like every Russian mobster in every Russian mobster movie Roscoe had ever seen. "I will tell them of my Uncle Yuri. Yuri is in Siberian prison since I was small boy."

"You're full of shit," Jarlsberg said, laughing. "So is Uncle Yuri."

Kooz raised an eyebrow and lowered his voice. "Do

you know what happens to man who calls Uncle Yuri full of shit?"

Roscoe sighed, dragging a hand through his hair. Tempting as it was to let Kooz put the fear of God into these kids, he gave the idea a pass. Ultimately, turning this sinking ship around was his responsibility. He was the team captain. The leader. And, according to his teammates and family and basically everyone who'd ever spent more than five minutes with him, a nice fucking guy.

Probably explained why he kept going home alone at night. *Too* nice, they all told him. Even the women themselves.

Especially the last one, right before she packed up and bailed, two nights before he'd planned to propose.

It'd been a few years, but he'd only just gotten rid of the ring. He'd kept the damned thing locked in a box in his closet all that time, like some old relic to happier days.

Roscoe took a deep breath, shook off the funk. What did he have to complain about now? He had great friends and a big, closer-than-close family. Loved his city, his job. Got to spend his days on the ice, teaching kids how to shoot and score and charge down the rink. That's what it was all about.

"Thanks, Kooz," he said. "I'll take it from here."

"Sure you're up for this, Mr. Sunshine? Or would you

rather go get a manicure?" Henny nailed him in the shoulder, but real concern flickered in his eyes.

"Got one last week. Hasn't even chipped yet." Roscoe wriggled his fingers in Henny's face, his mood brightening. Yanking his helmet into place, he knocked it once and said, "Let's roll."

Roscoe and Kooz scooted down to the net, zooming around the cluster of kids gathered in front of it, herding them like cattle into a tightly packed group. Henny and the D-men fell in line behind them with a puck, the five of them passing it back and forth, showing off some stick work.

But damn, those kids were a tough bunch.

"What about us?" one of them shouted, and the others nodded along. Number sixty-one again, Roscoe noticed. The alpha. Every group had one, and Roscoe knew from experience with his nephews that kids like that would set the tone for the whole pack. "When do we get sticks?"

"Not yet." They weren't ready for gear, that was for sure. They hadn't even mastered the basics yet; most hadn't even paid attention during the safety drill.

"Come on," sixty-one whined. "We came to play hockey, not watch from the sidelines. Let us make a move here, Feathers."

Feathers?

Before that moment, Roscoe hadn't realized teen boys could actually *giggle*.

Before that moment, Roscoe hadn't realized his teammates could giggle, either, but Henny and Kenton were quickly challenging that assumption.

Roscoe looked over his shoulder at Henny. "Did he just call me—"

"Feathers?" Henny could barely contain himself. "Yeah. Yeah he did."

"What is American saying?" Kooz asked. "If your feather bra fits?" Bastard really got the kids going with that one.

That's it.

Ignoring his boys, Roscoe skated up to the kid who'd just given him his new moniker. "Name?"

The kid sniffed, jutted out his chin. "Nick Harper."

"So you've spent some time trolling me on YouTube, Nick Harper." Roscoe said. "That where you learned your stand-up routine, too? Pretty amateur, if you ask me."

"At least I don't wear a bra, bro."

Everyone laughed at that, even Roscoe. Damn, these kids didn't miss a beat.

"That a fact?" Roscoe asked, keeping his tone light. Teasing was all part of the game, and as long as they all kept things good-natured, he'd play along. "Seems to me, hanging out on the Internet all day doesn't leave much time to work on your weak-ass game."

The kid's cheeks turned red behind his face shield, but to his credit, he didn't back down. "I got plenty of game, Feathers."

"Yeah?" Roscoe got right up in his face. Smiled that sunshine grin of his. And handed over his stick. "Don't keep us in suspense, sixty-one."

Nodding once, Nick took the stick, zoomed down to the blue line at the other end of the rink. Henny followed, passing the puck good and hard.

The kid actually caught it, right in the sweet spot of the stick. Kenton went after him, but Nick was quick, dodging and weaving, charging down the ice. Kooz positioned himself in the net, ready to block.

The rest of the kids were cheering Nick on, shouting as he slipped past Kenton and Henny. He got in position for the shot, wound up…

Out of fucking nowhere, another kid swooped in with a stick and stole the puck, right from under Nick Harper's nose.

"Who's that?" Roscoe asked, impressed.

"Forty-four," Jarlsberg said.

Roscoe pulled the roster from his pocket, scanned the list. Reggie Heinz. Fifteen years old—a year younger than Nick Harper. Fast as hell, too.

The kids on the sidelines went wild again, whooping and hollering as Nick and Reggie fought for the puck. They chased each other around the net, stealing and blocking, but their antagonism quickly morphed into mutual respect. Soon they were passing like real teammates, testing each other's skills and limitations, uniting together in a quest to get that puck into the net. It was a damn thing of beauty, and as the kids zoomed together toward the goal zone, Roscoe's heart warmed at the sight of it.

Nick got in position for the shot, catching Reggie's perfect pass. He arched his stick, took the shot hard and straight...

No dice. Kooz dove and blocked the puck—good thing, or Roscoe would've benched his ass for letting two kids beat him on the first day—but hell, Roscoe cheered anyway. These kids knew their stuff.

Holding out his hands for the sticks as they skated back toward him, Roscoe nodded at them, acknowledging their skills. "Alright, sixty-one. You've got some moves. You too, double-fours."

Both kids beamed.

"Damn straight we do." Nick punched Reggie's shoulder.

"I can teach you guys a few more," Roscoe said, "if you'll let me."

Roscoe stuck out his hand. Reggie shook right away. Nick hesitated only a moment, then reached out. Roscoe went in for the shake, but Nick fist-bumped, and Roscoe totally fumbled the follow-through.

Roscoe laughed. "Maybe you can teach me something, too, slick."

"We'll see about that, old man." Nick gave him another fist bump and a big, genuine smile. Reggie hadn't said a word, but he hadn't stopped grinning, either.

These kids were happy. No hiding it.

And just like that, the whole morning turned right around.

The kids just needed to play—to be kids. Let off some steam, expend some of that pent-up energy before they got serious with all the rules-and-regulations bullshit. Roscoe had his own reasons for being there, but for the kids, this wasn't the NHL. Wasn't a job.

"Alright." Roscoe clapped once, turning toward the rest of the group. "Everyone grab a stick. Let's play some hockey."

The kids erupted in cheers, damn near killing each other to get to the box where they'd stashed the rest of the equipment.

Since Nick and Reggie seemed to know their way around the rink, Roscoe paired them up with Kenton and Jarlsberg to help out some of the younger kids, then sent Kooz and Henny to scope out the rest of the crew, gauging their skill level and physical fitness so they could assign official positions before the photographer showed up.

Roscoe kept his eyes on his star players, Nick and Reggie. In their short time together on the ice, they'd already bonded, already had that connection that allowed them to communicate wordlessly in a game.

"Left winger and center, I'm thinking," Henny said. He'd left Kooz with the less experienced group and joined Roscoe in watching the standouts.

"You called it," Roscoe said. "Nick's got a bit more technical finesse, but Reggie's faster. His heart is all in, too. Kid like that was born to play."

They both watched in awe as Reggie sped past, demonstrating a move for the others. He skated a little too hard, undisciplined and rough around the edges, but he was definitely talented with the stick. He switched from the left side to the right, equally adept at both. And when he faked out Kooz and made a shot that some of Roscoe's own pro teammates might've missed, Roscoe wanted to weep with joy.

Not that he was the type to get weepy on the ice, but still. The shot was fucking beautiful. Kooz would catch hell for the miss later.

"Nice work, forty-four," he called out. Then, to Henny, "Let's send him through the special backward crossover drill."

"Eva's?"

"Why not?" Roscoe asked. Eva was their skating coach, the kind of woman who took a special pride in torturing Tempest players as often as she could. She was also engaged to Tempest starting center Walker Dunn; the two were currently island hopping in the Caribbean, scouting out wedding locations.

"You want the kid to quit on us?" Henny asked. "My legs are still screaming from the last time Eva worked me over."

"Dude. She's been on vacation for two weeks."

"My point exactly."

"Let Reggie try," Roscoe said. "I need to see how hard he's willing to push."

"You're the boss." Henny called out to Reggie, and the kid skated over to them, barely winded from all the hard work he'd already done.

"You up for a challenge?" Roscoe asked.

"Yes, sir." The kid squared his shoulders, nodding so hard Roscoe thought his helmet might pop off.

"You familiar with backward crossovers?"

"Totally."

God, he sounded so young. Young and enthusiastic.

"I'd like to have you try our special version," Roscoe said. "It's like the backward crossover, but with a twist."

"More like a kick in the balls," Henny grumbled. "With another kick in the balls right after."

Ignoring him, Roscoe explained the deal, then sent Reggie off to give it a try.

Kid fucking nailed it. Not only that, but he swung back around for two more runs.

"Is it weird that I wanna adopt that kid?" Roscoe asked Henny.

"Totally weird."

"Look at him," Roscoe said. "When was the last time you saw a fifteen-year-old kid with stamina like that? Not to mention stick control."

"You want a kid, pops? Make your own." Henny laughed and nodded toward the seats, where a few parents had gathered to catch the rest of practice. "Maybe one of the hockey moms will help."

Roscoe barked out a laugh. "Yeah, *there's* a brilliant idea."

"Glad you think so. Because here comes your future baby mama." Clamping a hand on Roscoe's shoulder, Henny jerked his head toward the tunnel, where a blonde woman was stomping toward the rink.

Even at this distance, Roscoe could see the anger in her eyes.

One of those kids was in serious trouble.

"Christ. I'd better take care of this," he said to Henny. "Can you help the guys out there? I want Nick on left wing, Reggie on center. See what the other guys think about the lineup. Then you need to get them calmed down for the photo opp."

"On it," Henny said. Then, just before he skated off, "Hey. I was just kidding about the baby mama thing, douche bag. Don't get any bright ideas."

Too late, though. One look at those plump, heart-shaped lips as she came out into the light, and Roscoe's head was *swimming* with ideas, each one filthier than the last. So much for being a nice fucking guy.

Now that *is a hockey mom I'd like to f—*

"I'm here to pick up my kid," she said, skipping right over the pleasantries. Her short blonde hair was wind-blown and wild, her face pink, her blouse pulled back off one shoulder, revealing a blue bra strap. "Reggie Heinz?"

"I, uh…" Roscoe blinked, forcing himself to pay attention. Reggie Heinz, his new starting center. Best kid on the team. And the one with the hottest mom he'd ever laid eyes on.

"There," the woman said, pointing to the ice. "Forty-four. Also known as Grounded for Eternity."

Oh, fuck. Roscoe hoped the eternal grounding didn't apply to hockey practice.

"Sure," he said. "We've still got about twenty minutes on the clock, though. We're waiting for the photographer."

"Photographer?" Her light brown eyes widened in shock.

"Didn't you sign the release? It should've been in the packet you filled out this morning."

At this, she laughed, sharp and cold. "No. No I didn't."

Roscoe waited for her to say something else, but she folded her arms over her chest, her jaw clenched.

"Are you okay to wait," he asked, "or do you need to—"

"No. Now would be best." She forced a smile, but it wasn't real. Whatever Reggie had done, the poor kid was in deep shit. Like, wait-till-I-tell-your-father, you're-never-leaving-the-house-again kind of shit.

Nodding, Roscoe turned toward center ice and blew his whistle. "Double fours," he called out, waving. "Bring it in."

The kid looked up and skated toward Roscoe, then froze at the sight of his mother.

"You are in *serious* trouble." The woman took a step out onto the ice. Soon as her foot touched down, she lost her balance.

Roscoe saw it coming a mile away. He lunged forward and grabbed her arms, steadying her right before she went down. They were closer now, so close he could smell the faint scent of her shampoo, like lemons and sugar, cookies left out in the sun.

It took her a second to realize what had happened.

"Thank you," she finally said, a little breathless.

With a cocky grin, he said, "Not as easy as it looks, is it?"

"You can say that again." For a moment she seemed to forget about Reggie, whatever screwed-up thing he'd done to invoke her ire. She was clutching Roscoe's arms, looking up at him through dark lashes, her eyes sparkling under the arena lights. They weren't just brown, he saw now, but amber, ringed in dark honey and flecked with gold. She smiled at him—a real one this time—a little shy, a whole lot sexy, and absolutely worth the wait. It was easily the most beautiful smile Roscoe had ever seen; it took every ounce of brain power he possessed just to remember his own damn name.

"You okay now?" he asked softly.

"I... I think so. I'm not really a fan of ice rinks."

"I see that." He smiled softly. "Name's Roscoe LeGrand. I'm heading up the youth clinic."

"Reggie's mom," she said. "Um. Ally Heinz."

They were in their own little world now, all the sights and sounds of the arena fading into an indiscernible buzz as Roscoe continued to stare into her eyes.

"Nice to meet you," he said.

"You, too."

After a second that stretched out like an hour, he finally said, "Well, Reggie's mom, you're welcome to keep holding on to me, but eventually we'll need to go home, and driving like this could be a challenge. I'm up for it if you are, but—"

"Oh my God, I'm so sorry." The woman—Ally—blushed again, another smile appearing on her face. Roscoe could've stared at that mouth all day.

"Mom?" a small, desperate voice squeaked out from behind a face shield, breaking the spell between Roscoe and Ally. The kid's voice sounded nothing like the fierce player Roscoe had seen on the rink. "Don't freak out. I can totally explain."

Ally's smile vanished, ice rushing back in where the warmth used to be.

Game over.

She righted herself, straightening her shirt and turning all her attention on the kid. "You'll have plenty of time to explain later. Right now I want you to take off that helmet and apologize to Mr. LeGrand for wasting his time today."

Roscoe wanted to tell them both it was unnecessary, but if he'd learned anything from his years of summer vacations with his parents, four brothers, one sister, five siblings-in-law, and all his nieces and nephews crammed into a five-bedroom cottage and a couple of pup tents, it was this: never come between a mama bear and her cub. Especially when the cub did some dumb-ass shit to piss off his mama.

"We're waiting," Ally said.

"God. Fine." The kid took off the helmet, shaking out a head of long, honey-blond hair the same color as Ally's. "I'm sorry I wasted your time."

Roscoe stared into a pair of bright blue, tear-filled eyes, trying not to show his utter shock.

Reggie, number forty-four, the player he'd already pinned all his hopes on for the youth cup and for all the youth clinic summers to come, was a girl.

Just how fast will things heat up between Roscoe and his sweet, sexy hockey mom? Find out in BIG HARD STICK! Grab your copy now.

ACKNOWLEDGMENTS

Thank you, dear readers and reviewers, for your continued encouragement and support, and for falling so hard for my hockey boys. You make writing these icy, angsty love stories fun!

Buckets of gratitude and sparkly magnets to Lili Valente, Lauren Blakely, Michelle St. James, Kara Schilling, Janice Owen, and all the ladies in the Boneyard. Writing books would be a whole lot harder without your guidance, expertise, and cheerleading (and occasional butt-kicking, as needed).

Finally, all my love to my own best-friend-to-loverboy husband, who appreciates sparkly magnets and hockey romance novels *almost* as much as he appreciates naughty nacho night. ;-)

ABOUT THE AUTHOR

Romance author Sylvia Pierce loves writing about kick-ass, headstrong women and the gorgeous alpha guys who never see them coming. She believes that life should be a lot like her favorite books—smoking hot, with happy endings and lots of temptations, twists, and trouble along the way. She lives in the Rocky Mountains of Colorado with a strong, sexy husband who appreciates her devious mind, loves making her laugh, and always keeps her guessing. Like the heroes in her stories, Sylvia's man didn't see her coming... but after twenty-plus years together, he's finally figured out who's boss!

Visit her online at SylviaPierceBooks.com or drop her an email at sylvia@sylviapiercebooks.com.

f facebook.com/sylviapiercebooks
g goodreads.com/SylviaPierce
a amazon.com/author/sylviapierce
BB bookbub.com/authors/sylvia-pierce